With a divorce in the works, Annabelle Jones heads out to Southern California, the land of sun and starting over. She wants to prove to herself and her young daughters that she still has what it takes to turn heads as a swimsuit model—that she doesn't need a man to take care of her. Until an accident forces her to rely on the hunky, yet mysterious man next door...

Nathan Cooper is trying to revive his own career. Once a top left-handed relief pitcher, he tried to get over a hidden injury with the aid of banned substances. Not only was he caught and suspended, he was traded and missed out on winning the championship. Now he's a free agent without a contract, and that means life is ready to play ball...

Visit us at www.kensingtonbooks.com

Books by Kristina Mathews

Better Than Perfect
Worth the Trade
Making A Comeback

Published by Kensington Publishing Corporation

Making A Comeback

More Than A Game Series

Kristina Mathews

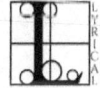

LYRICAL PRESS
Kensington Publishing Corp.
www.kensingtonbooks.com

Lyrical Press books are published by
Kensington Publishing Corp. 119 West 40th Street New York, NY 10018

All Kensington titles, imprints, and distributed lines are available at special
quantity discounts for bulk purchases for sales promotion, premiums, fund-
raising, and educational or institutional use.

Special book excerpts or customized printings can also be created to fit
specific needs. For details, write or phone the office of the Kensington
Special Sales Manager:
Kensington Publishing Corp.
119 West 40th Street
New York, NY 10018
Attn. Special Sales Department. Phone: 1-800-221-2647.

First Electronic Edition: July 2015
eISBN-13: 978-1-61650-999-6
eISBN-10: 1-61650-999-6

First Print Edition: July 2015
ISBN-13: 978-1-60183-462-1
ISBN-10: 1-60183-462-4

Printed in the United States of America

To my grandmother, who passed down her love of books to me.

Acknowledgements

I'm truly grateful for the overwhelming support I've received from family and friends since I started this journey of becoming a romance writer.

Chapter 1

Today was a good day. A glorious day. Sitting at the stoplight in the Southern California sunshine, Annabelle Jones did a drum solo on the steering wheel of her convertible Mercedes. She didn't care if people stared at her singing along to "Don't Stop Believing." She hadn't stopped believing, and look at her now, fresh off her first modeling job since filing for divorce. So it wasn't the cover of *Sports Illustrated*, still, it was a job. Something she could be proud of. Her daughters could be proud of her.

It wasn't about the money. The income she earned from this modeling job was more about pride. Having something to offer the world, even if it was just her face.

Annabelle wanted to show her daughters that a woman didn't need a man to take care of her. She could stand on her own two feet, and return to the career she'd given up when she married Clayton Barry. She might not fly off to exotic locations or work with the world's most famous photographers, but she was working.

She lifted her face to the sun, soaking in its warmth. It was as if the fog of the last few years had finally lifted. Nothing but blue skies ahead for her and her six-year-old twin daughters.

Today's shoot was just the beginning. Her agent had two more jobs lined up for her before the end of the month. He'd also scheduled her to attend the televised celebration of the fiftieth anniversary of the *Sports Illustrated* Swimsuit issue. She hadn't been able to make the photo shoot last fall in New York for the magazine, but he thought making an appearance on the live show would give her plenty of exposure.

Hopefully, she'd be able to juggle it all. Part of what appealed to her about today's job was that it was close enough that she'd be able to shoot for a few hours and still get home in time to meet her daughters when they got off the school bus.

Annabelle glanced at the clock. If the light didn't change soon, she wasn't going to make it to the bus stop in time.

The song ended and Annabelle turned down the volume. She'd started listening to Journey during the Goliaths' World Series run. So the song was five years older than she was, the message still rang true. It was about hope. Starting over. Believing.

The traffic light turned green, and she pulled into the intersection. A flash of yellow appeared out of the corner of her eye. She turned in time to see an SUV blow through the stoplight. Before she could react, the vehicle struck her Mercedes just behind the driver's side door.

Her head slammed into the side window. Glass shattered and she looked down at the blood on her blouse. A thousand black pixels danced before her eyes.

And then nothing.

* * * *

Nathan Cooper was almost home. He'd gotten his miles in, had lunch at his favorite restaurant, and he'd spent the early part of the day working his shoulder to the point of fatigue, but not pain. What a concept. How many times in the last two years had he told himself to toughen up? Work through the pain? He'd been in denial enough to believe he could overcome the injury to his shoulder by working harder, longer, stronger.

When that hadn't worked, he'd tried herbal supplements, powders, creams, and potions—just about anything that promised one more inning, one more pitch. He'd been desperate enough that he'd believed in the so-called experts until he couldn't be sure what he was putting in his body.

He slipped his hand under his collar to run his fingertips over the tiny scar. He should have started with the surgery. It would have saved him a whole lot of time and trouble. Hell, it might have even saved his career.

Standing at the corner, he waited for the school bus that had been sitting there idling for almost ten minutes. But he hadn't seen any passengers unload. The red flashing lights were to stop vehicular traffic. On foot, he could go around the bus, but he was determined to be a model citizen. To keep from making another mistake.

Finally, the doors opened and two little blond girls waved to him. The bus driver nodded, and the girls bounded off the bus.

"Miss Nora said we couldn't get off until we had an adult waiting for us. I told her you were our neighbor." They were five or maybe six years old. He'd seen them next door, playing with their mother, heading down to the beach. This one wore jeans, running shoes, and a San Francisco Goliaths sweatshirt. Not exactly a popular choice in this part of the state, but they had won the World Series last October. Without him. "I'm Sophie. This is Olivia. We're twins."

Olivia was pink, from the giant pink daisy clipped into her hair to some kind of tutu she wore over leggings tucked into pink cowgirl boots. She moved closer to her sister and looked up at him almost as if she thought he was the big, bad wolf.

"My sister's shy." Sophie gave her twin a shove. "Say 'hi' to our neighbor."

"Hi." Olivia looked down at the ground. Her little cheeks turned the same color as her tutu.

"So do you know where our mom is?" Sophie was not shy at all.

"No. I'm afraid I don't." He knew who their mom was. Annabelle Jones. *The Annabelle Jones.* One of the hottest models to ever grace the cover of *Sports Illustrated.* Damn.

He'd taken one look at her picture and fallen instantly in lust with her perfect combination of girl-next-door sweetness and a rocking hot body. Blonde, blue-eyed and… well, *built* was quite an understatement.

When the real Annabelle Jones moved in next door, he'd kept his distance. Partly because she was the picture of perfection in the pages of a magazine. She was his fantasy. Untouchable. Flawless. He didn't want to see her taking out the trash in her pajamas. Not even in silk pajamas from Victoria's Secret.

But mostly, he didn't get too close to her because he didn't want her to get too close to him. He didn't want her to figure out who he was. And how he'd let down his teammates, his sport, and his fans.

So he'd smiled and waved when they saw each other on the street, nodded politely when she'd suggested they get together for coffee sometime, but he always found an excuse to put her off.

"She's s'posed to meet us at the bus stop, but she had a job." Sophie put her little hands on her hips. "I thought she asked you to come instead."

"No. I haven't talked to her today." He'd spoken to her maybe a half dozen times since he'd received her mail by mistake. She hadn't recognized him, so he'd pretended not to recognize her. He had grown his former military-cut hair out, and was contemplating a beard. She was as gorgeous as always, and way out of his league.

"That's okay. I know where the key is." She shrugged and grabbed her sister's hand to start walking home.

"Sophie!" Olivia's eyes widened. "We're not supposed to cross the street without a grown-up."

"He's a grown-up." Sophie tilted her head in his direction.

"Yeah, but he's not our grown-up." Olivia snuck a glance up at him before turning back to her sister. "He's a *stranger*."

"You're not a stranger, are you mister?" Sophie looked at him with an innocent, trusting expression. "We've seen you talking to our mom and stuff."

"I'm Cooper, from next door." He had no business taking charge of two little girls. But he couldn't exactly leave them there at the bus stop. "Let's go find your mom."

He checked the traffic, looking both ways. Sophie took his hand without hesitation as they started to cross. But it was when Olivia slipped her tiny hand in his that he realized just how fragile trust was.

When they got to the house, Annabelle's Mercedes was still missing from the driveway. Sophie marched up the steps and tried the door. It was locked. She trotted around the house to the back door. Cooper had no choice but to follow.

"Sophie, you shouldn't show anyone where Mom keeps the key." Olivia's trust wasn't complete. She was fine with him helping them cross the street, but drew the line at him knowing where they kept the spare key.

"I'll close my eyes." He stood between the girls and the driveway, closed his eyes, and listened as Sophie rummaged through the flowerpot next to the back door.

"I got it." The little girl proudly held the key in her hand. He tried not to notice the frog figurine that had been knocked over. Not the most secure place to keep a key. But then, he supposed having a hide-a-key anywhere wasn't a good idea. Especially for a woman living alone with two young girls. A protective instinct rose inside him.

This was already more than he'd bargained for. It was one thing to get them off the bus and help them cross the street. He didn't want to follow them into their home, but they were too young to be left alone. The only other choice would be to take the girls to his place, but that wasn't an option. He had a lot of weights lying around and nothing kid-friendly to eat. What little kids liked almonds, avocados, and kale?

He followed the two girls through the back door into their kitchen.

It was a warm, friendly space, with hand-picked flowers in the window over the sink, candid photos and the girls' drawings pinned to the fridge. A bowl of fruit sat on the center of the round kitchen table. He could almost smell cookies baking, but he knew the oven wasn't on. No one was home.

"So, do you girls have homework?" The cozy, happy-family vibe of the kitchen didn't fit with the idea of a woman who would forget her children at the bus stop. But then again, maybe this happened all the time, and that was the reason Sophie was so comfortable going off with a near-stranger.

"No, silly. It's Friday." Sophie laughed and dragged a chair over to the pantry. She stood on it to help herself to a snack.

Cooper glanced at Olivia. He had a feeling she'd call her sister on any unauthorized snack choices.

Turned out the girl grabbed the kind of snack he'd choose for himself—a jar of organic peanut butter and whole grain bread. She carried them over to the counter and pulled a butter knife out of the drawer.

"Do you need any help?" Cooper offered. He felt like he should be doing something. Here he was in Annabelle Jones' kitchen, supervising snack time for her daughters. He wondered if she had a phone book, but even if she did, chances were she wouldn't have put her own cell number in it.

"Nope." She opened a drawer at the bottom of the cabinets and pulled out two pink plastic plates and matching cups. She gave her sister a look and Olivia grabbed a gallon of organic milk out of the refrigerator.

The cordless phone on the counter rang. Caller ID showed *Jones, Annabelle.* He picked up, hoping Annabelle wouldn't be too freaked out that a man answered instead of one of her daughters.

"This is Officer Garcia with the California Highway Patrol." A concerned male voice came on the line. "Am I speaking to Mr. Jones?"

"No. Miss Jones is not married." At least, her husband wasn't living with her. And he'd heard she'd filed for divorce. Cooper felt his stomach knot. He instinctively turned away from the girls.

"Is there someone in her immediate family I can speak to?"

Cooper took the phone out to the back porch. He kept an eye on the twins but didn't want them to overhear what was obviously bad news.

"Her immediate family members are minors. I'm caring for her young children." He called up the kind of steady nerves he'd needed coming into a game with the bases loaded and nobody out. "Tell me what I need to know."

"Miss Jones has been involved in a traffic accident. She's being transported by ambulance to University Trauma Center."

Cooper sank against the porch railing as the officer relayed the address of the hospital. He pulled out his own phone and searched for the phone number.

After hanging up with the CHP officer, he checked in on the girls and saw they were happily chatting as they ate their peanut butter sandwiches and washed them down with cold glasses of milk.

Taking a deep breath, he dialed the hospital. Claiming to be Annabelle's brother, he was able to find out the extent of her injuries. He hung up after discovering she'd been brought in with lacerations to the face, bruised ribs, and a concussion. They would release her if she had someone who could stay with her to observe for any post-concussion complications.

With a heavy heart, he walked back into the sunny kitchen.

Two innocent faces looked up at him. They trusted him. They needed him.

"Your mom has been in a car accident." He used the gentlest voice he could find. He didn't want them to worry. He was doing enough of that for all of them. "She's going to be okay, but we'll need to pick her up from the hospital."

Sophie blinked back tears but held her head high.

Olivia slid off the chair and threw herself at him. She clutched his legs, holding on with everything she had.

"It's going to be okay." He patted her back, hoping to God he was telling the truth.

* * * *

Annabelle hurt. Everywhere. Her ribs, her back, her neck, and her left shoulder throbbed in pain. But most of all her head hurt, the worst headache she'd ever had. She tried to open her eyes, but could only see out of her right eye. Her other one was covered. Trying to focus with just one eye made her dizzy. Trying to sit up made her dizzy. Even lying still made her dizzy.

Where was she? She looked around slowly, hoping the nausea would pass, or at least not get any worse. There was a heavy industrial-type curtain dividing the room in half. Along one wall stood a sink with foot pedals below and hand sanitizer above. An uncomfortable-looking couch stood against the other wall. The bed she was lying in had railings and a remote attached to the side. She could raise or lower the foot and head of the bed and call for assistance. A tube coming out of her arm was hooked up to a bag of some kind of fluid. Machines beeped softly behind her.

She'd been in a place like this before. She just couldn't remember why.

Babies. There were babies before, one for each arm. Her babies.

Was she still in the hospital with the twins? No. She could picture them, much bigger. Walking. Dancing. Starting school. They were definitely old enough to go to school.

Was she having another baby? She looked down at her flat belly. No. That wasn't why she was in this place. This… Oh, why couldn't she remember what it was called? Why couldn't she remember anything?

A man stepped into the room. He was a tall man. A strong man. An *oh-my-God* very good-looking man. His long-sleeved gray T-shirt hugged broad, well-sculpted shoulders. Black athletic shorts hung low on his hips, almost clinging to muscular thighs. His dark brown hair was a little longer than she preferred, but she couldn't help but wonder what it would be like to run her fingers through it. His lips were thick, sensuous, and framed by dark whiskers—thicker than stubble, but not quite a full beard. His green-gold eyes swept over her with concern and something else. What was it called? That feeling of wanting…or needing…*something*?

Annabelle swallowed. Her throat was dry, too dry to speak. She reached for a glass of water from the bedside table. Even with one eye, she liked what she saw. But she couldn't remember who he was. He wasn't a stranger, she knew that much. Could feel that much.

"Come in." Her voice sounded raspy and harsh. But maybe that was the way it always sounded.

He hesitated before entering, turning back to the hallway, he ushered two little blond girls into the room. Her daughters. *Thank God.* She recognized them. Olivia. And Sophie. The two bright lights of her life. The reason she fought through… What had happened to her? She closed her eyes, trying to recall the details.

There was screeching, crunching of metal, shattering glass, and blood. So much blood.

She remembered the blood.

Her daughters crept carefully into the room, eyes wide as they took in her appearance. She must be a real mess. Sophie clutched the man's hand. No. It was Olivia. Sophie never wore pink. Or did she?

"Mommy, you look like a mummy." Sophie skipped over to the side of the bed. The child's energy bounced off her in waves. "Maybe I'll call you Mummy from now on. Like I'm British."

Her daughter's laughter filled Annabelle with joy, taking the edge off her pain and confusion.

Olivia scooted closer to the man. He must be someone close to them. Olivia was slow to warm to people. She wouldn't just reach out for someone if he wasn't special.

So who was he? And how did she ask without looking like an idiot, or worrying her girls?

"How are you feeling, Annabelle?" She recognized his voice. It was familiar, comforting, and every bit as sexy as the rest of him. They way her name rolled off his tongue made her believe he was a lover. But she was married. No, divorced. Everything was mixed up in her head.

She reached for her water again, took a long swallow, and watched him watch her.

"I'm a little sore." She tried to smile but her skin felt tight. Especially over her left eye. The one covered in a bandage. "But I'm alive."

He smiled, his lips curved almost sinfully, and his gaze roamed over her banged up body as if he knew what she looked like under the sheet.

If he wasn't her lover, he wanted to be.

How could she even think about things like that? After what she'd been through? And with her daughters right there in the room.

"Mr. Cooper said to be careful when we saw you." Olivia peeked out from behind his legs. "And not to bounce the bed. He said to ask before giving you a hug."

"Just Cooper. You don't have to call me mister," he said to Olivia, but he didn't take his eyes off Annabelle.

"Can I give you a hug?" Olivia asked, her voice more cautious than usual.

"Of course." Annabelle braced for the contact. The man, Cooper, picked her daughter up and gently set her on the bed. Olivia gave her a small squeeze and she felt warm tears against her face. "It's okay, baby. Mommy's okay."

Chapter 2

Cooper was shocked by the sight of Annabelle lying in that hospital bed. Her usually flawless skin was pale and her face was half-covered in bandages. Her silky, golden locks hung matted and limp on the pillow. Her luscious lips had quivered as she'd invited him into her room.

She looked him over with the one eye not covered in gauze. Maybe she recognized him, maybe she didn't. She'd drawn her brows together as if she was trying to figure out how she knew him, but she'd winced at the small movement.

He wondered, not for the first time, if coming here had been a mistake. The girls needed to see their mother, but if he was so shaken by her appearance, he worried they would be even more freaked out. Still, they'd driven all this way, just under the speed limit, and he'd kept glancing back wondering if he'd strapped them into their booster seats correctly in the back of his Escalade.

The moment the girls stepped into her room, Annabelle's face had transformed. A beauty no camera could capture lit her up at the sight of her daughters. Love. Pure and simple.

"Thank you for bringing them here to see me." Annabelle reached for his arm, and just the slightest touch sent electricity through his entire body.

"No problem." He shrugged. Just last week he'd turned down another invite for coffee or chai tea. He didn't want to get involved, and yet he couldn't just walk away.

"I don't have anyone else to…" She glanced over at her daughters, who had moved off the bed and were entertaining each other on the couch. "We're still pretty new in town, and I don't have many friends here yet."

"You've got me." He'd spent the better part of the last year trying not to feel anything. Now he felt too much. Annabelle Jones was real. And she needed him.

"Yes. I've got you…" She glanced at her daughters again, then crooked a finger at him, inviting him to come closer.

He moved toward her, and she tugged on his arm, pulling him down so she could whisper in his ear.

"Who are you? I mean, I know you, but I don't know how I know you." He could tell she was disturbed by the lack of recognition.

"I'm your next-door neighbor," he whispered back.

"Oh." She closed her eye and sank into the pillow. After a slight shake of her head, she opened her eye and swept her gaze over him. "Are we, uh…"

"We're friends." He figured a little white lie was necessary here. Especially since he had her children with him.

"Friends." She sighed. "Okay, that's good."

"Is there someone you want me to call? Your… husband?"

"No. Not him. He's…" She brought her right hand up to her forehead, as if pressing on it could stimulate her memory. "We're no longer married."

"Still, he might want to know you've been in an accident." Not that Cooper wanted to be the one to tell him.

"No. He wouldn't. That I'm sure of." She shook her head hard enough to make her wince.

He leaned even closer, so there was no way the girls, who were giggling and squealing, could overhear. "Is there a reason you don't want your ex-husband to know what's happened to you? Is it violent? Abusive?"

His stomach clenched at the thought of that man hurting her or her daughters.

"No. No, that's not…" She exhaled, briefly closing her eyes. "He's not around. He's…"

Her face contorted in pain…or confusion.

"Do you want me to get the nurse? Do you need something for the pain?"

"No. It's just…foggy." She rubbed her forehead. "Foggy…like San Francisco. No, he's not there. He's…oh, what's that place? The sun sets on the wrong side of the beach."

She drew a shape on the sheet, like a long finger.

"Florida? Is your ex-husband in Florida?" Of course he was. The hearing. Her ex-husband was testifying in the biggest steroid scandal in recent history. He'd been an investor, a silent partner who was now willing to spill his guts in an attempt to keep from losing his fortune.

"Yes. Florida." She gave him a weak smile. "That's the word I was looking for. It was there…but out of my reach. Like so many things. Just. Out. Of. Reach."

She sank back against the pillow, exhausted by the effort. Annabelle had been in a serious car accident. She'd suffered a concussion and simple tasks were difficult for her. He'd had a concussion once, after being hit by a line drive. It had scared the crap out of him. One minute he felt fine, sitting in the clubhouse after the game, and the next, he couldn't tie his shoe. The weirdest part was that he'd managed to tie one of them, but couldn't for the life of him remember how he'd done it.

"Thank you for bringing the girls here. I'm sure you had much better things to do than hang out in a hospital with your neighbor."

"Hopefully, they'll release you soon." He wondered if he should try to get some information. Maybe he could use his persuasive skills at the nurses' station. Once upon a time, he'd been pretty charming. But that was before he'd become a disgrace. Now he wasn't sure that his status as a Major League ballplayer would get him an advantage, or get him kicked out of the hospital.

"I'm sorry to keep you waiting." She closed her eyes, wincing once again. "But thank you for coming."

"No problem."

A quick knock on the door and the doctor entered the room.

"Ms. Jones, I'm Doctor De Rosa." She gave a professional smile to Annabelle, but Cooper got the feeling he wasn't welcome.

"Why don't I take Sophie and Olivia to get something to eat?" That would give Annabelle privacy and give him something to do. Besides, he was hungry.

"There's a cafeteria on this floor. Just go down the hall and to your left," Dr. De Rosa said.

"Great. Thanks." He turned to the girls. "Should we go check out the cafeteria?"

"Sure." Sophie hopped off the sofa and was ready to go.

"Okay." Olivia glanced at her mother as if she needed assurance it was okay to go off with him.

"Be good, girls." Annabelle smiled and nodded her approval.

"Do you think they gave Mommy weird drugs to make her talk funny?" Sophie asked once they sat down in the nearly deserted cafeteria. The twins each ordered a slice of cheese pizza and Cooper grabbed a large salad with a grilled chicken breast.

"If they did give her medicine, it was to help her body heal." Cooper wasn't sure how to explain the difference between healing medicine and drugs that could wreck your life. "Sometimes medicine can have side effects. But it's important to take them when the doctor tells you to. Only when the doctor tells you to."

"Yeah. One time we had ear affections, and we had to take this disgusting medicine." Sophie chattered away. "It tasted like pink poop."

"Sophie!" Olivia was apparently offended by her sister's strong language.

"So you've tasted pink poop?" He couldn't help it. The kid was a hoot.

"No. Of course not, silly." Sophie laughed, and the sound went straight to his chest. "Miss Ramirez tells us to write *juicy* sentences. Not boring *I like cats, I don't like medicine* sentences."

"Miss Ramirez?"

"She's our teacher." Olivia added with a starstruck note in her voice. "But I don't think she's really a teacher."

"Oh really?" He suspected he was getting in over his head.

"I think she's really a *princess*." Olivia was breathless with awe. "She's just pretending to be a teacher until her Prince Charming comes along."

"And then she'll go back to being a teacher when she gets a divorce." Sophie joined in the conversation, but instead of romantic ideals, she had a more jaded take on things. "That's why Mommy had to get a job. 'Cause she got divorced."

Yep. Definitely in over his head.

"How come girls have to give up their job when they get married?" Sophie asked thoughtfully.

"They don't. Some women choose to stay home with their babies. Maybe that's why your mom quit modeling, so she could look after the two of you." He really had no idea what motivated Annabelle to quit at the height of her career. For a guy who couldn't figure out his own motivations at times, he wasn't in any position to judge others.

"So now we're big girls, she can be a model again?" Olivia asked.

"Sure, why not?" He shrugged. "Your mom can be anything she wants to be."

"I want to be a princess when I grow up," Olivia announced. "Or a teacher."

"I don't want to be a princess. I want to be a baseball player." Sophie said with confidence. "Or maybe I'll be an owner like Auntie Hunter."

"Or like Daddy." Olivia had a note of sadness in her voice. "Before he moved to Florida."

Where the sun sets on the wrong side of the beach.

* * * *

"So how are you feeling?" Dr. De Rosa asked as she took Annabelle's vitals.

"I want to go home." She hated feeling trapped, dependent on others. "I just want to sleep in my own bed."

"You've had a serious head injury." The doctor didn't need to remind her of that. She felt the dull thud every time she moved her head. "I'm going to ask you a few questions before we can release you."

"What kind of questions?" Annabelle wasn't feeling up to taking some kind of test. Especially if her release was dependent on getting the right answers.

The first few questions were straightforward. Her name, age, and occupation. She only stumbled a little on the occupation question. For a long time, she'd been nothing more than a wife and mother.

"I'm a model," she finally answered. "Or at least, I was."

She reached up to touch the bandage on her face. "How bad is it? I know it will leave a scar, but…"

It felt like her face was cut from her left temple to her jaw. That's where it hurt the most. But she might have a smaller cut or two above her eyebrow and across her cheek.

"I won't lie to you. It's going to look pretty bad right now. There will be a lot of redness and swelling. You won't look like yourself for a few days." The doctor offered a sympathetic smile. "But you'll improve steadily over the next several weeks."

Annabelle wanted to see, but had a feeling she wouldn't like what she saw.

"Let's take a look, shall we?" The doctor pulled up a chair and started unwrapping the gauze around Annabelle's head. "Not bad. It looks like a clean wound."

"But it will leave a scar?"

"Yes, I'm afraid so."

"That's not going to help my modeling career." Annabelle hated how disappointed she sounded. Almost whiney.

"Tell me about what happened today," the doctor said as she applied a fresh bandage. This one was smaller, and it didn't cover her eye. "What do you remember about the accident, and what you did earlier in the day?"

Annabelle recalled snippets of time. Sitting in a chair having her makeup done. Wardrobe changes. Bright lights and the clicks of the camera. A typical day as a model. She'd done her first *Sports Illustrated* issue when she was only nineteen. Had it been ten years already? Somehow today's shoot had felt new and exciting, like the first time, only better. Her agent had set her up on a photo shoot with a small upscale boutique in Aurelia Beach. The ads would run in a regional magazine, distributed at restaurants, hotels, and businesses throughout Orange County, giving her plenty of exposure. She'd hoped it would be enough to re-launch her career.

She sank back against the pillow, trying to gather more details from the foggy corners of her mind.

"I was on my way to a photo shoot." It was like that dream. The one where she was running in slow motion, only instead of her feet, it was her brain that felt stuck in quicksand. "No. I was on my way home. I had done my job and I was going to meet the school bus."

"But you didn't meet the bus?"

"No. I saw a flash out of the corner of my eye." And then crunching metal. Broken glass. So much blood. "It must have been the car that hit me."

Annabelle closed her eyes, hoping the picture would form in her mind. But she was tired. So tired.

"Can I go home?" she asked again, weary of the hospital. Of the questions that seemed much harder than they should be. "I just want to go home."

"Do you have someone staying with you?" the doctor asked.

"My daughters live with me." She sensed that wasn't the right answer, but it was the honest one.

"I'm afraid I can't release you unless you have a responsible adult who can keep an eye on you for the next twenty-four to forty-eight hours."

"I can't think of anyone who could stay with me." If she was in San Francisco, she could call Hunter. No, she was still on her honeymoon. They would be coming to Aurelia Beach in a few days on their way home.

"What about the man who is here to pick you up?"

"Cooper? He's my neighbor." And she couldn't just ask him to stay overnight with her. Not when she was such a mess.

"He'll need to stay with you. Next door isn't close enough."

"I couldn't impose like that." Especially since she wasn't sure where they stood. He'd said they were friends, but there was something more between them. Something she couldn't act on.

"Okay, then we'll just admit you overnight."

"No. Wait." If she didn't go home, who would watch her girls? If she couldn't ask Cooper to babysit her, she certainly couldn't ask him to look after her children. "I'm sure he'll stay with me. I'll ask him."

Chapter 3

It was nearly nine o'clock by the time Annabelle had been cleared to go home—on one condition—he would have to stay with her overnight. How many times had he imagined spending the night with Annabelle Jones? But this wasn't exactly the scenario that had fueled his fantasies.

It was a good thing he'd thought to bring her a change of clothes. Hers were ruined in the accident. Cooper thought he'd been practical in selecting a soft velvety yoga outfit for Annabelle. He figured she'd want to be comfortable. And he hadn't wanted to spend too much time going through her wardrobe. It was bad enough he'd had to look in her underwear drawer, but since he didn't possess the ability to teleport her clothing to the hospital for her, he'd had to pack by picking up her things and putting them in a suitcase. He'd thrown the first pair of underwear he found into a small duffel bag along with a tank top, some socks, and the light blue yoga pants with matching jacket.

He'd found a pair of slip-on walking shoes. It was the kind of outfit he'd seen on plenty of women in Target at eleven on a weekday. Casual, comfortable, and just right for running errands and grabbing coffee after their morning workout.

On Annabelle, it was sexy as hell. The soft fabric hugged her every curve. She'd pulled the hood up over her head, probably trying to hide her injury. It only made him want to slowly lift the veil of her hoodie and kiss every single stitch.

Sophie and Olivia were extra careful around her. He'd warned them she might be sore, so they should be gentle. He was surprised at how well they'd followed his suggestion.

"Thank you for coming to pick me up." She turned away from him, so that the left side of her face was in the shadow of her hoodie. "I don't know how I'll ever repay you. For this and for staying with me."

"What are neighbors for?" He shrugged, not wanting to think about how she could repay him. When she was recovered from her injuries, of course, he would never take advantage of her in her fragile state.

"Loaning me a couple of eggs, picking up the newspaper when I go out of town for the weekend." She gave him a half smile. He wasn't sure if it was because the other side of her face hurt or because she was unsure of herself. "Not picking me up from the hospital, bringing me a change of clothes, and spending the night with me."

"What can I say? I'm an excellent neighbor." He flashed his cockiest Nathan Cooper grin. The one he'd used for interviews, pickups, and most famously, his shutdown strut.

Damn. He wasn't that man anymore. The last interview he'd done had been given with the somber expression of a ballplayer who didn't know if he'd ever pitch again. He knew pain. He knew scars. And he knew this was the worst time to even think about trying to get Annabelle into his bed.

"I don't know, you do play your guitar late at night." She gave him a teasing smile. A moment of connection passed between them. She'd been listening to him when he sat on his porch, picking out tunes, trying to figure out what he was going to do if baseball wasn't in his future.

"I'll try to keep it down."

"I like your music. It's...comforting." She lowered her voice, as if she was sharing a secret. "It makes me feel... Like I'm not so alone."

He didn't like thinking of her as being lonely. He didn't want to think of her as anything other than the image of perfection that had graced the covers of a magazine. But here she was, not only human, but very vulnerable. With her bandaged face, blood-matted hair, and need for supervision for the next day or two.

"I'm glad you like my music." He felt a sense of pride knowing it brought her a small comfort.

Cooper followed as a hospital employee pushed Annabelle's wheelchair to the exit. The girls walked softly beside her, like twin guards. "I'll go get the car."

He returned with his Escalade. After making sure all his passengers were buckled in, he pulled away, feeling as nervous as a first-time father entrusted with a newborn.

Both Sophie and Olivia fell asleep on the way home. He carried each of them up the stairs and dropped them on top of their coordinating bedspreads.

"Thank you," Annabelle whispered. "I'll get them undressed and into their pajamas."

"I'll run next door and grab a toothbrush. Maybe a change of clothes."

"You don't have—"

"Yes. I do need to stay here. Doctor's orders." He slipped out and raced over to his place to grab his toothbrush, a clean T-shirt, and a pair of athletic shorts that could double as pajamas. On a whim, he grabbed his guitar—just in case—and hurried back to Annabelle's.

Cooper let himself in through the back door and felt just a little like he was making himself too much at home. He tiptoed through the kitchen and into the living room. No sign of Annabelle. He debated going upstairs, but wondered if maybe the twins had awakened and were getting into their pajamas.

Upon hearing the shower turn on overhead, Cooper settled himself onto the sofa and flicked on the TV, keeping the volume down low. He could watch basketball without the sound, especially since he really couldn't care less about the sport. It was just something to do to kill the time while he waited for Annabelle to finish her shower.

Damn. The last thing he needed was to picture her naked, water sluicing off her near-perfect body. Even with the inevitable bumps and bruises she must have sustained in the accident.

A loud thud jolted him out of his fantasy. He shot up from the couch and took the stairs three at a time.

"Annabelle!" His hand was on the doorknob to her bathroom, but it wouldn't turn. "Annabelle, are you all right?"

"I dropped the shampoo," she called through the locked door. "Sorry if I startled you."

"Are you sure you're okay?" His heart was hammering, not convinced that she should be in there alone. And it had nothing to do with his fantasies.

"Yes. I'm just a little clumsy, I guess."

"Well, I'll be right here if you need anything." He slumped down on the edge of her bed, adrenaline still shooting through his system.

He sat there, his thighs trembling in fear. What if she slipped? Or fainted? What if she became overcome with the heavy steam and just slid into unconsciousness? A million worst-case scenarios filled his mind. He was just about ready to say to hell with it and break down the door, when he heard the water shut off. The glass door slid open, and he could just make out footsteps as Annabelle must have stepped from the shower.

He let out the breath he'd been holding since he sat down. She was conscious.

And most likely naked.

Breathe in. Breathe out.

Cooper tried to steady his heart rate as he'd done on the mound so many times. But he hadn't stepped foot on a baseball field in months, and he was too wound up for too many reasons.

* * * *

"Oh, you scared me!" Annabelle was startled to find Cooper sitting on her bed. Good thing she'd slipped on her robe instead of just waltzing out of her bathroom naked.

"I said I'd be here if you needed me." He raked his hands through his hair, obviously just as uncomfortable being there as she was having him there. "Isn't that the whole point of this sleepover?"

She cinched the belt around her waist tighter, all too aware that she was naked underneath. Her heart rate spiked as she thought about having a sleepover with this man under very different circumstances.

"I…I think the guest room is all set." She crossed the room, hoping he'd follow. "I haven't had anyone stay there, but there should be sheets on the bed."

"I can take the couch."

"No. I couldn't have you do that." She opened the guest room door and made her way to the bed to check for fresh linens. "You wouldn't fit. The sofa is less than six feet long, and you're, what six-one, six-two?"

"Six-three." He shrugged, as if his size was something of an inconvenience.

"You wouldn't be comfortable on the sofa." She turned down the comforter, relieved to find crisp cotton sheets underneath.

"Are you going to be comfortable having me in the room right next to you?"

"Why? Do you snore?"

"Not that I know of." He gave her a smile that made her all too aware of how close he would be.

"Well, that's good." She wasn't going to tell him she was uncomfortable having him so close. That she hated having him hover over her. She couldn't even take a shower without him standing guard outside her door.

It would be different if he was naked and hovering over her, or taking a shower with her. If he was spending the night because he wanted to, not because he had to. But maybe that was the biggest reason she didn't want him here.

"There's a bathroom down the hall." Annabelle stepped toward her room. "I'm going to go brush my teeth, so if you hear me drop the toothpaste…"

"I'll come running." He offered a faint smile. "Just to make sure it's not your head."

"I figured as much." She was just going to have to get used to the idea that he was there. So close. Too close. "Are you going to wake me every two hours?"

"The doctor said three." He stepped back, giving her a little breathing room.

"I'm sure I'll be fine." She didn't like the idea of having him come into her room every few hours, waking her up just to make sure she was alive. But it was better than him having to sit down with her daughters explaining that mommy wasn't going to wake up. She shivered at the thought.

"Maybe you should get your pajamas on." He must have thought she was cold, standing there in her robe. "I'll get myself settled in here."

And probably set an alarm for every three hours.

She slipped out of the guest room and went to her own bedroom. Shutting the door, she contemplated locking it, but thought she'd better leave it unlocked. Just in case. Annabelle grabbed her favorite sleep shirt, an extra-long tee with a picture of Minnie Mouse on it. It wouldn't be easy getting it over her head, her shoulder was so stiff, but she wasn't about to ask Cooper for help. The attraction between them was already a problem, she didn't need him dressing her. Or undressing her. At least, not while her head was so fuzzy.

Since he would be visiting her at least twice during the night, she decided she'd better wear pajamas instead. She didn't need to worry about kicking off the covers and having him see her underwear.

After brushing her teeth, Annabelle settled in for a long and restless night. She was exhausted, but worried the thought of Cooper checking in on her would keep her from getting any sleep.

A soft knock on the door was followed by Cooper calling out to her, "Annabelle, is there anything you need?"

"No, I'm good." She sighed, wishing he didn't have to be there. And that he didn't have to be so good-looking. Especially since she was such a mess.

"Can I come in?"

"Sure." Annabelle pulled the quilt higher, covering all but her face.

"Is there anything I can do for you before I turn in?" He stood there as if he wanted to be anywhere else.

"Could you…" She felt so stupid even asking, but she didn't want to take chances. "Could you read the instructions on the pain medicine the doctor gave me? I want to make sure I'm not taking the wrong dose."

"Sure." He picked up the prescription bottle that stood on her nightstand. He didn't even have to squint to read the tiny print. "Says here to take two pills with a full glass of water, every eight hours as needed for pain."

"What about side effects?" She rarely took anything stronger than the occasional Advil or Alka-Seltzer Cold.

"Don't drive or operate heavy machinery. May cause drowsiness…"

"Maybe I shouldn't take it." She glanced toward her daughters' bedroom. She didn't like the idea of being knocked out with them just down the hall. "If you're supposed to wake me up in three hours, it seems like a bad idea to take something that may cause drowsiness."

"But you need your rest."

"I'll try it without the pills, but if I can't sleep, I'll take one." She grabbed the bottle from him, feeling like she'd regained at least some illusion of control.

"One more thing…" He hesitated as if he was afraid to ask. "How do you want me to wake you?"

"I'm a pretty light sleeper." Especially if she didn't take the meds. "I'm sure I'll wake up when you open the door."

"If not?" He shrugged. "Should I call your name? Tap your shoulder?"

"I'm sure none of that will be necessary." She happened to glance at his mouth. The several days' stubble would probably wake her up if he brushed a kiss across her lips.

She shook her head to get rid of the unwelcome thought, but winced as pain pounded behind her temple.

"Are you sure you don't want to take the pain pills?"

"I'm a mother. I can't be comatose with young children in the house."

"I'm here." He leaned just a little closer. "I won't let anything happen. To you, or your daughters."

And for some reason, she believed him.

* * * *

Cooper waited for half an hour before finally taking a quick shower. He threw on his clean T-shirt and shorts and tried to make himself comfortable in the guest room. Annabelle was in the next room, and in two and a half hours, he would need to creep up to her bed and gently wake her.

Waking up next to her had been a long-time fantasy, but not like this. Especially since he had the feeling she didn't want him there. He just hoped it was the situation and nothing personal. Then again, if she'd known who he was, she wouldn't have continued to invite him over. She certainly wouldn't have let him stay.

Still, he had a hard time falling asleep. Especially when he knew he'd have to wake up in two hours. Wake up and creep into Annabelle's bedroom, tap her on the shoulder, and then tell her to go back to sleep. Then he would repeat the whole process at least once more before morning.

He should have just jogged around the bus.

But then where would Annabelle be? At the hospital still? And what about her daughters? Would the bus driver have eventually let them off, having a schedule to keep? Or would she have kept them on the bus, returned to the school, and tried in vain to reach Annabelle?

It seemed as if he'd only blinked twice before his phone chimed, sounding the alarm to check on his patient. He roused himself out of a fairly comfortable bed, even if it was only a queen-sized mattress. Stumbling across the room, he ran his fingers through his hair and braced for the task ahead of him.

He pushed Annabelle's door open. Moonlight filtered through the sheer curtains that hung on her windows. Curtains that offered only the smallest amount of privacy. He'd seen her shadow from his porch. Could make out the shape of her figure as she'd moved around at night. He'd tried not to look up when her bedroom light had been on, but she was Annabelle Jones.

She was sleeping soundly. He could see the soft rise of her chest, hear the barest trace of a snore. She looked so peaceful. So beautiful. He hated to wake her, but that was why he was here.

"Annabelle." He touched her shoulder, gently shaking her. "Annabelle, honey, wake up."

Honey. What was he thinking?

She responded with a soft moan, and it was all he could do not to slide into bed with her.

"Annabelle, you need to wake up." His heart rate started to spike and not in a good way. He should have paid closer attention to the doctor's instructions. How many times should he try to rouse her before calling 9-1-1?

She rolled over, facing him, and opened her eyes. Blinking, and then rubbing her eyes, she looked at him as if she didn't know why there was a strange man in her bedroom.

"Annabelle, it's me, Cooper." He took a deep breath. "I'm here to make sure you're okay after your accident."

She drew her brows together and winced. Her hand moved to the bandage on the left side of her face.

"I'm okay." She yawned. "Just a little sore. And tired."

She dropped her hand and rolled onto her back.

"Well, I'll let you get some rest."

"Thank you." Her eyes fluttered closed and she drifted off to sleep.

He stood there crouched at her side for a few minutes, fighting the urge to brush her hair off her face. To touch her in some way.

Clenching his fists, he stood up and backed out of the room. It was going to be a long night.

He shuffled back to bed, reset the alarm, and tried to get comfortable amongst the feminine pillows and subtle scent of lavender and Annabelle.

Yeah, it was going to be a really long night.

Chapter 4

Annabelle was tired, sore, and a little disoriented after being woken up twice during the night. Or was it three times? She wasn't sure, she just knew that every time she felt like she was finally resting, that man came into her room. And each time, it took her longer to fall back asleep. It wasn't from the head injury, though. It had more to do with the gentle concern in his voice. The electric, yet cautious touch as he shook her shoulder.

And the dreams. Oh, the dreams she'd had during the night. It was a strange combination of fear and longing. She'd dreamed of being in the car, of something coming toward her, careening out of control. But then she'd find herself on a gurney, naked, with her sexy neighbor playing doctor.

She knew it was pointless, especially in her current state. She'd taken a long, hard look at herself in the mirror this morning. What she saw wasn't pretty. Not by a long shot.

The gash ran from her temple to her jaw. Another cut slanted over her eyebrow, and a third extended toward her cheek. She looked like someone had carved a large letter K in her face. There was not enough makeup in the world to cover that scar. Her modeling days were indeed over.

She tried to let that thought sink in. She'd walked away from the job once before. She could do it again.

It wasn't about the money. At least that's what she'd tried to convince herself. She'd taken a cash settlement over future alimony. With the sale of Clayton's share of the Goliaths, there was plenty to live on. She just wished she could feel better about taking it. Her short-lived modeling career had provided the only income she'd ever earned. The rest had come from Daddy. And then Clayton. If it wasn't for her children, she would have been tempted to tell him to take his money and shove it.

Instead, she'd put most of it away for her daughters' future. College. Travel. Whatever they'd need.

What she'd wanted to give them more than anything was someone they could look up to. Or at least someone they could be proud of. She'd wanted to show them that they could be more than just spoiled little rich girls. True, modeling wasn't exactly saving the world. But it was the only job Annabelle had ever had.

She'd have to think about that after she got the girls their breakfast. At least she could still be a mother. She hadn't done too bad in that job. Her daughters were happy, healthy, and adjusting better than expected with all the changes they'd gone through in the last few months.

She'd been plagued by guilt for making the girls change schools in the middle of the year, but they had all needed a fresh start. At least they loved their new teacher. Both girls were absolutely smitten with Miss Ramirez. They'd come home from their first day engaged in a heated debate over whether she looked more like Jasmine or Pocahontas from their favorite princess movies.

Her daughters didn't seem to mind the move from the big city of San Francisco to the small coastal town of Aurelia Beach. They liked living half a block from the ocean. Being able to build sandcastles practically in their backyard was a definite plus.

Heading downstairs, she heard her daughters' voices coming from the kitchen.

"Is that your guitar?" It sounded like Sophie. "Will you play for us?"

"Sure." Cooper was still there, apparently about to perform a breakfast concert.

"Do you know 'Let It Go'?" Olivia loved that song. Maybe a little too much, she sang it over and over and over.

"I know 'Let It Be.' I'll play that for you." Cooper strummed his guitar and sang The Beatles' classic.

Annabelle closed her eyes and leaned against the wall at the bottom of the stairs. He had an incredible voice. Soulful. Sensuous. And downright sexy.

She needed to steady herself before facing him in the light of day. She tried to brush her hair back off her forehead, but it caught in the antibiotic ointment. Man, she was a mess. At least she looked better than she had last night. And even without the pain pills the doctor gave her, she felt better, too.

"Good morning." Annabelle tried to put on her most sunshiny face. "I'll get breakfast going for you here in just a jiffy."

"We already ate." Cooper looked up from his guitar. "They helped me find the cereal. And I made coffee. I hope you don't mind."

"No. That's great." She was a little thrown by how he'd just made himself right at home. Or maybe it was because Clayton had never made breakfast for his daughters. Not once. Not even when she'd had the flu and could barely get out of bed.

"Can I get you anything?" Cooper stood, setting his guitar on the kitchen table. "Cereal? Coffee?"

"No. I'll get it." She wasn't sure she could eat just yet. Her stomach was a little queasy. Maybe some coffee though, to clear her head.

As if coffee would do the trick.

She poured herself a cup and sat down.

"So, I'll hang around until you've had your shower, then I'll head on home." Cooper picked up the empty cereal bowls and carried them to the sink. "I figure you could use a little time to yourself. Unless you need me to stay."

"No. I'll be fine. You've done enough already." Annabelle didn't want to be a burden. "Surely you have better things to do."

"Nothing that can't wait." He rinsed the dishes and put them in the dishwasher. "But I don't want to get in the way."

"I'll try not to drop the shampoo." She took a sip of her coffee, torn between wanting him to go away and just wanting him. "That way you won't have to come running."

"I'll try not to overreact." He slid into the chair next to her. "But I do take my responsibilities seriously."

"I'm not your responsibility." The last thing she wanted was to be taken care of.

"Until you're back on your feet, I feel like I should at least be close by."

She stood up, nearly knocking the chair over. "See, I can stand just fine. I can walk, and shower all by myself. I can even take care of my daughters."

He glanced at the girls, who were sitting there, eyes wide. They'd never heard their mother raise her voice before. Annabelle had spent too much of her life putting on a happy face, pretending that life was perfect.

"I'd like to think you'd be able to take better care of your daughters if you take care of yourself first." He looked at her with genuine concern, and there was something in his tone of voice that made her think he wasn't being condescending. "I'll feel better if I know you'll rest and ask for help when you need it."

She wasn't sure what bothered her more—that he was right or that he'd discovered one of her biggest weaknesses. She'd never been very good at asking for things. Sure, she seemed to have it all, but not because she asked. A lot of what she'd been given was more because she had a hard time saying no when someone offered.

Until now. Why was she so resistant to having Cooper's help? Was it because she was trying to start a new life? Or was she worried she'd fall for him, and like she'd done in her previous relationships, give up her identity?

"Well, I know where to find you." She took her coffee and headed for the shower. Cooper's voice carried upstairs over the sound of his guitar. He was doing a good job of keeping the girls entertained. She tried to be grateful for that, but they didn't need to get too attached to him either.

She showered quickly and without dropping so much as a sliver of soap. Dressed in comfortable clothes, with hair up in a plastic clip, she was a far cry from the heavily made-up and styled look she'd had at the photo shoot.

Warily, she tried to recall more details of her job yesterday. It was still fuzzy, like faded photographs. A snapshot here of a silky blouse being draped over her shoulders. Flashes of sound, the whirr of the camera, the photographer's voice.

No, it wasn't the photographer's voice she recalled, it was Cooper's. Had she spoken to him that morning? Just how close were they?

She tried really hard to remember more of the man who lived next door.

Annabelle remembered being six years old and desperately trying to get her father's attention. She'd put on fashion shows, dance routines, and acrobatics. Daddy had barely looked up from his business reports.

She remembered being a teenager. When boys and men had started to notice her, to appreciate her looks, her figure. Maybe there was something worthy about her after all. She'd started competing in pageants and had made third runner up for Miss Texas. And she certainly remembered the thrill of being approached by a real agent. Had she ever considered modeling?

At least her father had taken time out of his busy schedule to look over the contract and make sure it was legitimate. No daughter of his would be exploited or paid less than she was worth. But once the contract had been signed he'd dismissed her, just like always.

How could she remember everything she'd tried to forget, but she couldn't remember Cooper? The doctor had told her it wasn't uncommon for long term memory to come back quicker than more recent events. Still, she should recall more details about her hunky next-door neighbor.

She could picture him running up the beach, sitting on his porch, and playing his guitar. She even recalled peering through his window and seeing him lifting weights. But she had absolutely no recollection of interacting with him.

* * * *

Annabelle had sent Cooper home not long after her shower. It was Saturday, so she didn't have to worry about getting the girls ready for school. That was one less thing to think about. She was now grateful the girls took the bus to school. She hadn't planned on it, but when she'd gone in to register them, the school secretary had mentioned the bus forms and Sophie had been so excited about the idea of riding the bus, she'd decided to fill out the forms, figuring once the novelty had worn off, they'd go back to the usual routine of having her drive them.

One of the things she'd hoped for with this move was to let her daughters live as close to a normal life as possible. That included public school, especially since the local elementary was one of the best in the state. She wanted to give them chores and an allowance. Maybe someday get a puppy, so they could learn responsibility.

They spent the morning picking up where their neighbor had left off, trying to take care of her. They made her toast after Cooper left, with peanut butter and honey. Why not? It wasn't like she had to worry about every calorie she consumed anymore.

The doctor had warned her to get plenty of rest. No more than two hours of any type of cognitive activity until she was headache-free for twenty-four hours. That included reading, watching TV, or using the computer. She could gradually increase her time by small increments after each twenty-four hour period with no symptoms.

She'd been given similar guidelines for physical activity. She could take short walks on the beach, gradually working her way up to her normal workout routine. Annabelle wondered if she'd ever feel normal again.

Although she usually enjoyed listening to her daughters' constant chatter, today the sound caused pressure to build behind her eyes.

"Why don't you put on your favorite princess movie?" She hated to plop them in front of the TV on such a beautiful sunny day. "Mommy needs to rest a bit."

They argued over which movie to watch, but when she told them they could watch both, it solved the problem quickly.

She was just going to close her eyes for a few minutes.

* * * *

A quick run on the beach was just long enough to get Cooper's heart rate up, but not long enough to let go of the troubling image of Annabelle's injuries. Her beautiful face. It looked like someone had used her face to record a strikeout, a backward K, meaning the batter froze and struck out looking as strike three crossed over the plate.

Damn. He should be thinking about baseball, the game that he'd played since he was nine. The game he thought he'd do anything to keep playing. He rubbed his shoulder. The pain was only in his head now. Man, he'd been an idiot, thinking he could outsmart his body, outsmart the league. They weren't supposed to test him until after he reported to spring training.

Too bad his number had been called for the random off-season test. His mistake had cost him fifty games. It had cost him his confidence. Instead of the healing powers of science, all he'd gotten from FITNatural was a weakened shoulder that he'd injured in his first appearance after being traded to St. Louis.

A simple arthroscopic surgery had fixed his shoulder. A slight tear of the rotator cuff. Physically, he felt stronger than ever. But he couldn't pick up a baseball. The thing that had brought him such satisfaction, millions of dollars, and more women than he knew what to do with now taunted him. Every time he touched a ball, he felt his throat close up, as if he'd swallowed the damn thing. He couldn't breathe. It made him sick. No, he made himself sick.

He would have preferred to do his workout at the gym, but he didn't want to be that far away from Annabelle, in case she needed him. His home gym had the basics. He could get a good workout without leaving the house. He hit the weights sitting in his spare room, lifting a little more weight than he'd been doing. Just to test the shoulder.

Cooper hated that there was a small part of him that hoped he'd feel a sharp pain, a sign that his shoulder was shot. Then he wouldn't have a choice but to turn down the remaining offers that came his way. If he hadn't already dropped the ball.

* * * *

Cooper took a chance and picked up Thai food for dinner. He chose a variety of dishes, ranging from mild for the kids to moderately spicy for his tastes. He figured if the girls wouldn't eat any of it, there was always peanut butter.

He knocked on the back door. For some reason, he was more comfortable using the kitchen entrance rather than going to the front door.

Olivia greeted him with a pink bow in her hair and a sweet smile on her face. "Shhh. Mommy's sleeping."

He stepped into the kitchen, closing the door quietly behind him. "How long has she been asleep?"

"We watched two princess movies." Olivia didn't seem to realize that might be a little too long. "But we were really good and didn't wake her up to ask if we could watch another one."

"Maybe I should check on her." He put the takeout containers on the counter. "Why don't you and your sister set the table for me? We'll need plates, forks, and cups."

"Okay." She skipped off to find Sophie.

Cooper approached the couch where Annabelle was sleeping and knelt down next to her. She was breathtaking, even with the ugly gash across her face. He was tempted to wake her with a light kiss on the forehead, on the right side, where her skin was still flawless.

Heaving a sigh, he gently touched her shoulder instead. Just as he'd done during the night.

"Annabelle." He spoke softly, not wanting to startle her. "I brought you some dinner."

She moaned.

Oh hell. All the blood rushed straight to his groin.

Focus. Think of anything other than waking up next to her.

"Annabelle, honey, you need to wake up."

Her eyes fluttered open. A look of confusion was quickly followed by one of embarrassment.

"I must have fallen asleep while the girls were watching a movie." She sat up, looking around as if she wasn't sure where she was.

"You've been out for a while." He didn't want to show too much concern, didn't want her to hear the worry in his voice. He'd already gotten the message loud and clear, she didn't want to be coddled. "How are you feeling?"

"Fine." She ran her hands over her face, wincing when she touched the stitches. "I'm just a little tired is all."

"I guess that's to be expected." He offered his hand and she took it as he slowly lifted her to a standing position. "I hope you like Thai food."

* * * *

"That sounds perfect." Even if she wasn't sure how much the girls would eat, she could always make them a sandwich later.

She was surprised to find the table set with the plastic plates and cups she kept in the bottom drawer for the girls to use for snacks.

Cooper pointed out which entrees were mild and which ones were more flavorful or even spicy. It all smelled delicious. Her stomach rumbled at the smell of garlic, curry, and basil.

"Who wants to try some sticky rice and lemongrass chicken?" She hoped her daughters would be polite enough to try one of the milder dishes.

Surprisingly, they both seemed eager to experience new flavors.

"Would you like some curry, Annabelle?" Cooper held a serving spoon ready to dish out the spicy combination of meat and vegetables.

"Yes, please. I'll have a little of everything."

He spooned a serving of each dish on her plate and then heaped double portions for himself.

"What's that?" Sophie pointed to one of the spicier dishes.

"It's called evil jungle noodle," Cooper explained. "It has lots of yummy vegetables and rice noodles and red curry sauce."

"That's a funny name." She laughed. "Could I try some?"

He nodded and placed a small spoonful on her plate.

"Is it spicy?" Olivia asked cautiously.

"A little. But you might like it." He spooned a few bites onto her plate, too, away from the rest of her food.

They ended up trying a little of everything. Sophie liked most of it, but Olivia preferred the milder dishes. Just the fact that they'd tried all of it was a testament to how impressed they both were with their neighbor.

After the meal, Cooper stood and started collecting the plates.

"You don't have to clean up," Annabelle protested. She rose stiffly out of her chair. "You've done enough already."

"I've got it." He carried the dishes to the sink and rinsed them before loading them into the dishwasher. "I'll take care of cleaning up in here, if you take care of the cleanup with those two."

"Thank you." Annabelle was impressed by the way he just did what he could to help. He didn't complain or wait for direction. He just came in, got the job done, and was ready for the next time she needed him.

As much as she hated to admit it, she did need him.

She couldn't drive. She couldn't shop for groceries. Heck, she couldn't even stay awake through a Disney movie. The only thing she could do was accept help and hope that he didn't feel like she was taking advantage of him.

Annabelle followed Olivia and Sophie upstairs. They were already in the bathroom and undressed by the time she made her way up to the second floor. Everything hurt, every muscle, every bone. At least her headache was better. It only hurt when she moved too suddenly.

She turned on the water in the tub, testing the temperature before letting the girls get in. At least they were old enough that she didn't have to squat down next to the tub to bathe them. Now she just had to hand them the bottle of shampoo and they could wash their own hair.

They were probably old enough take their baths without her supervision, but she still liked having this time at the end of the day when they chatted about what went on in their lives. She knew it wouldn't be long before they would demand privacy. Soon enough, they would share their secrets with each other and keep them from her.

She'd have to enjoy helping them into their jammies and reminding them to brush their teeth while she still could.

"Okay girls, crawl in bed while I find a story to read." She approached the bookshelf, wondering how long this ritual would last. They were already reading simple books they brought home from school. Miss Ramirez had recommended the *Biscuit* stories about a cute little puppy, and the girls were gobbling them up like candy.

"Can Cooper sing to us again?" Olivia asked.

"Yeah. Can he?" Sophie nearly leaped out of bed in excitement.

"He's done a lot for us already…" Annabelle hated to ask for more.

"Please?" both girls begged.

"I'll ask him." She hoped her daughters didn't get too attached to their neighbor. But she had a feeling it was already too late.

Cooper was more than willing to sing to her daughters. He'd brought his guitar and her heart swelled as she watched her daughters smile and clap and sing along with Cooper's songs.

Finally, Sophie and Olivia nodded off to sleep.

"Thank you," Annabelle whispered as they crept out of the girls' bedroom. "You've been terrific. They're absolutely smitten, you know."

"Please. I'm no Prince Charming." He stood in the hallway, looking uncomfortable. "I'm just a regular guy."

"No. You're more than that." She wondered how much they'd shared. But she was afraid it would hurt him if he knew she couldn't remember.

"Look, I sang a few songs. It's not like saving lives or something."

"You're too modest." She wished there was some way to show her gratitude. "Too good to be true."

* * * *

Oh hell. She thought he was one of the good guys. He'd been afraid of that. He really needed to set her straight.

"You don't even know me." He thought for sure she'd have recognized him by now. She had been, by the laws of community property, one of his former owners. Even with his longer hair and beard, she should have recognized him as one of the Goliaths players.

"Oh no." She looked horrified. "You're someone famous, aren't you? You're a rock star, or something?"

"No. I'm not a rock star." It was all he could do not to laugh. But she sounded so sincere. "I have played with a few bands you've probably heard of. Filling in here and there, you know, a couple of charity events, or a last minute replacement when the regular guitarist was sent back to rehab and well…the show must go on."

"So what do you do?"

He'd known the question would come up eventually.

"I'm a professional beach bum." He offered a grin that once-upon-a-time made women swoon. "Actually, I'm between jobs at the moment."

"Oh." Her expression changed and she looked disappointed. Or maybe she was embarrassed for him. "I guess that makes two of us."

"You're a beach bum, too?"

"I am now." She tried to smile. Half of her face cooperated. But the left side couldn't quite pull it off. "And I'm also between jobs. I was hoping to resurrect my modeling career, but…"

She closed her eyes. It must be difficult for her to give up on a dream before she was ready.

He stood there, wondering what he could do to help. Even as he knew he'd already done too much. He'd already inserted himself into their lives more than was good for any of them.

"Well…" She let out a sigh and wiped her hands on her thighs. "The guest room is still made up for you."

"Thanks." He had a feeling she didn't want him there. Or maybe she did. It was hard to read the expression in her blue eyes.

"I guess I'll see you in a couple of hours." She started for her room.

"If you don't mind, I'd like to stay up for a while. Maybe watch a little TV." Try to take his mind off spending another night so close to Annabelle.

"Sure. Make yourself comfortable." She hesitated, as if there was something else she wanted to say, and broke eye contact. When she glanced up again, she had a look of confusion on her face. "Did we… I mean, have we ever…"

He stepped closer. Couldn't help himself. Gently, he reached up and stroked her right cheek. "No, Annabelle. We've never... Trust me, you'd remember if we'd ever gone to bed together."

He flashed a teasing grin, acknowledging the sexual tension between them.

"Oh. Good." She sounded relieved, and maybe a tiny bit disappointed. She shook her head again, but it wasn't in disagreement. More like she was trying to shake things loose. Or into place.

"I am such a jerk." He would have hit himself upside the head, but that would have been even more insulting. "You really don't remember."

"I remember more than I did yesterday, but no..." Tears shimmered in her eyes. "I don't recall a lot of things."

He squeezed his hands into fists to keep from reaching for her.

"Do you remember the accident?"

"No. Not really. Just blood and shattered glass." She shook her head slowly. "I don't remember much about any of that day. I don't remember taking the girls to school, or driving to my photo shoot. I do remember someone doing my hair, my makeup. Kind of like snapshots, but it's like I lost the whole day."

He shoved his hands in his pockets.

"I don't..." She bit her lower lip. "I don't even remember how we met."

Something in the tone of her voice made him reach for her.

"I got your mail by mistake." He placed a gentle hand on her shoulder. "So I brought it over. We chatted a few minutes, and you invited me in for some chai tea, but I declined."

"Why did you decline?"

"Oh, lots of reasons really." Most of them selfish. "I didn't want you to think you could come over anytime and borrow a cup of sugar. I don't keep sugar in the house."

"I see." She nodded, but she didn't look convinced.

"Look, Annabelle." He let out a frustrated sigh. "I know who you are. I have every one of your magazines. I keep them in a drawer next to my bed."

"Oh." Her hand came up to the scarred side of her face.

"You've always been my number one fantasy." He might as well get it all out. "I wanted to keep it that way. I didn't want to see you as a real person. With feelings, ideas, and imperfections."

"Sorry for ruining your fantasy." She turned and walked away.

He didn't want to hurt her, but she was getting too close. And he was getting too comfortable here.

He'd tried to tell her he was no Prince Charming.

Chapter 5

Annabelle washed her face and got ready for bed. She avoided looking in the mirror as she smoothed a thin layer of antibiotic ointment over her cuts. She didn't want to see just how imperfect she'd become.

Her appearance had always been the one thing she could count on. The only thing she could control. Sure, she'd been blessed with her blond hair, blue eyes, and a body that fit the current standard of beauty. But she had to work at keeping it up. While her girls were in school, she'd spend a couple of hours on the treadmill, running along the beach, or doing yoga. The alternative would be to not eat, and she didn't want to set that kind of example for her children. She tried to focus on eating the right kinds of foods, more lean proteins and vegetables, fewer carbs, and keeping her portions small. She didn't push her diet on her daughters, she wanted them to grow up being able to enjoy food. Not fearing it.

She had to maintain her highlights. Although born blonde, her hair had darkened over the years. When she was young and carefree, she just had to spend hours in the sun and it would lighten to an almost platinum by mid-July. Now she spent a small fortune on highlights, conditioning treatments, and sun protection to keep her hair color from fading.

Her skin didn't stay flawless without creams and serums, scrubs and sunscreen. Always sunscreen. She'd spent so much time and money on keeping her skin perfect.

A lot of good that did her now.

She'd never be the girl on the cover of a magazine again. The one her neighbor kept next to his bed.

She wasn't quite sure how she felt about that.

He wasn't the first person to see her only as she presented herself in magazines. She got that. Those images were about fantasy. It was about glamour and glitz and yes, sex. She didn't want to think about how long it had been since she'd last had sex. Two years? Longer than that?

She didn't want to think about sex, but with her hunky neighbor so close, she couldn't help it. If she didn't need his help she'd send him home. But even next door was too close.

Annabelle walked slowly and carefully downstairs to get a glass of water.

"Is everything okay?" He switched off the basketball game he must not have been really watching.

"Yes." She started for the kitchen but then switched course and sat down next to him. Not too close, but close enough to notice his scent. Warm. Masculine. And incredibly sexy. "I was wondering how you ended up bringing the girls to the hospital."

"Right place at the right time, I guess." He shrugged, as if it was no big deal for a near stranger to just step into their lives so suddenly. "I was coming home from my afternoon run. The bus driver wouldn't let them off without an adult to walk them across the street. They recognized me and I think it was Sophie who persuaded the driver to let them off."

"Thank you." She smiled. It sounded like a Sophie thing, convincing the bus driver that their neighbor was a close friend. "I wonder what would have happened if you hadn't been there."

"I guess they would have gone back and the school would have called your emergency back-ups."

"I don't have anyone local. Except my agent." Who she needed to call in the morning and let him know she wouldn't make the next two shoots he'd lined up for her.

"Well, you've got me."

"So, you're over the 'keeping the fantasy' problem?" She teased.

"Yes. I'm glad I got to meet the real you." There was a genuine quality to his voice. He meant it.

"Do you really have my magazines next to your bed?" The idea both embarrassed and excited her.

"Yes." He squirmed. Just a little.

"And do you…uh, use them?" She felt a blush heat her face. "I mean, I know you're not a teenage boy or someone who would have trouble getting a date. But I haven't seen any women leaving your place since I moved in."

"I thought you didn't remember me." He smiled, just enough to show he was teasing her.

"I don't remember interacting with you much. But I do remember seeing you. Listening to you play your guitar. Watching you run along the beach. Wondering about you."

"So you've been stalking me?" His grin widened playfully.

"No." Her cheeks grew warmer. "I just appreciate the view."

She turned away, embarrassed by her admission as well as the fresh scars on the left side of her face.

"Annabelle." His voice was gentle yet commanding.

She turned to face him.

A smile tugged at the corner of his lips. He reached up and swiped a strand of hair that had stuck in the ointment on her face, tucking it behind her ear. His long, strong fingers lingered there, in that delicate spot, before sliding down her jaw line. He lifted her chin just enough to make her look into his eyes. Desire blazed in the green-gold depths before he leaned closer and kissed her.

His lips were soft, playing hers tentatively, as if he was searching for the right note. But once he found it, he plunged wholeheartedly, finding the rhythm, making her body sing.

She moved with him, picking up on the unsung music of his lips. Sweet harmony thrummed through her body. His hands rested on her hips as he deepened the kiss. She pressed against him, and he slipped his hands beneath her shirt. He stroked her lightly, her skin on fire as he moved his hands higher and higher. His grip tightened as he moved toward her breasts. His right hand grazed her ribcage and she groaned as pain shot through her.

"Oh, Annabelle." He dropped his hands. "I'm so sorry. I hurt you."

"It's okay." She wanted to deny it, but the bruised ribs throbbed in a way that was as far from sexy as she could imagine. She eased away from him, grimacing at the pain and the embarrassment of leading him on.

"No. It's not." He heaved a heavy sigh and raked his hands through his hair. "I should go."

"No. Please. I need you to stay." She tried to smooth her T-shirt back into place. But it hurt. Almost as much as her heart. She wanted this man. This near-stranger who sang like an angel and kissed like the devil and did her dishes and looked after her daughters. She wanted him, but she couldn't have him. Not when her body was bruised, and her head was befuddled, and her divorce wasn't yet final.

"You're so beautiful." He looked at her, his gaze taking in every inch of her, lingering on her breasts before resting on her face. "You're so beautiful it hurts. I knew I couldn't trust myself around you."

"My children trust you." She couldn't let him walk away so easily. "I trust you with them."

"I would never hurt Sophie or Olivia." There was a desperate honesty in his voice. "But you... God, Annabelle, you're every fantasy I've ever had."

"So you do use my magazines?" She laughed. For the last ten years, she'd been trying to convince herself that the idea of strangers getting their kicks while looking at her magazine covers was just a myth. That there weren't men or boys using her picture to fuel their fantasies. But this man had admitted it.

"I don't need the magazines." He reached a trembling hand to touch her knee, almost as if he was making sure she was real. "Your face is burned into my soul."

"Oh."

"Do you know how many times I've slept with a woman and pretended she was you?"

"I don't think I want to know."

"You're right. You don't." He closed his eyes and leaned back against the couch, letting out a frustrated groan.

"I should get to bed." She pushed herself off the couch, but swayed with a rush of dizziness.

"Let me help you." Cooper stood, taking her arm and steadying her. "I'm here to help you heal. That's all. I can't be anything more."

She nodded, somehow knowing he was lying to both of them.

* * * *

Too bad he'd never been a Boy Scout, then he'd know how to help a woman up the stairs without wanting something for himself. He tried to think of the last time he'd done something, anything, without expecting something in return. Even his long-standing work with the Harrison Foundation had been more about furthering his career than helping kids. He did the pitching clinics to endear himself to the community and the organization, not because he thought a week spent with him and his teammates would give some poor kid a shot at making it as a ballplayer.

When he donated large sums of money to various charities, he considered it part of his job. The team and the league had their pet causes and he'd wanted to be seen as a team player. A Goliath on and off the field. The tax write-offs helped, too.

So, it was hard to convince himself he was helping Annabelle just to be neighborly. He wanted something from her. Wanted it real bad. So it was perfectly fitting to find himself guiding her to her bed, knowing full well he couldn't join her.

Penance. That had to be what this was, payback for all the selfish shit he'd pulled in his life. He'd never been a particularly religious man, but he couldn't help but wonder if there was some higher plan in delivering the one woman he'd always wanted to the house next door. There was a catch, of course. The pretty packaging came with a warning. *Fragile*. But wait, there's more! Two vulnerable little girls, innocent children who'd already been subject to the breakup of their parents' marriage, a move, and the scare of finding their mother in a hospital bed with tubes in her arms and bandages on her head.

Annabelle Jones was most certainly payback for all the things in his life that Cooper had gotten so easily. Pretty much everything he'd ever wanted, and a whole lot he didn't. He'd been given more than his fair share.

And now, as he tucked Annabelle into her bed, he realized the irony.

"Can I get you anything?" He was going to give if it killed him.

"No." She shook her head, wincing at the effort.

"Okay, then." He stood, ready to go to the guest room and stare at the ceiling all night.

"Wait." She sat up. "Could you bring me a glass of water?"

"Sure. No problem." He inched toward the door.

"And could you…" Her cheeks tinged pink, making her look almost angelic. "Could you sing to me? Like you did for the girls?"

"Sure." Angelic. Devilish. Either way, she was torture. "Water and a song."

He went downstairs for his guitar and a glass of water.

When he got back to Annabelle's room, she was already asleep. He set the water glass on the bedside table and watched her for a little longer than was healthy. Kissing her had been a mistake. She'd been hotter and sweeter than any of his fantasies. He'd never get the taste of her out of his system.

A cry from down the hall startled him. He crept quickly and quietly to the room the twins shared.

"Mommy! Mommy! Don't die." One of the girls cried out in her sleep. He could just make out the image of Olivia tossing and turning in her pink bed.

"Shhh. It's okay." Cooper knelt next to her bed. "Mommy's sleeping. She's fine, she's going to be just fine."

Olivia sat up, blinked a few times, and then threw her arms around his neck. "Mommy's car was on fire."

She buried her sobs in his neck.

"It was just a dream." He patted her back and spoke gently. "Just a dream, sweetheart."

Slowly, her sobs subsided. She sniffled and wiped her nose on his T-shirt. But he didn't mind. Not one bit.

"Will you sing me a song?" Olivia asked. She was wide awake and bright eyed now. "Please?"

"I don't want to wake your sister." But he knew he'd give in.

"It's okay." Sophie stirred in her light blue and yellow bed. "I had bad dreams, too."

"I know a song you might like." Cooper positioned himself on the floor between the two beds. He sat cross-legged with his guitar in his lap. He sang softly, in the words of Bob Marley, entreating them not to worry about a thing.

He sang as many uplifting, hope-affirming songs as he could think of off the top of his head. Mostly classic rock ballads he was sure the six-year-olds had never heard of, but they seemed to enjoy the music. Then, after the girls had fallen asleep, he plucked at a melody that had been playing around in his head. A song that sounded like longing for something just out of reach. He had no lyrics yet, but knew the song would be titled "Annabelle."

Chapter 6

Was that bacon she smelled? Annabelle woke feeling stiff and sore, but a little more clear-headed than yesterday. And she was definitely hungry. She pulled her hair into a quick ponytail, brushed her teeth, and headed downstairs.

Cooper was helping Olivia and Sophie make breakfast. Both girls were covered in flour and standing on a chair at the stove making pancakes. Cooper even had a spot of flour in his hair. Who would have thought a pink and white polka dot apron could make a man look so sexy?

"Good morning." He offered a sleepy smile as he turned off the gas burner. "I hope you're hungry."

"I am." Annabelle made her way toward her daughters and kissed each of them on the top of their heads. "Did you girls help make breakfast?"

"We made pancakes," Olivia said proudly.

"And bacon and chocolate milk." Sophie also beamed with pride.

"I made coffee, too." Cooper went over to the coffee maker and grabbed the pot. "Would you like some?"

"Yes please." She got the half and half out of the fridge. She'd given up the sugar, but not the cream. A dash of cinnamon helped.

"Did you sleep well?" he asked.

"Mostly." When she wasn't reliving the kiss and the way he'd pulled away so quickly afterward.

"Did you take anything for pain?"

"No. I'm afraid of feeling even more fuzzy-headed. And the over-the-counter stuff doesn't really help." She took a sip of her coffee, sighing at the rich flavor and aroma. "Besides, it's mostly just muscle aches. I'll feel better in a few days."

"I have this lotion I've used for sore muscles. It's all-natural, safe, and legal." Cooper's lips curled slightly at the last word. "It's got lavender, eucalyptus, rosemary, and a few other essential oils. I can run next door if you're interested."

"That would be great." Annabelle smiled at his never-ending thoughtfulness. "But eat first."

He helped the twins plate the pancakes and arranged the bacon on a paper towel-covered platter. The syrup was already warmed and placed on the table with the butter. After pouring himself another cup of coffee and waiting for Annabelle and the girls to sit down, he took the chair across from her.

"This is delicious." Annabelle savored her first bite. "Oh my goodness, you didn't make them from scratch did you?"

"Yeah." Cooper shrugged, as if it was no big deal. "I try to avoid processed foods as much as possible. I used whole wheat flour, organic buttermilk, and cage-free eggs."

"You'll have to give me the recipe. Or else come by every morning and cook for us."

"I do need a job." Cooper winked at her. "But I don't think you could afford me."

Something crackled between them. Attraction, sure, but there was something more. He had a secret. And it wasn't about the stack of magazines he kept by his bed.

"So how much do you charge?" She took another bite of the delicious whole-wheat pancakes.

"I recently turned down an offer for three million." He said it in such a way that she didn't think he was kidding.

"That's a little pricey for pancakes." Maybe he was a celebrity chef, and that was why he was so comfortable in her kitchen.

"Well, I'll start on the cleanup." Cooper rose, taking his empty plate and cup to the sink. He loaded the dishwasher and set the skillet in the sink to soak.

She watched him, fascinated by this man and his mysterious background. Judging by his build, he could be an athlete, but why would he keep that hidden from her? Most of the athletes she knew were only too happy to brag about themselves.

Olivia, who was happily licking syrup off her fork, would suggest that he was a prince, in hiding from being forced to marry a girl he didn't love. Oh dear, she really needed to wean that girl off her princess fantasies. They were becoming contagious.

"Mommy, can we go to the beach today?" Sophie asked. She was finishing off her third piece of bacon.

"Maybe this afternoon." If she felt up to it. But she didn't want to keep the girls inside all day, watching TV.

"Can Mr. Cooper come, too?" Sophie asked.

"I have some things I need to take care of." He turned from the sink. "Maybe some other time."

"Oh, okay." Annabelle hated to hear the disappointment in her daughter's voice. She hated her own disappointment even more. She was getting far too used to having him around.

"But I'll be at the bus stop when you girls get home from school tomorrow." Cooper offered a sincere smile. "I'm sure your mom will need to take it easy for the next few days. I'll be here as backup, okay?"

"Okay." Sophie's smiled widened.

Olivia stood and carried her plate to the sink. She handed it to Cooper with such admiration in her eyes, Annabelle was starting to think the princess obsession would quickly turn into a Cooper obsession. Or maybe that was her own fear. She could get attached to this man far too easily.

"I'll run and grab that lotion for you." Cooper wiped his hands on a dishcloth once the last of the dishes were loaded into the dishwasher. "You can use it after your shower."

"Yeah. Thanks. Are you going to stay and make sure I don't drop the bottle?" Annabelle swallowed, tempted by the thought of him rubbing the lotion on her sore muscles.

"I think you can manage." He folded his arms across his chest. "You did make it through the night just fine."

"Yeah. Just fine." Except for the longing that had kept her from getting enough sleep. He hadn't come into her room during the night. Was he also afraid of the sizzling attraction between them? That kiss. If it wasn't for her injuries, it could have easily burned out of control.

* * * *

Cooper went back to his place, took a long shower and tried not to think about Annabelle doing the same next door. He had to get the woman out of his head. Maybe he should have taken that offer from Toronto. Canada would be a lot better than somewhere like Japan and it would get him away from the lovely Annabelle Jones.

But if he wasn't here for her, she'd have no one. Or her ex-husband would have to take care of her. He couldn't let that happen. He hadn't spent too much time around Clayton Barry, but he didn't trust the man. The last time he'd seen his former owner had been shortly before his suspension. He'd made a compliment to Barry about his wife and the look on the other man's face was almost enough to make Cooper believe he'd been behind his surprise drug test. But that would be counterproductive, since Cooper's downfall had resulted in FITNatural's downfall, and the loss of large sums of money for Mr. Barry.

Maybe he felt a little guilty about his crush on Annabelle. He wanted to blame her husband for a mere coincidence. Because if she was his wife, he'd have a hard time with any man who even looked at her.

It was time to get back to work. He should hit the gym, find a mound to throw off. But he couldn't leave Annabelle and the girls alone. Those kids were something else. They'd chatted all morning while they were making breakfast—about their teacher, their favorite movies, and even how they got to see their Uncle Marco win the World Series, even though he wasn't really their uncle.

They talked a little bit about their dad, but it was clear they were much closer with their mother. They did mention he'd met them in Dallas for Christmas and had promised to take them to Disneyland when he finished his "hearing test" and sold his "vitamin company." He could only assume they meant the hearing for FITNatural and its involvement in the steroid scandal that had started with his own suspension. He wasn't about to correct them.

What would Annabelle think when she found out he was the one who'd brought her husband's side business to the attention of the league? And how much was the dissolving of the company going to hurt her and her children financially?

Had he truly believed his agent's assertion that turning in evidence against FITNatural would convince the league to reduce his suspension? Not when the new commissioner had taken office with the vow to clean up baseball "once and for all."

At least the union had prevented the hundred-game suspension for first-time offenders from passing before last season, but he was certain increases were coming. Not that it would have mattered. He'd missed that many games after all, with the fifty-game suspension and then the surgery that ended his season three days after the trade.

Cooper took his frustration with the whole mess out on his weight bench. He turned up the music and started lifting. More than he'd been lifting, but he had added frustrations to work out, especially with Annabelle so close. So close, yet so far out of his league.

The iPod shuffled to a quieter song and he thought he heard the doorbell.

Shit. Annabelle or the girls needed him. He dropped his weights and nearly sprinted to the door.

"Hi." Annabelle stood on his doorstep with a smile and the bottle of healing lotion. "I tried this stuff on my shoulder and it works. It really works."

"Good. I'm glad." He was also relieved she wasn't here for an emergency. "It's all-natural. Really, not just as an advertising claim. It's made by a little old lady from—"

"Pasadena?" She interrupted him with a wide grin and a twinkle in her beautiful blue eyes.

"No. Mendocino." Why did she have to be so great? Funny and sweet and appreciative. Why couldn't she be more like her ex? A spoiled, rich asshole.

"And have you met this little old lady personally?" She still had a smile on her face. Or most of her face, the left side didn't quite go up as much as her right, with the giant gash on her face.

He clenched his fists to keep from reaching for her. "Yes. I have. She was at a farmer's market and she charmed me into buying a whole case of the stuff."

"Well, I'm glad you did, because it really does help." Annabelle moved toward him, as if she wanted to come in. Or tell him a secret. "But I can't reach my back. Would you mind?"

Oh hell.

He stepped back so she could come in. She smelled of lavender and rosemary and eucalyptus and something even sweeter.

A hard rock song blasted from his weight room speakers.

"Let me go turn that off." He moved down the hallway and she followed.

Annabelle stopped in the doorway of the dining room he'd converted to a home gym and laughed. "Is that me? I don't remember them doing a poster of that cover."

"*They* didn't. I had it done." It had been ten years ago and he still hung the framed picture in every place he lived. "A buddy of mine worked at this place that could turn anything into a poster for twenty bucks."

"Twenty bucks, huh?" She gave him a look that might have been disapproving, if not for the way her eyes crinkled at the corners and her lips twitched trying to hold back a smile. "That's some pretty expensive artwork."

"I paid another thirty for the frame." He stood there feeling every bit the twenty-one-year-old who'd been so obsessed with Annabelle he'd convinced his friend to risk his job in making the poster when he didn't have the rights to the photo.

"Fifty bucks, huh. Quite an investment."

"I was young. I wanted to class up my first apartment." He wondered briefly if she would have been interested in him back then. Would she have even looked twice at an up-and-coming ballplayer who thought he was the next hot prospect?

"I was even younger." She approached the poster he had hanging over his weight bench. There was something almost wistful in her tone. "I was so young."

He watched her study herself and wondered what she must be thinking. Probably that he was some kind of stalker and she would be calling her lawyer when she got home.

"So you really do use me." She laughed, turning around to show an amused grin on her face. "Does that help you add cardio to your workouts?"

"Huh?" He was surprised at how lightly she was taking this.

"You know, getting your heart rate up?" Her gaze drew over him, settling just below his waist. "Among other things."

"Look, Annabelle, I didn't mean to…"

"To what? Get off on my picture?" Her gaze narrowed. "Objectify women?"

"I just liked the photo. I liked it a lot, so I had it blown up." He felt like a real jerk. "And I kept it because it reminds me of a time in my life when I didn't really know what the hell I was doing."

"And you think I did?" She laughed again. "I was so young. So naïve. It's hard to believe I'm the same person."

He moved closer to her. Couldn't help himself.

"Annabelle." His voice sounded funny to his own ears—strained—as if he couldn't believe he was standing here, with her, having this conversation with the one woman he'd always dreamed of. But she was real, and she was upset. "Look I'm sorry about the poster. I'll take it down."

She shook her head and stepped away from the picture.

"So could you rub this lotion on me?" She looked up at him, with such desperation in her eyes he wouldn't have refused if she'd asked him to pour gasoline on himself and set himself on fire.

He took the bottle of healing lotion, poured a generous amount in his hands, and took a deep breath when she turned around and lifted her shirt so he could apply it to her back.

"You're not wearing a bra." He was screwed. Totally screwed.

"Too constrictive." She groaned as he applied the lotion. "My ribs aren't broken, but they still hurt like you wouldn't believe."

"I'll be gentle." He rubbed slowly, gently, up and down her back. The moans of pleasure she made were almost his undoing.

She turned slightly and his hand slipped over her left breast.

Oh sweet lord.

"Not as perky as they once were." She looked up at him with fire in her eyes. It wasn't a mad kind of fire, not even an insulted kind of fire. But the most dangerous kind of fire. Desire.

"They're perfect." He dropped his hand before things could get any more out of control. "You're perfect."

"You think so?" She had just a hint of doubt in her voice. "Clayton offered to have them done. After the twins were born. He even booked the appointment, to celebrate their first birthday. Can you believe that?"

Cooper just shook his head. What kind of man couldn't appreciate a woman like Annabelle?

"I guess I wasn't good enough for him anymore." Her voice held a small quiver of regret. "Well, I should get back to my girls. They're watching a movie and I hate to use the TV as a babysitter."

He grunted, not trusting himself with words. He wanted her now more than ever, but she deserved so much more than he could give.

"Oh, thanks for the lotion." She gave him a shy smile. "Can I keep it?"

She held out her hand and he placed the bottle in her palm.

"I'm glad you have that poster." She nodded toward the wall. "It makes me think you're not all alone over here."

She smiled one more time before turning and walking out his front door.

* * * *

As she walked the short distance to her house, Annabelle shook her head. He had a giant poster of her first swimsuit cover. She should have been offended. Six years ago, she would have been offended. Back when she was struggling with her identity as a new mom and wife to the man who always introduced her as the "former supermodel." A man who had made it painfully clear he no longer found her attractive. She wasn't joking about the boob job Clayton had tried to give her as a *gift* once the twins were weaned. He'd hinted that he would be more than happy to pay for a tummy tuck at the same time.

Six days ago she might have been offended. But then again, the whole purpose of that picture was to sell magazines. The kind of magazine people kept, not tossed aside after reading the articles. He'd not only kept the magazines, he'd had the cover blown up into a poster he'd carried around for ten years.

Maybe she should be flattered. Her neighbor still found her attractive. That much was very clear. Even though she was no longer nineteen, with perfectly perky breasts and flawless skin. She gently touched her stitches. She'd have to go back to the doctor to have them removed in a couple of days. And she'd have to ask Cooper for a ride. Unless she wanted to take the bus. Hopefully the doctor would clear her for driving again. But…

She closed her eyes trying to remember something, anything from the accident. What if she couldn't get behind the wheel? She lived in California. She needed a car. Sure, she could hire a service, but she'd never really liked the idea of a stranger driving her around. And stepping out of a limo to pick up a few groceries seemed a little much.

Annabelle had really hoped to reestablish her modeling career before the end of the new year. She'd hoped for a reliable income stream so she could save the settlement money for the girls' future. They would go to college. She'd make sure of it. Her daughters would have choices that she'd never had.

They wouldn't have to rely on the wrong man. Or even the right man, who happened to come into their lives at the wrong time.

"Mommy, can we go to the beach now?" Sophie was less content than her sister to watch movies all day long. "*Please.*"

"I think we could go for a little while. Maybe pack a picnic lunch." Annabelle was feeling much better thanks to Cooper's magic lotion. The one made by the little old lady from Mendocino.

"Are you sure we can't invite Cooper?" Her daughters were almost as smitten with the man as she was.

"No, sweetie. He's been great. I just don't want him to feel like we're imposing on him too much."

"Oh." Olivia's expression was one of mock understanding. Then she tilted her head to the side. "What's 'imposing'?"

"It means getting in his way, disrupting his life."

"Were we imposing on Daddy?" Sophie asked. "Is that why he moved to Florida? Did we erupt his life?"

"Oh honey. No." Annabelle pulled her daughter into a hug. They were quickly joined by Olivia. "No, you girls had absolutely nothing to do with your father and I getting a divorce."

They may have been the reason they'd gotten married in the first place, but they had nothing to do with the divorce. If anything, they were the reason she'd stayed as long as she had.

"Sometimes he'd get mad when we erupted his work." Sophie needed more assurance.

"Interrupted." Olivia corrected her sister. "A volcano erupts, like the one that killed the dinosaurs."

"A steroid killed the dinosaurs." Sophie argued. "Not a volcano. It was a big rock from outer space that crashed into the ocean making them all drown."

"Girls. Do you want to go to the beach or do you want to argue about why the dinosaurs became extinct?" Annabelle loved the way they each stood their ground, like two little scientists arguing over theories. They were already smarter than she was. Or at least, they were smarter than she'd ever been encouraged to be.

"The beach!" Both girls stopped their argument and rushed upstairs to get their swimsuits on. It still amused her to think they could wear swimsuits in January. There was only about a ten to fifteen degree difference in temperature, but it felt so much warmer down here than in San Francisco. They often wore fleece sweatshirts to the beach in San Francisco even in the summer. And they didn't swim in the ocean. Sure they'd dip their toes in the water, explore tide pools, and fly kites at the beach. Swimming was something they did at the tennis club.

Still, she grabbed the girls' sweaters. Just in case.

The excitement on her daughters' faces was reassuring. Moving down here had been the right thing to do. Even if her modeling career wasn't going to take off. The change had been just what they'd all needed to be happy, healthy, and healing.

Chapter 7

Even knowing Annabelle had promised to take her daughters to the be ach that afternoon, Cooper felt a jolt straight through him at the sight of them enjoying the sun and the sand. Annabelle was stretched out on one of those low-slung beach chairs with a big floppy hat protecting her delicate skin. Olivia, wearing a pink swimsuit, and Sophie, in green, were happily digging in the sand just above the waterline.

He couldn't not stop by and see how they were doing.

"Hey, how's everything going?" He stood above her with the sun on his back.

Annabelle held a hand up to shade her eyes, even though she wore those oversized sunglasses that were practically required gear in Southern California.

"Good." She smiled when she recognized him. "Just soaking in the fresh air and sunshine."

"Well, enjoy." He turned back toward his house but Sophie ran up to him holding a ball and a glove.

"Will you play catch with me?" she pleaded. "Olivia just wants to build castles, but I want to play catch and Mommy's gotta rest."

He swallowed, looking down at her earnest expression. She wanted to play a game of catch. Something that had once come as natural to him as breathing.

"Please?" She tilted her head to one side, big blue eyes shining so much like her mother's.

"Sure. I just need to grab my glove." He swallowed the twenty pound rosin bag that had lodged in his throat.

"You can use Olivia's" She held out her sister's tiny brand-new glove—a Christmas gift, maybe.

"Don't think so." He knelt down, inspecting the stiff unbroken leather. "It's too small, for one thing. And I'm left-handed. I wear my glove on the other hand."

"Oh." She sounded slightly disappointed. "I thought it was because it's pink."

"I'll be right back." He stood up, patted her on the top of her head, and jogged back to his place.

He opened the hall closet where he kept his equipment, shoved in the back where it couldn't mock him. He unzipped the bag and reached for his trusted companion. He held the leather up to his nose and inhaled. For the first time in a long time, the smell didn't make his stomach churn. It was familiar. Comforting, even.

He put it on. Yep. It still fit. Fit like a…like an extension of his hand. He punched the pocket, just as he'd done thousands of times. When he didn't see spots dance in front of his eyes, he figured he could do this. He could play a simple game of catch.

Cooper grabbed an extra ball and zipped up the bag. He toed the closet door closed and headed out the front door feeling as if his left arm wasn't a thousand pounds heavier than it should be.

"What took you so long?" Sophie stood with one gloved hand on her hip, the other dangling at her side, the ball nestled in her palm.

Had to slay a few demons, milady.

"Took me a few minutes to find my glove," he lied. It was his courage he'd had to rummage around for.

"Well let's go then, we're burning daylight." Sophie popped the ball into her glove as if she'd been born to play. He could picture her with a wad of bubble gum in her mouth and her cap pulled low over her forehead.

Crouching down a few feet in front of her, he held his glove up, ready for her to make a soft toss. He'd spent a few years working with kids as part of the Harrison Foundation's minicamp. But those kids had been a little older, like nine to twelve. And they hadn't been miniature versions of Annabelle Jones.

Sophie did an exaggerated windup, curled her gloved hand in front of her, scrunched her face up with all the seriousness of the most hardened veteran, and hurled the ball toward him. It sailed over his head and he jogged off after it.

He could hear Annabelle's laughter behind him as he picked up the ball. He brushed the sand off on his shorts and then prepared to throw a baseball for the first time since his surgery. For the first time since he'd blown out his shoulder in that disastrous appearance in St. Louis.

Okay, so a soft toss into the glove of a six-year-old was hardly the same as the mid-nineties fastball he'd wielded so effectively in his prime. But if he couldn't get past his mental block, his prime was over. His career would be over.

He held the ball, feeling the raised stitches as he turned it over in his palm, trying to find the right grip. He glanced over at Annabelle who watched with hopeful anticipation. She reached up and touched her own stitches, almost subconsciously, as if she didn't realize she was doing it.

Cooper tossed the ball softly to Sophie. It landed in her glove and she clapped her hand over it.

"I caught it." She squealed in delight. "I caught it. Did you see that, Mommy? I caught it."

Annabelle clapped and watched Sophie throw the ball back to him. This time she underthrew it and he had to lunge forward to snag it just before it hit the sand.

"That's great, honey." Annabelle praised her daughter's triumph. What she didn't realize was that it was an even bigger accomplishment for him.

A few more tosses back and forth, and he no longer felt like a fraud. He could pick up a ball and his arm didn't fall off. His head didn't explode, and an angry mob didn't come after him with pitchforks calling him names.

Cheater. Imposter. Loser.

"Can I play, too?" Olivia abandoned her sandcastle and picked up her pink glove. Soon they were engaged in a three-way toss. Eventually the two girls became more comfortable playing with each other and he faded into the background.

He stood there marveling at the joy the two of them found in a simple game of catch. It wasn't about money or fame or winning at all costs. It was about having fun. They were *playing* ball. Something he'd forgotten how to do a long time ago.

Baseball had once been something he played. Because it was fun. It got him out of the house. Away from his father's anger, his sister's nagging, and the fear that he'd somehow been the reason his mother had left.

At some point, baseball had become more than a game. It had become his ticket to making something of himself. It had been a long shot, but for someone like him, it had been everything.

And he'd pissed it away.

"It's hot." Sophie drew her gloved hand across her forehead. "Can we go in the water?"

"Yeah, can we?" Olivia hadn't been playing as long, but she seemed just as eager to cool off.

It had to be at least seventy degrees out. Not exactly sweltering, but warm enough to dip their toes in the water.

"Sure. Just don't go in too deep," Annabelle warned.

They dropped their gloves and the ball on the beach blanket and dashed off toward the water.

* * * *

"Would you like to sit down?" Annabelle craned her neck to invite Cooper to join her.

"No. I'm okay." He seemed distant as he looked out over the ocean.

"Well, then can you help me up?" She reached out her hand. "I'm getting a stiff neck trying to talk to you."

"Sure." He grabbed her hand and pulled her into a standing position.

"How tall are you again?" She stretched, her muscles tight from sitting for so long.

"Six-three."

She filed the information into her memory, along with the fact that he was left-handed, and all the other little details she'd noticed about him. He liked Thai food and classic rock. He played his guitar on his porch at night and had turned his dining room into a home gym. The man bought all-natural healing lotion from the farmer's market and kept old magazines in his bedside drawer.

She focused on the little bits of information she knew about him. Maybe she was afraid of forgetting. Or maybe she was afraid of finding out his secret.

"Thanks for playing catch with Sophie and Olivia." She looked over at him, noting how he held his glove almost reverently.

He glanced down at the well-worn mitt and smiled. "Anytime."

He tossed it on the blanket next to the girls' gloves and stretched his arms overhead.

Oh my. His shirt stretched across his broad chest and clung to sculpted shoulders. The high tech fabric was designed to wick away moisture, but there were a few spots darkened by perspiration. A slight breeze tickled her nose and she could smell him. The salt from sweat and the sea air. A faint scent of leather that seemed to fit him. And that certain something that was unique to him alone.

Desire swept over her like a rogue wave. She wanted this man. This mysterious yet kind, strong but gentle man who'd come to her rescue and played with her daughters.

She swept her gaze out over the water, trying to get her thoughts back to where they belonged.

"Oh, Sophie's getting a little too far out." Her gut tightened. She should have been keeping a better eye on her children instead of letting her mind wander to where it had no business going.

"I'll get her." Cooper moved with an astonishing quickness. One minute he was standing next to her, sending off powerful pheromones. The next he was racing into the ocean, scooping Sophie up just as a giant wave came crashing over her.

She sputtered and coughed and clung to his neck. Olivia ran up to him from where she was playing in the shallower water. She threw her arms around his waist and followed him and her sister up the beach to dry land.

"You saved her." Olivia's eyes were wide with fear and awe. "You're a hero."

"Th-th-thank you." Sophie's voice was thick with fright. She buried her head into his neck, sobbing.

"You're fine." He patted her wet, matted hair. "Come on, let's get a cold drink and then we'll go back out. This time, I'll show you how to dive under those big waves."

He lowered her to the blanket while Annabelle reached into the cooler for Sophie's water bottle. She wasn't sure if she liked the idea of him taking Sophie back out there, but realized that he was only trying to get her to face her fears.

Besides, he'd be right there with her. He would protect her. And Olivia, too.

Sophie emptied her water bottle, calming with each swallow.

"Are you ready?" Cooper stood tall and strong, extending a hand to both girls. He walked slowly toward the surf with her daughters. They both stared up at him with rapt attention, as if he held all the secrets to the universe. They would believe anything he told them. If he told them they could become mermaids, they'd grow tails and swim away.

He eased them back into the water. A couple of times, the girls clung to him when the bigger swells reached their knees. But he was patient and steady and strong. Eventually the girls let go of his hand. They frolicked in the surf, jumping and squealing, and having a blast. And yes, they did learn how to dive under the bigger waves, popping up like otters on the other side.

They played in the water for about twenty minutes before Cooper chased the girls back up the beach. He tore off his wet T-shirt and

Annabelle gasped. Just loud enough that he heard her and gave her a naughty little smile when she tossed him an extra towel.

"Thank you," she mouthed as she turned to dry off her daughters.

"Anytime." The way he looked at her—no, he looked right through her—she got the feeling he was talking about taking off his shirt, not saving Sophie from the ocean and then keeping her from becoming afraid.

"Stay for dinner?" She couldn't help but ask.

"What are you making?"

"I don't know yet. I'll have to check my pantry." She realized she hadn't done her usual Saturday grocery shopping.

"I'm sure between the two of us we could cook up something tasty."

"Yeah. I'm sure we could." But nothing edible.

* * * *

His hands were trembling by the time they got all the beach stuff packed up and carried back to Annabelle's house. They hung the wet beach towels over the porch railing and stomped off as much sand as possible before going through the back door into her sunny kitchen.

"Let's see…food." Annabelle tossed her sun hat on the counter and pulled open the refrigerator. She bent over at the waist, rummaging through her available produce. "I have some chicken breasts. And carrots…"

He tore his eyes away from her perfect ass. Glancing around her kitchen, he spied some lemons in a bowl on the counter.

"We could make soup." He had some kale that was starting to wilt. And he always kept onions, garlic, and some organic chicken broth in his pantry. "I have some vegetables we could throw in there. Maybe some barley."

"Barley?" Annabelle gave him a quizzical look. "For chicken soup?"

"I guess your kids aren't big barley fans."

"No. They probably won't eat much of the vegetables either." She put the chicken and carrots on the counter and crossed the room.

"I imagine the kids would prefer pasta." He tried to avoid processed foods, choosing whole grains when possible.

"Yeah, I think I have some Annie's." Annabelle pulled a purple box of organic macaroni and cheese out of the pantry. "Could we use this?"

"I'm not sure about the cheese packet, though."

Laughing, she walked over to him and gave him a shove. "Don't be silly. I'll save that to make a double batch next time."

"I'll run next door and grab a few things." Such as the vegetables and a quick, cold shower. He almost wished he had a bottle of wine to bring over, but then he remembered Annabelle had suffered a head injury.

And this wasn't a date.

So what was he doing combining Annabelle's chicken with his vegetables? Was he trying to merge their two households and create some kind of family?

No. Stupid to even think such a thought.

He couldn't leave them to starve, though. Yeah, right. Like Annabelle couldn't pick up the phone and have anything she wanted delivered. She wasn't helpless. She didn't really need him. He was just convenient, an easy solution to a problem, a quick fix.

He just hoped she wouldn't come to regret using him.

Chapter 8

It was far too comfortable working side by side with Cooper, making homemade chicken soup. Who would have thought adding lemon zest, thyme, and kale could turn a plain soup into something special? She was starting to think three million would be perfectly reasonable to hire the man as a personal chef.

He'd actually got her children to eat green vegetables and ask for seconds. She'd more than expected them to pick out the chicken and the pasta shells and leave the rest behind. They normally didn't eat anything green—not even green Skittles.

Once again, she handled the bathing, and Cooper took care of the kitchen cleanup. He was just wiping the counter when she came back downstairs.

"I'll run over and get my guitar." He folded the towel and hung it on the oven door handle. "For bedtime songs."

"They're already asleep." Annabelle brushed her hair off her forehead. "They had a busy afternoon."

"Yeah. They did." Cooper leaned against the counter. An awkwardness rose between them now that they both realized they were essentially alone.

"I can't thank you enough…"

"Stop." He moved just a little bit closer. "I've heard this one already. I'm no hero."

She inched toward him, her heart beating faster. "You saved Sophie. That makes you a hero in my book. "

"I'm sure it looked like a bigger wave than it was. Sophie's a pretty strong girl." The space between them seemed to dissipate. "Like her mother."

"I'm not that strong."

"Yes you are. You're stronger than you think."

"I wish that were true."

"Annabelle." He said her name with a breathless intensity. Sexy. Exotic. Almost musical.

"I like the way you say my name." She smiled, tilting her head slightly. "I've always thought my name was a little, oh, I don't know, kind of silly."

"Silly?" He raised an eyebrow, as if the idea was ridiculous.

"You know, frivolous." How could she explain? "No one expects much of me. Other than to look pretty and not say much."

"Like a picture in a magazine?"

Yes. Exactly.

"Annabelle." He said her name again. But he was very serious. "You are so much more than a pretty face."

Her hand went to the side of her not-so-pretty face. She winced as her fingers grazed the stitches.

Cooper bent his head and brushed the lightest of kisses on her left temple.

Her eyes fluttered closed when he moved his lips across her cheek. Finally his lips found hers. He was very serious now as he slipped his tongue into her mouth.

She wrapped her arms around him, pressing her body against his. There was nothing silly about what was happening between them, nothing superficial. Oh no, things were about to get very deep.

Annabelle reached up to pull him closer, clutching his hair in both hands. She thrust her tongue into his mouth, taking control of the kiss. She wanted this. Needed this.

His arms circled her waist. Slipping his hands beneath her T-shirt, he caressed her lower back, careful not to bump her ribs. She arched into him, wanting to get closer. Wanting to feel him, to feel everything.

Cooper broke the kiss. "Are you sure you want this?"

She answered by capturing his mouth, kissing him harder, deeper than before.

"I'm not this great guy you think I am." He pulled away again, his breath ragged. "I'm not a hero, you know."

"You got my kids to eat vegetables." She moved in to nuzzle his neck. Enough with the *I'm such a bad guy* stuff.

"Annabelle." He groaned when she flicked her tongue across the skin just behind his ear. "I don't know how long I'll be here. If I get a job... I could end up moving across country. Or even..."

She tried to shut him up by kissing him on the mouth. He gave in for a moment but pulled back again.

"I'm not looking for anything long-term, if that's what you're worried about." She realized they weren't going to get anywhere until he was sure of her expectations. "Hell, my divorce isn't even final, so…"

"You're a married woman." He took two steps back, but it might as well have been two miles.

"Only on paper." She shook her head. "My marriage has been over for a long time, but the state of California hasn't figured that out yet."

"Look, I can't… I can't be that guy." He moved toward the door. "I'm sorry, Annabelle."

This time when he said her name, it was with such regret she wondered if she'd ever see him again.

* * * *

The next morning, Cooper stood at Annabelle's front door four heartbeats away from panic. He'd knocked three times and rang the doorbell twice. No answer. He was about ready to call 9-1-1 when he heard footsteps behind him.

"Cooper, can I help you with something?" Annabelle was coming up the walk, her face a little flushed. It could be embarrassment over what happened last night, or maybe it was from exertion.

"I thought you might need me to drive Sophie and Olivia to school."

"They take the bus." She tilted her head slightly.

Right. He knew that.

"Oh, okay." He stood there waiting for her to tell him to get lost. She didn't need him anymore. Not after last night.

He started down the porch steps, but only got as far as the sidewalk that ran in front of both of their places.

"Hey, about last night…" He turned back, putting one foot on the bottom step. "I'm sorry."

He waited, hoping she wouldn't tell him to go to hell.

"I'd invite you in for some tea, but I'm all out." She gave him an apologetic smile.

"Annabelle." Just saying her name made his heart do this funny little stutter. It was almost like coming into a game with runners on and nobody out. He could save the day or he could end up making things worse. "Can I explain?"

She shrugged and unlocked the front door.

He followed, part of him wishing he didn't give a damn. He'd had the chance to make love to Annabelle Jones. But he'd blown it. He was just trying to do the right thing and he'd ended up hurting her.

"So…" She tossed her keys into a colorful bowl on the side table. "Explain."

Where did he start? He glanced at the bookcase. Scattered amongst the many paperbacks and knick-knacks were photos of the twins. Their smiling faces, so innocent and trusting, staring back at him.

"My parents split up when I was eight." He shoved his hands in the pockets of his jeans. "My mom left. She left me and my sister and my dad to run off with some guy she'd known only a few weeks."

"I'm so sorry." Annabelle shifted, leaning toward him but not quite reaching for him.

"I can't be that guy." He hated how much it still hurt. And pissed him off that she'd chosen some stranger over her family. Her kids. She'd chosen a guy she ended up leaving for the next guy. And then the next…

"I didn't leave my husband for you." She crossed her arms over her chest. "I married him for my father. Stayed with him for my daughters. But leaving him? That was something I did for myself."

She turned her back toward him.

Yeah. He'd just made the situation worse. Like hanging a slider right over the plate.

"I'll go." He took a step toward the door.

"No. Wait." She placed her hand on his arm. But it wasn't the friendly touching she'd done last night. "I really am out of tea. And I need to pick up some milk and cereal and a few other things. I could use one of those online grocery services, but I like to be able to check out the produce for myself and…"

"I need to head to the store anyways." He felt like he did when the long ball he'd just dished up sailed foul by just a few inches, relieved to get another chance. "You can tag along."

"That would be great." She tried to fake a smile, but it seemed like too much effort. Especially with the stitches on the left side of her face.

"When do you go back to the doctor?"

"I'll make an appointment for later this week to get my stitches out."

"Let me know what time."

"I can find another way…"

"I don't mind." He hated the realization that he'd pushed her away. "I'd be more than happy to take you."

"You're not afraid I'll think you're some kind of hero?" Her smile returned, the real one. The one that had just a bit of devil behind the face of an angel.

"I think we both know I'm not." He moved toward the door. "So when do you want to head to the store?"

"How about now?" She gave him a challenging stare. "I'll just grab my purse."

"Sure. I'll meet you in my driveway." He let himself out so he could grab his car keys.

He was somewhat relieved that she still needed him. She couldn't possibly want him, not after last night. But at least she still needed him. And there was a part of him that preferred it that way.

Once upon a time, he'd had no problem with hooking up with a woman for short term mutual satisfaction. No strings. No promises. He was a relief pitcher—come in on short notice, get the job done, and get out as quickly as possible. It worked for baseball and it worked for women. Or it had.

Now he'd completely lost his mojo. He couldn't let things take their natural course with a beautiful, willing, if not quite single woman. And until yesterday he couldn't even pick up a baseball.

He'd tossed the ball around with Annabelle's daughters. Not that it was in any way physically challenging. But he'd gotten past a mental block. He didn't feel bile rise in the back of his throat at the smell of glove leather. His fingers didn't burn when he touched the raised red stitching on the ball. And his vision didn't blur when he brought the two together. Ball to glove. Glove to chest. Shifting his weight to make the motion that had once come as natural as breathing.

If he could manage a game of catch, maybe he could manage to spend the next few days with Annabelle. Just until she got back on her feet.

Then he could focus on his game. His career. Then he could get back to his real life.

When Annabelle didn't appear within a few minutes, he started to worry, and walked up the back steps, ready to knock on the kitchen door. He peeked through the window and saw Annabelle on the phone. Relaxing, he went back to wait for her at his car. He leaned against the black Escalade as if he had all day.

Hell, he did have all day. He had less than a month before teams would start reporting to spring training. Without him. He should have taken Toronto's offer. But at the time, three million had been a slap in the face. If he hadn't screwed up, he could have easily asked for five. If he'd been healthy and clean he would have gotten it, probably before winter meetings had started in December.

He had plenty of time on his hands. Time in which he might have to start thinking about a second career. Music seemed the obvious choice, but he wasn't sure he wanted to ruin it by turning it into a job. He enjoyed playing an occasional gig, but really his music was something he did to relax, to relieve the pressure of a long season in the bullpen.

"Sorry." Annabelle swept down the steps wearing her trademark oversized sunglasses and another form-fitting warm-up suit. This one was a pale pink, softly hugging her every curve. "My agent called and I needed to get him up to speed."

"No problem." He knew what it took to keep an agent from freaking out, especially when having to report a physical setback. "How did it go?"

She stepped back. He almost expected her to retreat into her house.

"He wished me well and he pretended not to hear the part about my face being scarred beyond repair."

"You might heal just fine." They both knew that wouldn't be the case. She'd still be beautiful, of that he had no doubt, but hardly photo-worthy. He had a better shot of re-signing with the Goliaths than she did of getting another modeling job. "Maybe there is some kind of cream or oil you could try to eliminate the scarring."

"I'll never be the same." She brushed an imaginary strand of hair off her face. "But I guess I'll just have to move on."

"Annabelle…"

"Don't say my name. Please. Not like that." She stood, waiting for him to unlock the passenger door.

"What should I call you then? Hey you? Ms. Jones?" he asked. "Or should I call you Mrs. Barry?"

"Not that." She folded her arms across her chest. "Anything but that."

"Okay…"

"I never took his name." She stared off over his shoulder. Or that's where she seemed to be looking, it was hard to tell under her dark shades. "I used my career as an excuse, but I guess I always knew it wasn't a sure thing. Our marriage."

It was none of his business, even if he felt less guilty knowing her marriage hadn't been the happiest.

He pressed the button to unlock the door and held it open while she climbed in. Then he went around the front of the SUV and got behind the wheel.

"So can you get everything you need at Whole Foods or will we need to make more than one stop?" He stabbed the key into the ignition, not wanting to look at her. She was too beautiful. Too fragile. Too everything.

"I guess we'll find out soon enough." She clicked her seatbelt into place, wincing slightly as she strapped the belt over her hips.

He checked the mirrors before pulling into the street. This was going to be one hell of a long day.

* * * *

That wasn't as awkward as she'd feared it would be. Annabelle had stocked up on enough groceries to last more than a week, if the organic produce held up that long. Cooper had left her to complete her shopping on her own, but she'd noticed he never strayed too far. He kept enough distance that she didn't feel like he was hovering, but he remained close enough that he could come to her rescue if she needed him.

Fortunately, she was tall enough not to need his help reaching for items on the top shelf. And she even managed to keep from slipping in some spilled juice. No surprise that Cooper had immediately alerted the manager after she wheeled her cart around the mess. It gave her an extra five minutes to wander three aisles over and catch her breath. She hated being so dependent on him. But she couldn't very well carry on with no food in the house. She had her pride, but her daughters came first. They needed fresh fruit and milk. They needed food for their lunches and afterschool snacks.

"Do you need any help getting everything put away?" Cooper had insisted on loading her groceries in the back of his SUV and carrying all seven bags into the house.

"No. I can manage." She was more than ready for a little space. Especially since he'd made it very clear they could only be friends. The only benefits would be his chauffeur service. "I need something to keep me busy anyway."

"Well, let me know if you need anything." He stood near the door, acting as if he didn't quite want to leave.

"I know where to find you." He was too close. She wished he would leave already, so she could stop trying to be brave and strong. "Besides, I have to call the insurance company, the doctor's office…"

"You will let me know what time your appointment is." It wasn't a question, but a demand.

"Don't you have things to do besides be at my beck and call?" She was starting to get irritated.

"Nothing that can't wait."

"I thought you were looking for a job." She crossed her arms over her chest, hoping he didn't notice her wince when she bumped her ribs. "Or are you trying to play me?"

"I'm not trying to play you, Annabelle." A look of regret passed over his face. "I would never use you like that."

He wouldn't use her any other way, either.

"Well, good." She relaxed her stance, letting her arms fall to her sides. "Because if you're hoping to get a piece of my fortune, you can forget it."

"I don't want your money." He moved closer, his voice lowering. "I could never take money I didn't earn."

There was something about the way he spoke that made her wonder if he was talking more to himself. She knew he'd made a lot of money in his former career, but got the feeling he wasn't proud of his wealth. Maybe he'd worked for a corporation that was involved in something he was morally opposed to. Exploiting child labor, for instance, or taking a homophobic stance on same-sex marriage.

Or maybe he'd inherited his money, perhaps from the mother who'd abandoned him at eight years old.

"Well, thanks again for the ride." Annabelle knew she was in no position to press him for more information. Whatever it was, he was convinced it made him a bad guy, even though his actions had shown just the opposite.

"What are neighbors for?" He gave her a half-smile and took a step back.

Neighbors. She'd just have to get used to the idea that's all they'd be.

She sighed as she watched him head back to his place. He sure did fill out a pair of jeans. And the way he tortured that T-shirt, stretching it to the max. But she'd learned a long time ago that having a beautiful body didn't guarantee happiness.

Chapter 9

"Coop! It's about time you dragged your sorry ass down here." Bruce Sanders met him at the door of Sanders Baseball Academy. He pulled Cooper into a hearty embrace and slapped him on the back a couple times for good measure. "I was starting to wonder if you were just blowing me off. Like my facilities aren't good enough for you."

"I've been working out at home, mostly." Guilt at avoiding his friend and former teammate gnawed at him.

"Keeping a low profile, huh?" His buddy gave him a friendly shove on his good shoulder. "Don't have to worry about being interrupted by fans or groupies?"

"I haven't had to worry about either in a long time." The two of them had been in the minors together. They'd been battery mates. Sanders had been one hell of a catcher and mentor. "The Colonel" was a mastermind behind the plate. He studied hitters and was always ready with a battle plan. Cooper didn't think he would have developed as a pitcher without Sanders' help.

"Well, let's get you back on track." His friend welcomed him with another hearty back slap. "Get you back on the mound where you belong."

"I just want to throw a little today." Cooper waited for his stomach to clench at the thought. But he felt fine. Almost normal. "Work my way up to getting back on the hill."

"You haven't been throwing, yet?" Sanders gave him a skeptical look. They both knew he was behind schedule if he wanted to show up to spring training in any kind of playing shape. If he could manage to get a contract.

"Been focusing on building my strength." Or avoiding the possibility that he'd never be the same pitcher. "The doctor is very pleased with the repair. Says I should have no trouble returning to full strength by the time the season starts. But the worst thing I could do would be to rush my recovery."

Sanders gave him a stare. He could smell bullshit a mile away.

"What's really going on, man?"

"I'll tell you everything"—Cooper rolled his shoulders, anxious to get started— "after I make my throws."

"Okay. I'll get Brandon to suit up. My nephew's playing college ball, now. He's one hell of a catcher." Sanders had adopted the boy when his sister was killed in a boating accident.

"You could probably handle me," Cooper joked. A collision at the plate had ended The Colonel's career shortly after being called up to AAA ball. He'd been so close to his dream. Cooper sometimes wondered how he managed to live with himself. "I'm not throwing hard. Yet."

"Still, I'll let the kid warm you up." Sanders led the way through the facility to the back, where there was plenty of space to warm up. "He's better than I ever was. And he's got a couple of weeks before he goes back to college. He's a sophomore, so he thinks he knows everything. He needs to spend a little time with someone who's been there."

"You don't want me as a role model for the kid." He was no hero. Not by a long shot.

"We'll talk. After you warm up." Sanders shook his head. He'd been trying for years to get Cooper to at least consider joining him as a consultant once his playing days were over. He really wanted Cooper to become one of his coaches for his year-round baseball academy. He had a good staff of former minor league players. Guys who'd almost made it, but for whatever reason hadn't gone all the way.

Cooper had made it. And he'd pissed it away.

"Sure." He stretched his neck and shoulders, trying to get loose, and trying to get Annabelle out of his head. She was a married woman. But even if she wasn't, she deserved better than a guy who'd been so careless with the gifts he'd been given.

"Nathan Cooper." Brandon approached Cooper with his hand extended. "My uncle's told me a lot about you."

The young man stood a little taller than his uncle—probably six-one—a nice looking kid with a bright future ahead of him.

"He's full of shit." Cooper shook the kid's hand. "Don't believe half of his stories about our playing days."

"Oh I know he exaggerated his accomplishments," the kid played along. "But you're the real deal, man."

Was.

"So you're trying to get back in shape, huh?" Brandon bobbed his head, trying to play it cool. "It's a real honor to be able to work with you."

Kristina Mathews

"Don't you watch ESPN?" He couldn't let the young man idolize him. "I've dishonored the game. I'm just trying to see if I'm not a complete fraud."

Brandon blew out a breath, as if he'd been sucker-punched, but he shook it off. "Let's get to work, then."

The kid wasn't rattled. He just grabbed his gear bag and began putting on his knee pads and chest protector. He stuck his hand in his catcher's mitt and crouched down behind the plate, pulled down his mask, and popped his fist into his glove.

It was now or never. Time to find out if he still had it. Cooper grabbed a ball from the bucket his friend had set next to the practice mound.

"I'm going to start slow," he announced. "I haven't thrown much since the surgery."

"Sure." Brandon nodded, but remained in the ready position. The kid was a gamer.

Cooper stood a few feet in front of the rubber. His legs were a little shaky, but they held him upright.

He threw a soft toss toward his target, not even close to full speed. The kid had to reach up to catch it, but he had no trouble making the grab. He stood and tossed it back. Cooper caught it, and without even having to think, he threw back. Toss after toss until he was almost comfortable. Almost. He still couldn't step up to the mound, though. He needed to get his muscles used to throwing in general before he could push himself to pitch.

But he was running out of time. There was less than a month until the first pitchers started reporting. And he didn't have a contract, or an invitation to camp. He didn't have shit.

But he had made a giant step forward. He was able to play a game of catch. A real game of catch with an up-and-coming ballplayer.

"Thanks." Cooper took one last toss from the catcher. "I think I'm good here."

"Anytime." Brandon removed his mask, and walked over to shake hands, but with Cooper's glove on his right hand and Brandon's mitt on his left, it was a little awkward. Both men removed their gloves at the same time. The kid tried to extend his left hand at the same time Cooper extended his right. They both gave a nod and Cooper patted Brandon on the shoulder.

"You're a good catcher, you'll go far."

"Thanks." Brandon smiled, almost as if he was embarrassed by the compliment.

"I mean it. I can see why your uncle is always bragging about you."

"It's his job." Color rose in the kid's cheeks. "He has to brag about me. But if we're lucky, I'll make up for him not making it."

Brandon nodded toward Sanders, who'd been watching the whole time.

"How old are you, kid?"

"Twenty."

"Going on forty." His uncle added with a father's proud grin. "And he'll make it. But not for me. He'll make it because he's good. Real good. And that's not just family pride talking."

"You've got talent." Cooper hoped the kid understood how rare and special he was. "Keep your nose clean. Respect the game. Respect those who came before you. And be an example for those who come after you."

"I'll do my best." Brandon stood with his mask tucked under his arm, looking much older and wiser than a twenty-year-old. Maybe it was because, unlike most kids his age, he knew it took more than talent to make it. It took hard work, dedication, and a whole lot of luck. He also knew it could disappear just like that. One play could end the dream.

Cooper wondered what would have happened if he'd been the one to have his career cut short just one step below the majors. He had no doubt that his friend would have been one hell of a big league ballplayer. And he would have walked away rather than do anything that would tarnish his legacy. He never would have been tempted by the dark side.

"Thanks again." Cooper couldn't even begin to explain how good today had felt. He was starting to think that maybe, just maybe, he could at least get an invitation to camp. At this point, making a team was only secondary to proving to himself that he could still perform.

"Anytime." Brandon started gathering the equipment, putting stuff away while the two older men headed toward the front of the building.

"Wanna grab a beer and talk?" Sanders asked.

"I haven't had a beer in over a year." He hadn't touched anything stronger than coffee since the suspension. "Trying to keep my nose clean."

"I still can't believe you got mixed up in all that." Sanders shook his head. They'd come up together. Watched guys try to gain an advantage. Try to cheat their way to the top. "You're the last guy I ever would have thought…"

"Yeah. Me too." He'd been one of the most vocal opponents of doping. "But I was desperate, man. I saw my career slipping away. My shoulder…"

"That bad?"

"No. that's the problem. It wasn't bad enough to need surgery—or so I thought. But it still hurt." Cooper ran his hands over his face. "I tried everything. Exercise. Yoga. I even tried acupuncture, but by the last month of the season, I could barely lift a beer after a game."

"Your trainers couldn't help?"

"I was cocky. Thought I could man up. Power through." What an idiot he'd been. "I'd been taking these nutritional supplements. Legitimate stuff. And they'd helped for energy. Stamina, if you know what I mean. I was off to a real good start."

"Yeah, you were lights out."

"I felt better than I had in years. So when the grind of a long season started wearing on me..." He swallowed the bile that rose in his throat at the thought of how he'd trusted his so-called friend at FITNatural. "It wasn't such a stretch to take the next step. I thought they had my back. It wasn't until after I'd started taking the stuff and it was working that I even stopped to think about what I was putting in my body."

Unable to look the other man in the eye, he ducked under his cap.

"You know how desperate we were to make it in the first place?" Cooper threw the question out. "That was nothing compared to how desperate I was to stay there."

He couldn't expect his friend to understand. Not when he'd had his dream robbed from him.

"Hell if there'd been a potion to regrow the bones in my ankle, I might have given it a shot."

"No, you wouldn't have. You were always a bigger man than the rest of us."

"Are you kidding me?" Sanders tone made him look up. "I would have drunk the blood of a unicorn for just one day in the majors."

"I just traded my soul. For what?" Cooper was tired of feeling sorry for himself. His former teammates were champions. "So I could finish my last full season two games back in the division? Three back in the wild card? I was running on fumes at the end of that season. Maybe if I'd been man enough to admit I wasn't right...who knows?"

"Don't waste your time second guessing yourself." Sanders had the voice of bitter experience. "Every time I think about what if... What if I hadn't been so damn competitive? What was one run compared to a career?"

The other man shook his head.

"At least you went out honestly."

"Honesty doesn't pay the bills."

"Neither does a fifty game suspension." Cooper was starting to think his days of making a living as a ballplayer were over. His phone hadn't exactly been ringing off the hook. Teams had to be pretty desperate to touch a guy with his reputation and questionable health. And what was that old joke about not wanting to belong to a club that would accept him? That's how he'd felt about the teams who'd been willing to extend an offer. If they were that bad, he didn't want anything to do with them.

Talk about cutting off his nose to spite his face.

"Maybe I should start thinking about what else I can do." Cooper rubbed his shoulder, more out of habit than any stiffness. "Maybe I could become a rock star."

"No, man." Sanders clapped him on the good shoulder. "You could come work for me. I always need pitching coaches, and you've got experience with that foundation camp."

"That was more about PR than anything."

"Tell that to the kids who fall in love with the game. The ones who spend their days at the ballpark instead of out on the street."

* * * *

After putting away the groceries, Annabelle had spent much of the day on the phone with her agent, the insurance company, even her mother. She'd offered to come out to California but they both knew it was only because that's what a mother should say.

Annabelle had made an appointment for having her stitches removed on Thursday, but she didn't intend to have Cooper take her. Her agent wanted to see for himself what damage the accident had done to her face, so he'd rearranged his schedule to drive her.

The whole thing was exhausting. She decided to lean back on the couch and close her eyes, just for a few minutes. But Cooper's scent lingered and she ended up more agitated than before. She couldn't get the man out of her head, even though he'd made it very clear he was only interested in saving her.

She didn't need him. She'd get clearance from the doctor and get a rental until she could repair or replace her car. She was leaning toward replacing the convertible with a safer model. Maybe one of those giant SUV's like Cooper drove. One that would leave her and the girls more protected.

Frustrated, tired, and still a little stiff, she walked down to the bus stop to meet the girls after school.

Cooper was already there. He'd promised the girls he'd show up. She wanted to be mad at him, but her stupid heart was happy to see him. He looked like he'd just come from a workout. A gray T-shirt clung to his muscular upper body. Black shorts hugged his strong thighs and hung low on his hips. Sweat glistened on his tanned skin.

Why did he have to be so damned good-looking? And why did her divorce have to take so long? She and Clayton had been over for a long time. She should have filed for divorce once she'd suspected he was traveling to Florida for something other than Goliaths' business.

How many other lies had she believed? The biggest had been that she'd somehow deserved a man like Clayton Barry. By accepting his money and everything that came with it, she'd accepted his treatment of her.

Well, no more. She wasn't going to let a man treat her any way she didn't want to be treated.

"Thanks for being here in case I got hung up," she called to Cooper. "But I got this."

"It's no trouble." He flashed a heart-melting smile. "I was just finishing up my run."

"Well, you can head on home, take a shower." The minute she said it, she knew it was a mistake. The image of him in the shower, naked, with water sluicing off his skin, popped up into her mind. Damn. Her skin heated as she imagined joining him in that shower. Soaping him up, rubbing him down.

He stared at her as if he could read her mind. Shifting his body, he cleared his throat.

"Well, I said I'd be here for the girls, so…" Right. He wasn't there for her. He was there for her daughters. The thought made her even more self-conscious.

"Look, I appreciate all you've done for us, but we're fine. Really," she said. "I can take care of myself and my children."

"Of course you can. But you also could use some support."

"I think I gave you the wrong impression when I told you I didn't have many friends here. I do. I just couldn't think too clearly when I was in the hospital." And he was standing there looking so gorgeous. "I was on the phone all afternoon, talking to my agent, my insurance company. I even got the police report detailing the accident."

"What did the police say?" Concern laced his voice.

"It wasn't my fault." She hated to admit how relieved that made her. "Some kid was texting and ran a red light."

Her throat tightened, thinking how something so simple had changed her life forever. Something she'd done herself on more than one occasion.

"Texting, huh?"

"Yeah." She couldn't help herself. She broke down in stupid, pointless tears.

Cooper put his arms around her and just held on while she cried. She cried until she couldn't cry anymore. Her eyes felt like they were full of sand and her throat was as raw as if she'd swallowed sea water.

"Annabelle." He spoke her name, so soothing and yet so irritating at the same time.

"I don't want to need you." Her words came out in a harsh whisper. "I don't want to need you, and I sure as hell don't want to want you."

She broke away from his embrace just as the school bus pulled up to the corner. Turning away from both Cooper and her daughters, she wiped what was left of her mascara from her cheeks. It wouldn't do for her girls to see her a mess like this. Once again, she had to stay strong.

"Mommy! Cooper!" Her daughters called out as they bounded off the bus.

"Guess what?" Sophie was bursting with excitement. "It's almost the hundreft day of school."

"Yeah, and we have to bring a hundred of something in a bag and then we get to count all the way to one hundred." Olivia was just as excited.

"Oh really? Like what?"

"Well…" Sophie stood with her hands on her hips and her chin tilted sideways and her lip caught between her teeth.

"Miss Ramirez put a note in our backpacks," Olivia informed them. "It's part of our homework and everything."

"And we get to do a play!" Sophie added.

"Sounds like fun." Annabelle took comfort in knowing that her daughters were so excited about their new school and their homework assignment. They didn't care if she was scarred, scared, and sore. She had to maintain a positive attitude.

"Is there anything I can do to help?" Cooper offered.

"We'll let you know." Annabelle was torn between being grateful for his assistance and being pissed off that he just wouldn't back off.

Olivia's backpack slipped off her shoulder and Cooper stooped to pick it up. He slid one strap over his own shoulder and the sight of a six-foot-three man with a pink princess backpack shouldn't have made her heart flutter and her insides quiver, but it did. When Olivia slipped her tiny hand in his much larger one, Annabelle knew she was screwed.

Sophie trotted along on his other side, both of them chattering and telling him all about their day. He smiled and nodded in all the right places, as if he was actually listening to them.

When they got to the house, the girls bounded up the steps. Cooper started to follow, but Annabelle stopped him.

"Can I have a word?" she asked.

"Sure." He stood there, with Olivia's backpack still strapped to his shoulder.

"Look, I know you promised the girls you'd be at the bus stop today," She hated having to be the bad guy, but she had to think about what her children needed, not only what they wanted. "But you need to stop just showing up like that."

He crossed his arms over his chest, pulling the T-shirt tighter over his biceps. The pink strap stood out even more against all that solid muscle.

"They're getting too attached." They weren't the only ones. "And I think it would be best if you kept your distance…"

"Yeah. That's probably a good idea." He frowned, clearly annoyed with her request.

"I just don't want them to get the wrong idea."

"Right." Was that hurt she heard in his voice?

"It's just that they've been through a lot these last couple of months." She wasn't sure why she felt the need to defend her position. To make him think it wasn't about him. "Their parents split up, their father moved across the country, they had to make all new friends at a new school…"

"And you don't want me to be one of their new friends?"

"That's not…" She could handle his friendship, if she hadn't wanted something more. "I just don't want them becoming too dependent on you. You mentioned you might not stick around, and they need stability right now."

"And what do you need, Annabelle?"

Him. Naked. Attending to her every desire. She felt a little flutter low in her belly—no it was much lower than her belly. She closed her eyes, trying not to picture him hovering over her, stroking her skin, driving deep inside her.

Sex. She needed sex. But he wouldn't give it to her. And she didn't want anyone else.

She swallowed. "I need to make sure my daughters don't get their hopes up only to be disappointed."

"Your daughters." He nodded, but they both knew she was hiding behind the girls. She was the one who was afraid of being heartbroken.

She should be used to it by now. Despite her beauty, her wealth, and her brief shot at fame, she knew more about disappointment than most people. She had an advanced degree in disappointment.

Chapter 10

Cooper had made it all the way to his bathroom before he realized he still had Olivia's backpack. It felt too comfortable carrying it for her. Hell, being with Annabelle and her daughters felt too comfortable.

Except for the tension between him and Annabelle. The kind of tension that could easily be relieved if he hadn't gotten all freaked out about her technically still being married.

But even if she wasn't, getting involved with her would be a bad idea. For all of them.

He knew he should take the backpack to Olivia, but he, too, needed some space. He needed a shower. He could still smell Annabelle on him from when he held her as she cried.

Damn. What kind of asshole texted while he was driving through an intersection? And how fast must he have been going to do that much damage to Annabelle's face?

Cooper couldn't stand the way some people didn't stop to think about the consequences of their actions. Especially not the guy in the mirror. He stood in his bathroom, the steam fogging up the room and he stared at himself. The guy who thought he could get away with it. There were plenty of guys who'd done it. Gone their whole careers on the juice, with carefully timed injections, or elaborate concoctions of counter-measures. One pill makes you taller and another makes you small. Some such shit.

All he'd wanted was to finish the season. He'd done that. Barely. He'd stayed off the stuff all winter. But he'd been nervous about doing the pitching clinic. He thought if he was going to risk his arm, he wasn't going to do it for a bunch of kids. He'd do it in spring training, with the team's doctors nearby. So he'd taken one more dose. Just to be safe.

Boy was he sorry.

Stepping into the shower, he knew he needed to stay away from Annabelle. She didn't need someone like him. Someone who'd been selfish and thoughtless and just arrogant enough to think he was doing the right thing. Just like he'd thought he was doing the right thing by looking after Annabelle and her daughters.

He should just walk away. But it was damned hard when he lived just next door. And she was so…everything he'd ever wanted.

Maybe it was time to move on. He could head down to Arizona, and try to find a team willing to take a chance on him. Now that he knew he wasn't going to have a heart attack if he picked up a baseball, he could risk getting on a mound. Even if he sucked, at least he'd know he'd given it his best effort.

Switching off the water, he reached for a towel. He dried off, got dressed, and then went downstairs to return the backpack.

He picked up the pink, princess-covered bag and something inside him twisted in a knot. He didn't want to stay away from Olivia and Sophie. They both had managed to sneak into his heart. Sophie with her determination and her fearlessness. And Olivia with her cautious, yet trusting nature. They were both so much like Annabelle.

All three of them were sweet, funny, vulnerable, yet strong. He didn't want to walk away from them. But he knew it would be for the best.

He knocked on the door, waited until he heard footsteps, then dropped the backpack on the porch and headed back to his place. It took all the strength he had not to turn around when he heard the door open.

It took even more when he heard Annabelle whisper, "Thanks."

* * * *

After dinner, baths, and bedtime, Annabelle tried to watch a little TV. But *American Idol* couldn't hold her attention. Not when the only voice she longed to hear had been banished from her home. Cooper had returned Olivia's backpack, but instead of intruding, he'd left it on the porch.

If only she hadn't been so stubborn. If only she hadn't been determined to be independent, she could accept his friendship without wanting more. They could have invited him over for dinner. The girls might have eaten their vegetables and they wouldn't have spent the meal bickering over who was going to bring what for the one hundredth day of school. They'd rejected every one of her ideas and ended up in tears worried they would fail Kindergarten if they didn't come up with not one, but two super-duper ideas.

After switching off the TV, Annabelle poured herself a glass of Chardonnay. She sat at the kitchen table, but the memory of Cooper in her pink apron just made her more anxious. He was a good man. The kind of man who was willing to stand by his principles even if those principles made her ache.

She grabbed a sweater and threw it on over her nightgown. Taking her barely touched glass of wine, she stepped out on the porch, hoping the night air would clear her head. She needed to take the advice of her daughters' favorite movie song and "let it go."

The minute she stepped outside, she realized her mistake.

Cooper was on his porch, strumming his guitar and singing a haunting song. She turned around, to go back inside, but she was mesmerized by the sound of his voice.

So much for getting the man out of her head.

Instead, she sat in the shadows, listening to him sing, and hoping he couldn't see her watching him.

His voice was deep, rich, and had a certain quality that tugged at something deep inside her. His songs made her feel more than she'd felt in a long time. Longing. Yearning. Wanting a connection that was just out of reach.

And if the passion he brought to his music was even a little bit sincere, he wanted it too.

She closed her eyes and sipped her wine. She finally got why musicians were so appealing—even the ones who might not be all that physically attractive—they drew out emotion. Made you *feel*.

Oh, she was feeling right now. After so many years of merely existing, she was feeling too much. And instead of retreating into her house, she moved closer, still hidden from his view, but she wanted to hear the words to the haunting song he was singing. She wanted to feel a little bit closer to the man who was just out of reach.

"Your name on my lips
Like a song in my heart
Annabelle, sweet Annabelle..."

She froze. He was singing about her. Like he wanted her. Only he didn't. He'd made that very clear.

Draining her wine, she made the decision to let him know what his song did to her. She set the empty glass on the porch railing and marched next door.

"What do you think you're doing?" Annabelle demanded.

"Trying to stay out of your way." Cooper didn't look up from his guitar.

"By singing about me?"

"It's how I relieve tension." He strummed a few chords, his attention on his instrument.

"Really? I thought you did that by lifting weights or running along the beach."

"Nope." He glanced up at her now, but his eyes were hidden in the shadows. "That's how I keep in shape. My music keeps me sane."

"Yeah? Well, it's making me crazy." Her heart was racing. She couldn't remember the last time she'd been this worked up.

"I didn't mean to disturb you." He fingered the neck of his guitar, and she couldn't help but notice his long, strong fingers. Fingers that could no doubt make her body sing. "I'll take it inside."

"Not good enough." She stepped closer. Close enough to smell his soap or shampoo or aftershave. Whatever it was, it drove her almost as wild as his voice. "I'll know you're singing. About me."

"Annabelle." He held his guitar between them, like a shield.

"Stop. Please." She inched even closer, placing her finger on his lips. "You're killing me with your song."

"Softly?"

"What?"

"Nothing. Just made me think of the Roberta Flack song." He played a few notes.

"I'm glad you find all this amusing." Her blood was starting to boil. How dare he make light of this? He was using his music to… Well, he wasn't using his music to seduce her, so what was he doing?

"Am I too loud? You don't like my voice? What exactly is the problem, Annabelle?"

"That song. It's about me."

"Yes. It is." He set the guitar down and leaned forward.

"Don't." She was shaking, her nerves humming like one of his guitar strings after he'd strummed it.

"Don't what?"

"Don't sing about me." She squeezed her fists, digging her perfectly manicured nails into her palms. "Promise you won't sing that song about me."

"I can't make that promise, Annabelle." Every time he said her name, it was like a sliver digging ever deeper into her heart. "Every song I sing is about you. Every verse, every note, it's about you. It's always been about you."

"But why?" She didn't get it. He wanted her, he didn't want her. He didn't want to get too close, yet he never strayed too far away. "You sing about me, yet you don't want me."

"Oh, but I do. I do want you. More than you'll ever know."

Under the glow coming from the streetlight, she could see into his eyes. He meant it. Every word. And he wasn't any happier about it than she was.

"Annabelle…" He didn't say anything more, just pulled her toward him and kissed her. Softly killing her with his lips, his tongue, his breath. He threaded his fingers through her hair, pulling her closer, but not close enough.

She wrapped her arms around his neck, pressed her body against his. He was solid. Strong. Hot. She wanted, no *needed* to touch and be touched. She couldn't feel her bruised ribs, couldn't feel pain in her shoulder. She could only feel the pleasure of his lips on hers, his hands moving down her back, his erection pressing against her belly.

A soft moan escaped her lips, encouraging him to deepen the kiss. She moved her hands down his shoulders, feeling his biceps, his forearms, then guiding his hands to her hips.

"Annabelle," he groaned as he cupped her ass, pulling the soft cotton of her nightgown up.

She arched into his touch, wanting more. Wanting everything.

He inched his hand closer to her sweet spot.

Yes. Please. Now.

He withdrew his hand and took a step back.

"I can't." His voice was shaky, desperate. "I'm sorry, Annabelle, I just can't."

"Because I'm not divorced." She smoothed her nightgown down over her trembling thighs. "Or is it because I'm ugly?"

"No. That's not…" With the gentlest touch, he brushed a strand of hair off her cheek. "I want you, Annabelle. I want you more than I've ever wanted anyone. Or anything. But I don't have any protection."

"Protection?" At first she didn't know what he was talking about. "Oh. Like a condom?"

"I don't keep them around. I haven't in quite a while."

"I see." She searched his face for some clue as to why a healthy, sexy, single man wouldn't keep condoms handy. "Why not?"

"It's complicated." Again, the mysterious secret loomed between them. She backed away, wondering if maybe there was something dangerous he was hiding from her.

"You weren't in prison were you?"

"No." He laughed. "Not prison."

"You're not married yourself are you?"

"No. Never been married. And I'm not gay."

"I didn't think you were." The night felt colder now, and she wrapped her sweater tighter around herself. "I should go. I'll let you get back to your guitar."

"Annabelle... I'm sorry."

She held up her hands. "Go ahead and sing anything you want. I'll just close my windows from now on."

"Wait." He looked like he wanted to tell her something else. Something important, but then he shook his head. "Goodnight, Annabelle."

"It could have been." She turned and walked toward her house.

* * * *

He needed to tell Annabelle the truth. Tomorrow. If he followed her tonight, he would just end up even more frustrated than he was right now. They both would.

Why hadn't he bought a box of condoms when he was at the store? Maybe because he was in denial about being able to stay away from her. Or maybe he thought she'd believed him when he said he couldn't be with a married woman.

Either way, he was an idiot.

She wanted him. That would change when she found out who he was and what he'd done.

Cooper picked up his guitar. No more would he sit on his porch and play. Not as long as Annabelle lived next door.

Damn. Shaking his head, he walked into his house. He couldn't find a comfortable spot to play, even though lyrics were swirling through his mind. About Annabelle. Her sweetness, her softness, her sauciness. She was beautiful and sexy and strong, even though she didn't always realize it. The way she'd marched over there, begging him not to sing about her. It would be like him begging her not to be so beautiful.

His music was his way of dealing with the powerful emotions going on inside him. The lust. The longing. And something more. Something that scared him. Scared him even more than the thought of not playing baseball anymore.

He could see himself settling down with Annabelle and her daughters. Making a family. Possibly even making another baby.

No. He couldn't bring a child into this world. Because one day he'd have to look that child in the eye and tell him or her, "Yes, your father did steroids."

Chapter 11

Annabelle's agent was right on time. She'd carefully applied her makeup, done her hair, and put on one of her most confidence-inspiring outfits. She wore black cropped tuxedo pants, a blue silk wrap top, and silver platform sandals. A chunky necklace and chandelier earrings completed the look.

"Victor, it's so good to see you." She blew air kisses across both cheeks and pretended not to notice when he winced at seeing the large K carved into the left side of her face.

"Annabelle, you're lovely as always." Victor kissed her back on the right cheek only.

He was shocked by her appearance. He tried to hide it, but it was there.

"Would you like some coffee? Tea?"

"I brought your favorite, nonfat chai tea latte." He probably had a list of all his models' favorites. It was his job to make each of them feel like they were his most important client. He was good. But no agent would be good enough to get her a job now.

"Thank you. I'll grab my purse and we'll be on our way." She faked a smile. "I really do appreciate you driving me to this appointment. I hope I'll be cleared to drive again. I hate having to rely on my friends to get around."

She was babbling, she knew it, but couldn't help it.

Annabelle followed Victor to his black BMW. It was a convertible, and she had a brief moment of panic just thinking about how exposed she'd be in the open vehicle. She slid into the passenger seat, clicked her seat belt, and reached for her latte. If the worst happened, then she would have matching scars on the right side of her face.

She and Victor made small talk on the way to her doctor's appointment. Gossip about people they knew in common, the business, superficial stuff. They didn't talk about the accident. They didn't talk about her disfigurement. And they certainly didn't talk about how her career was over.

Once they got to the waiting room, Annabelle felt a little self-conscious looking at the glossy magazines on display. *People, Glamour,* and of course, *Sports Illustrated.* Nothing more than reminders of the life she used to lead. The life she'd hoped to recreate, but now had to let go of. She wondered if it would have been easier if she'd been back at work for more than one day. If she hadn't felt the hope and excitement of starting a new job, it wouldn't be so deflating to lose that job. Maybe once she'd gotten back into the routine—the long hours, hot lights, and the arrogant photographers who believed they could bring out emotions that she'd long ago stopped feeling—she would have been able to let it go more easily.

Her agent kept himself busy on his smart phone. Good, he was at least getting some work done while she waited to have her stitches removed and get the all clear for getting back behind the wheel. For getting her life back.

She had a hard time focusing on anything. She'd picked up a magazine, one geared more towards home and family than the glamorous life she used to lead. But she wasn't really interested in organizing her closet, repurposing her clutter, or finding new ways to get her children to eat their vegetables.

She'd already discovered the secret to that last one. Have her hunky neighbor, Prince Charming in disguise, whip up a fabulous soup.

God, she needed to get the man out of her system. But the more she tried, the more she found herself unable to put space between them. And every time she tried to rationalize all the reasons she needed to keep her distance, the more she found herself drawn to him.

He was hiding something. About his past. Something important enough that he, too, tried to keep them from getting too close to each other.

They were both failing. His secrets, her scars, were no match for the chemistry between them.

Before she could overthink too much, her name was called. Victor glanced up from his smart phone just long enough to acknowledge that she was leaving the room.

The first stop was at the scale. Annabelle kicked off her sandals and stepped onto the torture device. She held her breath, and was surprised to find she'd lost five pounds. A lot of good it was going to do her now.

She followed the nurse into the exam room, sat down, and pushed up her sleeve so she could have her blood pressure read. She tried to relax as the cuff tightened around her upper arm.

"Looks good." The nurse flashed an encouraging smile before entering the numbers in her tablet. "The doctor will be in shortly."

Annabelle was left alone in the room. At least she didn't have to disrobe. Most of the damage was visible. She might have to lift her shirt so the doctor could examine her ribs, but they seemed to be healing quite well.

She didn't bother picking up a magazine. It wouldn't hold her attention, not when her thoughts flitted from the end of her career to the start of something with her hot neighbor. Her musical, mysterious, and magnificent neighbor.

She'd flat out asked him if he'd been in prison and he'd denied it. He wasn't married either. She believed him on both accounts.

A soft knock on the door interrupted her thoughts.

"How are you feeling today?" The doctor, a young, fairly attractive man, stepped into the room.

"Much better, thanks." Annabelle was grateful to be in street clothes and not some flimsy gown.

He glanced at the chart, nodding to give the impression he was studying her case carefully.

"Are you still suffering headaches? Confusion?"

"The headaches are mostly gone." As for the confusion, she knew that had more to do with her neighbor and less to do with the accident. "And I'm feeling much more myself lately."

"Good, that's good." The doctor set the chart aside and approached her. He examined her face, or rather her stitches. "The incision looks good. No sign of infection."

"But there will be a scar." It wasn't a question. She already knew the answer.

"It will fade over time, but yes, you can expect significant scarring from lacerations of this severity. Down the road, you may be able to have plastic surgery to lessen the appearance of the scars, but it's too early to tell how well they'll heal."

The doctor reached for his tray of instruments, and selected the necessary tools to remove the stitches, one tiny thread at a time. It seemed to take forever. She imagined her agent growing restless in the waiting room. But it wasn't as if she could take them out herself.

Finally, he was finished.

"What about driving?" Annabelle asked, resisting the urge to feel her skin where he'd been working. "I'm hoping to get back out on the road soon. Before my friends stop taking my calls."

The joke fell flat. She was a model, not a comedic actress.

"We have a series of cognitive tests to run through before we can clear you." He made it all sound so routine. "It's done on computer, so we'll get immediate results. I'll let them know you're ready."

"How long will this take?" She was getting antsy. "So I can let my ride know when we'll be finished."

"It should take from thirty to forty minutes. Depending on how you do."

"Thank you."

The doctor left and she pulled out her phone to text Victor and let him know they'd be here at least another hour.

Victor assured her that he was fine, he could catch up from anywhere thanks to modern technology.

Twenty minutes went by before another knock on the door was followed by the entrance of another person in a white coat.

"I'm Dr. Sherman." The young woman smiled and offered a hand. "I'm the psychologist who will be administering your test."

Annabelle shook hands with the new doctor and readied herself for whatever was coming next.

"There are several questions that will test your memory, cognitive processing, and reaction times," the psychologist explained. "It was originally designed for athletes, but we've found it helpful in assessing patients' ability to resume driving."

"I'll feel better knowing I can get back on the road safely." Annabelle hoped she was ready. She had been dependent on others for too long. She was ready to resume her independence.

* * * *

Cooper had finished another throwing session with Brandon. He felt pretty good even after throwing about a hundred tosses. Still not ready to get on the mound, but he was starting to believe it would be possible.

Progress.

"Looking good out there, guy." Sanders gave him a hearty clap on the shoulder. His right shoulder, not his pitching arm.

"Feeling good out there." And he meant it.

"You want to grab a burger and a beer?" his friend asked. "We've got a lot of catching up to do."

"I'll take you up on the burger." Cooper tossed his glove in his bag. "And the catching up. But I'll pass on the beer."

His friend raised an eyebrow, but didn't say anything. Good. Cooper didn't want to rehash why he felt like he had to go above and beyond being a good citizen. Avoiding drugs, alcohol, and driving over the speed limit. He paid his taxes early, made anonymous charitable contributions, and he always remembered to bring his reusable grocery sacks to the market.

But it wouldn't matter how "good" he was from here on out. He'd always be remembered as a cheater. There would always be that one guy in the crowd who'd call him out, heckling him, harassing him, and making sure he would never forget what he'd done to disgrace himself, his team, and the game.

"Suit yourself." Sanders shrugged, grabbing his worn cap from when they were Titans, the Goliaths' double-A affiliate. "You can drive, then."

"Sure, why not." Cooper shouldered his duffle bag and waited while his friend left instructions with his receptionist.

They drove to an out-of-the-way burger joint. It was old school. No sweet potato fries or low-carb options. Just meat, cheese, bun. Greasy shoestring fries came with the burgers and a variety of condiments were kept on the table. Four different mustards, relish, and of course ketchup and mayo.

Sanders ordered a beer and Cooper stuck with the sun tea brewed right there on the back porch, next to where the cook took his cigarette breaks. He'd been coming here long before he started worrying about every single thing he put into his body. And a little cholesterol was probably much healthier than the crap he'd ingested or injected a year ago.

"So the arm's good?" Sanders asked once they settled in with their drinks.

"As far as I can tell." Cooper took a sip of his tea, almost wishing he'd joined his friend in having a beer. "But I haven't really challenged it yet."

"Holding out until you get to spring training?"

"Just getting to the point where I feel like I can answer my agent's phone calls." If Stan ever had reason to call.

"Any bites?"

"I passed on Toronto." Mostly because he didn't want to travel that far only to fail.

"I'm sure something will come up." His friend didn't sound too optimistic, though. "There's always a need for lefties out of the pen."

"If I'm healthy."

"Any pain?" Sanders looked him straight in the eye. One of the few people who could ask such a personal question and get a straight answer.

"No." It still amazed him. "I lived with the pain for so long, I almost don't know what to do without it."

"Yeah, I can only imagine what that feels like."

They both had known their share of pain. A ballplayer got to a certain point in the season and there was always something that hurt. But they were expected to man up. Work through it. In the minors, giving into the pain might cost a player his shot at the big leagues. Once he got to the Majors, Cooper had felt the need to live up to his contract. They'd paid him a lot of money to be available every night.

"You think you're a hundred percent?" Sanders asked.

"Hard to say without throwing off a mound. Or facing hitters." Cooper wanted to believe he could come back, all the way. But the game was more than just a physical thing. There was the whole mental component. And that was a lot harder to rehab.

"You think you'll make a comeback?"

"I hope so." Cooper gave a pained grin. "I don't know what the hell else I'd do. I've played baseball my whole life."

"You know you could always come work for me."

"What about the kids? Their parents?"

"What about them?"

"Come on, I used PEDs. I got suspended. Who would put their trust in a guy like me?"

"Get over yourself." Sanders set his beer glass down on the table with such force that several people turned to look at them. "You're not a freaking priest. You're a baseball player. A guy who's been there. If you can help prepare these kids for the next step, whether it's college or the pros, that's all they give a shit about."

"I cheated."

"And you think that makes you special?"

"So you're saying it's no big deal?"

"No. You screwed up. Big time." His friend shook his head. "But if you can't get past it, no one will."

Cooper grunted, knowing that was his biggest obstacle.

"So, you want to tell me about the car seats in the back of your Escalade?" Sanders eyed him over his frosty mug. "You adopt a couple of kids or something?"

"Just helping a neighbor."

"I never thought of you as the single mom type." Sanders laughed. "She must be pretty hot."

"Annabelle Jones." Just saying her name got his heart racing.

"That hot?" Sanders nodded as if he was very impressed. Back in the day, they'd created a rating system for attractive women. The levels were "hot," "scalding," and "Annabelle Jones." The latter meaning a woman so far out of their league she might as well be Annabelle Jones.

Their food arrived and Cooper busied himself with his burger. He loaded the lettuce and tomatoes onto the meat and spread a thin layer of spicy mustard on the bun.

"Annabelle Jones moved in next door to me." Cooper held his burger, ready to take a bite. "With her twin daughters."

"You're kidding me? *The Annabelle Jones?*" Sanders took a big bite, moaning in appreciation.

"Nope. She's there. Right next door." Cooper bit into his lunch, but found it less than satisfying. "She's been in an accident. I've been helping her get around."

"Oh, come on, your fantasy girl moves in next door and you're just helping her get around?"

"Yeah. I'm just helping her and her kids out." He really didn't want to get into his relationship with Annabelle. Especially since he didn't have any idea what their relationship was. He'd tried to keep his distance, but each day he became more and more drawn to her. She wanted him too, but that would change when he told her the truth.

"Sure." Sanders nodded his head, but Cooper could tell he was skeptical. "And you're just tossing the ball around for fun."

"Look, I don't know anything about anything right now." The three bites of hamburger sat like a rock in his stomach. "I don't have a contract. I don't know if I can pitch even if I did. And Annabelle?"

He sank back into the vinyl seat. He was crazy about her. But it wasn't the image of her he'd carried around all these years. It was the real woman who made his heart pound, his pulse race, and his head spin fairy tales about one big happy family.

"You really like her?" His friend wiped his mouth with a napkin. "You're not just trying to live out your fantasy?"

"Look, we both know nothing is as good as it seems." They had both been kids with a dream of playing professional baseball. They had both lived with the reality of grueling schedules, sore muscles, playing through pain, and watching other guys move up faster. They had seen relationships fall apart and guys lose their focus because of demands from home.

"And we both know some things are better than you even imagined." Sanders gave him a hard look. The kind of look only a real good friend could give a man. "Remember your first day in the Majors? Was it as good as you'd thought it would be?"

"It was better."

"What about Annabelle? Is she as beautiful up close?"

"You have no idea." Cooper's chest grew tight. "But it's not her beauty that... She's great. Really great. She's smart, funny. She's a great mom. But she's not the kind of woman you just fool around with. Even if she didn't have kids. But she does. And..."

"Kids can complicate things."

"And husbands." Cooper wasn't sure if he could get past that. "She's in the middle of a divorce."

"So you're standing by, being a good friend, waiting for her to be available?"

"Shit. I don't know what I'm doing." Cooper ran his fingers through his hair. For the first time in his life, he cared more about what Annabelle needed than what he wanted. "I should just stay away. I'm no good for anyone right now. I don't have a job. And if even I did, it wouldn't be around here. Hell, if I'm lucky I'll end up in Japan or Korea."

"Would you take it?"

"I don't know." He was still young enough that a year or two overseas could land him back on a major league roster. But did he really want to go that route?

He had money saved. He had his investments in real estate, and the market was coming back around after several years of losing equity in his properties. He could take another year off. Figure out what the hell he was going to do after baseball.

After baseball. He'd never really thought about what would come next.

Now it was all he thought about.

When he wasn't thinking about Annabelle. And her daughters. And how the four of them seemed to fit together so well.

Chapter 12

Cooper had dropped Sanders off at the training facility. He hadn't meant to take so long at lunch and now he wondered if he'd forgotten what time Annabelle had her doctor's appointment. Maybe she hadn't said. Or maybe with everything that was happening between them he'd forgotten. But the twins would be getting off the bus in two hours, so he wanted to make sure one of them would be there.

He pulled into his driveway and started for the back door, but for some reason his instinct sent him around to the front of the house.

Sure enough, there was Annabelle, wrapped in a blanket on her front porch swing, staring off into the distance.

"Is everything okay?" He asked, even though he was pretty sure it wasn't.

"I can't drive." She didn't look up. Didn't move at all, she just continued staring out into some unknown place. "They gave me a test and I passed all but one section. I guess you're stuck with me a little longer."

"Hey, it's no big deal." He tried to keep his tone light. There was something in her voice that told him this was difficult for her. "I don't mind being your slave for a while longer."

"Thanks." She didn't sound all that grateful. She sounded resigned. Defeated.

"So can you appeal? Retake the test?"

"I can go back in a couple of days. But what if... No, I will get better. I have to." A little bit of the spunk he'd come to associate with Annabelle returned to her voice.

"I'm here if you need me."

"I don't want to need you." She looked up for the first time, and he could see her eyes were red-rimmed and swollen. Not any less beautiful to him, but it killed him to see her hurting.

"My whole life I've had to rely on one man or another." Apparently she had something to get off her chest. "First my father, and then my husband. I don't need another man to take care of me. I don't need another man to tell me what to do."

"I wouldn't dream of telling you what to do." He sat down next to her. "I don't want to take care of you. I mean, I do, but not because you can't take care of yourself."

She wrapped the blanket tighter around herself.

"I know what it's like to want to prove to the world, and to yourself, that you have all the answers. That you don't need to rely on anyone." Maybe he should tell her now. Who he was. What he'd done. "I've been in a situation where I thought if I just stayed strong and didn't admit weakness, I could overcome anything."

When she didn't ask questions, he kept talking.

"I screwed up. Big time." He never would have thought that Annabelle Jones would be the one person he wanted to confess his sins to. But he couldn't think of anyone else in the world he wanted to understand him more. "I tried to be a lone ranger. Tried to be so self-reliant that I forgot that life is a team sport."

She titled her head just slightly, as if she was seeing a piece of the puzzle fall into place.

"By the time I realized I need help, I ended up turning to the wrong sort of people." He raked his hands through his hair. He hated the fact that he'd screwed up so badly. But if he could help Annabelle in any way, it was worth it. "By the time I admitted I couldn't do it on my own, I was desperate. I took what I could get. And I relied on people who didn't have my best interests at heart."

"Do you have my best interests at heart?" Annabelle's voice was skeptical, and maybe a little bit hopeful.

"Absolutely." He reached up and brushed her hair off her cheek. "Hey, you got your stitches out."

"Yes. My agent took me earlier today." She gave him an apologetic smile. "My *former* agent. I didn't want to bother you."

"Honey, you could never be a bother for me." At first he was hurt by the fact she'd chosen someone else to take her to the doctor. But then he realized he could use it to his advantage. "But I'm glad you have options. You don't need me. You don't need me at all."

Cooper stood as if he was going to leave her.

"Wait." Annabelle reached out and grabbed his wrist. "Don't go."

He knelt down in front of her, taking her face between his palms. "Don't you know I would do anything you ask? Anything you need. Anything you want…"

"Anything?" She turned her face toward him. Lifted her chin and smiled. "Anything I want?"

"Anything." His heart hammered in his chest. "Unless you ask me to walk away and leave you alone."

Her face twisted in an expression he couldn't quite read. Maybe he'd said the wrong thing, but it was the absolute truth. Walking away from Annabelle would be a thousand times harder than walking away from baseball.

"I have a request." Her voice shook, as if she was afraid to ask for what she really needed. In that moment, he hated every man she'd ever had to rely on in the past.

"Your wish is my command."

She smiled and for a moment it felt like gravity ceased to exist. Gravity and reality and sanity.

"Make love to me." Her request was simple.

"Are you sure?" He knelt in front of her. "I'm not trying to change your mind. Or second guess you. I just… I just need to know you really want this. You really want me. I mean, you're Annabelle Jones and I…"

"You're a bum." She touched him gently on the shoulder, just above the tiny scar she probably didn't even know existed. "You're some guy I barely know. You don't know how long you're going to stick around. I've heard it all before. But I want you. Right now. You have everything I need right now. You've got a car and a great body. You can cook and sing. You're the perfect guy for me *right now*."

"Okay." He took her hand and led her inside. They didn't speak as they made their way upstairs to her bedroom.

She locked the door and then turned toward him with a smile.

"Are you afraid I'm going to try to escape?"

"I'm not taking any chances." She undid the tie on her blouse and it fell open, revealing a lacy bra holding up her spectacular breasts.

Cooper reached up and lightly ran his fingertips down her fresh scar. She winced.

"I'm sorry, does it hurt?"

"No. Not really." She gave him a weak smile. "I was just wondering why you touched me there?"

"I guess I'm just making sure you're real" He brushed his lips across her scar, wishing he could kiss her all better.

"Oh, I'm real." She laughed and moved his hand over her heart. "Feel that? It's as real as it gets."

She undid the clasp on her bra and dropped it to the floor. Her hands trembled as she reached for the button on her waistband and unzipped her pants, sliding them down her hips.

"Well, what are you waiting for?"

He answered with a kiss, soft and tender, becoming hotter and more urgent as they made their way to the bed. He lowered her to the mattress and slipped her panties off.

"Oh, Annabelle." She was stunning. Beautiful.

She closed her eyes and sighed. "Do you have any idea what your voice does to me?"

"I've got an idea." He dropped kisses across her skin. Taking her breast into his mouth, he slid his hand between her thighs. She was hot, slick, and wet. "I've got a real good idea."

Kissing his way down her body, across her firm, flat tummy, her soft, round hips, he nudged her thighs apart. Starting at her knees, he kissed his way back up.

Annabelle squirmed, giving him a view of exactly how hot she was for him. He moaned as he pressed his mouth against her center.

She clutched her fingers through his hair as he tasted and teased and tormented her with his tongue. He could tell she was getting close by the way she lifted her hips and moaned. God, she tasted so good. So sweet and hot and…"

"Oh…Cooper." She shattered against him. "Oh my gah… I hear bells."

He was feeling pretty damned pleased with himself until he realized he heard bells, too.

Ding-dong-ding, ding-ding-dong.

"Someone's at the door." She sat up. "Oh, how could I forget?"

Annabelle tumbled off the bed.

"Are you expecting someone?" Damn, he couldn't imagine worse timing.

"Yes. My friends are here." She scrambled toward her dresser and pulled out some clean underwear, a T-shirt, and some yoga pants. "I can't believe I forgot Hunter and Marco were stopping by on their way home. They're on their honeymoon. And oh, I must be a mess."

She hopped into her clothes, and yeah, she looked pretty ruffled. But gorgeous.

"You're beautiful." He did his best to smooth her hair back and forget about how close he'd been to being inside her. "Maybe they'll go away. Head to their hotel and call you later."

"No. They're staying here. I should..." She looked around the room, as if she was hoping to find an excuse for her flushed cheeks, her mostly satisfied glow.

She grabbed an empty laundry basket and started tossing clothes in it. "Here, carry this."

"I should go. Leave you to your company." He really hoped he could sneak out the back door without the evidence of his frustration.

"No. They'll want to meet you." She popped into the twins' room, to grab a few articles of clothing. "They'll want to know the guy who's come to my rescue."

She raced downstairs and he had no choice but to follow.

"Sorry I took so long," Annabelle said as she flung the front door open. "I was just getting some laundry together. And Cooper was helping me."

She stepped aside as Hunter and Marco Santiago entered.

"Put that down and come meet my good friends," Annabelle ordered.

"Nathan Cooper." Hunter stepped forward and offered her hand. "It's good to see you again. How's the shoulder?"

"It's good." He shook his former owner's hand and tried to smile. "Real good. Good as new."

Great, he must sound like an idiot.

"I'm glad to hear it." Hunter smiled as if she meant it. "Have you met my husband, Marco?"

"We've played against each other." And he was the man she'd traded Cooper for. "Didn't you hit a triple off me about three years ago?"

"Yeah. I remember that game." Marco stuck his hand out and gave a hearty shake. "I got lucky. That pitch got a little too much of the plate."

"Well, if I'd known this was going to be a big reunion," Annabelle's voice was tight, irritated. "I would have dressed for the occasion."

"Look, Annabelle..." What could he possibly say that would make everything all right? "I'll start this load of laundry and get out of your hair."

"Don't worry about it. You've done enough." She put her hands on her hips and glared at him. She hated him. Just as he'd known all along she would.

"Enjoy your visit." He smiled at Hunter and then nodded toward Marco. "Hope to see you on the field."

He let himself out and walked back to his place. He still had the taste of Annabelle in his mouth. A taste he'd savor even more knowing he'd never get a second chance.

He should have told her. Everything. But no, he'd blown it. He was an even bigger jerk than anyone thought.

Chapter 13

"So how was the drive?" Annabelle made small talk even though she was dying to know how Hunter and Marco knew Cooper so well. *Nathan* Cooper. Nope, she couldn't see him as a Nathan. Not even a Nate. He would always be just Cooper.

"Good." Hunter smiled as Marco slipped his arm around her waist. "Not too much traffic."

"So what's Nathan Cooper doing here?" Marco asked, his gaze narrowed in suspicion. "Don't tell me he's just doing your laundry?"

"He's my neighbor." Annabelle wondered what it was to him. "And he's been a huge help for me and the girls these past several days."

She couldn't even remember how long it had been since the accident. Her thoughts were so jumbled and her body was still humming from the pleasure their arrival had interrupted.

"Well, be careful around him." Marco crossed his arms over his chest. "I'm surprised you would get mixed up with the guy who brought the whole FITNatural thing to the public's attention."

"Oh, that." Annabelle pretended as if it were no big deal. That she knew the secret Cooper had been hiding from her. "I swear, if I never heard the name FITNatural again…"

She put on her million-dollar smile, or what was left of it, and invited her friends back to the kitchen.

"So tell me more about the honeymoon." Annabelle went to the stove to start a pot of tea. "I want to hear all about it. I've always wanted to see the country on a big, long road trip."

Hunter sat down and relayed all the details of their drive from St. Louis to Dallas, then Santa Fe to San Diego, and all the places in between.

When Marco went out to retrieve their luggage from the car, Annabelle brought up the subject she really wanted to discuss.

"So tell me more about Cooper." She held her breath, hoping Hunter wouldn't reveal anything too terrible. "I take it you know him from baseball."

"He was a Goliath for years." Hunter's smile seemed genuine enough. "He was one of our top lefty relievers, but… I still find it hard to believe he was using steroids."

Hunter shook her head in disappointment.

"He doesn't seem the type." Not that Annabelle knew him all that well, but from what she did know, he was one of the good guys. "He's so into natural foods and healthy living. At least since I've known him."

"Maybe he learned his lesson." Hunter sighed. "I have to believe he was one of those guys who only did it because he was trying to get over an injury. My father might have known more, but he was fighting his own battle. I think maybe Cooper didn't want to put any more burden on the team."

Annabelle felt like a petty bitch, thinking her problems with her love life were anything compared with what Hunter had gone through in the last year, losing her father to cancer, inheriting the team, and then selling her share so that Marco could remain a Goliath.

"The more I think about it, the more I believe he was just trying to make it through the season. They were all trying to make it to the end. We were so close. So close."

"I'm sorry your father didn't get to see your ultimate victory." Annabelle reached across the table to take her friend's hand. "He would have been so proud of you."

"Thank you." Hunter let go of Annabelle's hand and reached for her tea. "Something tells me you're not really interested in Cooper as a ballplayer, though. Is there something between the two of you?"

Was it that obvious?

"He's been a really good friend. A huge help for me and…" Hadn't she said that already? Her brain was so mixed up. "I don't think I would have made it through this without him."

"But you're more than just friends." Hunter gave her a knowing look. "Are there certain kinds of benefits?"

Both women laughed. It was the kind of moment shared between good friends.

"I've missed you," Annabelle admitted. "I'm glad I moved down here, but I've missed you."

"Well, you're always welcome to come to San Francisco for a visit," Hunter offered. "We've got plenty of room for you and the twins."

"Thank you." Warmth filled her. They made some vague plans to get together once the girls were out of school for the summer.

"So tell me, how are you getting along without the team?" Annabelle knew it must have been difficult for Hunter to sell, even if she'd done it for love.

"Well, it was hard to watch Johnny Scottsdale retire. But I wish him and Alice all the best." Hunter's face lit up talking about her first love. Baseball. "And I really hope that Dempsey can sign Bryce Baxter to a long extension. I think he might ask for a little more than I would be comfortable with, but he was World Series MVP."

"Afraid he'll make more than Marco?"

Hunter shrugged. "Money will never be an issue for Marco again."

They both knew that Marco had grown up poor, the son of a single mother.

"So, how is Marco getting along with his father?" His father was one of the wealthiest men in Texas, but he'd abandoned Marco and his mother before he was born, only to reunite with her during the World Series.

"Baby steps." Hunter gave an exasperated sigh. "But at least he's trying. He wants to have a baby, so that should give me leverage. If I tell him I won't let him become a dad until he makes amends with his own father…"

She sighed again, but it was a different kind of sigh. A dreamy, hopeful one.

"Are you pregnant?" Annabelle was happy for her friend. Truly.

"No. Not yet. I don't want to even start trying until after the season starts." Hunter had a happy glow about her. "I'd hate to go into labor while Marco was on the field. Can you imagine?"

"So you're really done with the Goliaths?"

"Well, I'm done with the front office." Hunter had a wistful tone in her voice. "I guess I'm just a player's wife now. I can still do charity work and support the team by supporting my man."

"Will you travel with the team?"

"We'll have to see." Hunter shrugged. "I've never not been a part of the Goliaths. Even in college, I kept a close eye on things. Maybe I'll get lucky and get pregnant right away and have something else to focus on."

"I hope everything works out for you. I really do."

"I hope everything works out for you, too." Hunter cast a quick glance toward Cooper's house.

"I've got a pretty good feeling it will."

Marco returned with a kiss for his bride.

"So what are you girls talking about?" he asked.

"Oh not much." Hunter accepted his kiss on the cheek. "We were just comparing stats on a couple of ballplayers we know."

His cheeks darkened, he must have thought they were talking about him. He'd dated Annabelle a long time ago. He'd been her first lover, but they had never been serious.

"So how well do you know Cooper?" Annabelle put him on the spot.

"Not that well. We never played together, except for one All-star game." Marco shifted a little in his chair. "He seemed like a good guy, but…"

"The steroid thing." Annabelle was already sick of the subject. "Is there anything else I should know about him? Is he a major playboy? A bad tipper? I know you guys gossip worse than teenage girls sometimes."

"No." He shook his head. "He had a pretty good reputation around the league. We were all shocked when his suspension came down. It was kind of like finding out Santa wasn't real."

"Don't you dare say that in front of my children." Annabelle felt comfortable teasing him. He was such a good-natured man. Kind of like her next-door neighbor.

"I won't. But sorry, I can't help you with any real information about Cooper."

"So your initial warning was what? Habit?" Hunter joined in the conversation.

"Yes, dear. I'm a protector. You know that about me."

"Yeah, I do." Hunter laughed and kissed his neck.

Annabelle smiled, happy for the two of them. And relieved to find out that other than the one big mistake, Cooper seemed to be the kind of man she could count on.

She averted her gaze, to give the lovebirds a little privacy, and noticed the clock on the oven. It was time to pick the twins.

"I've got to go meet the school bus." Annabelle stood abruptly. "You two make yourselves at home. I'll be back in about a half an hour."

She rushed out the back door, and headed toward the bus stop at as fast of a pace as she could manage.

She needn't have worried. Cooper was there, looking out for her girls once again.

"Hey. Glad you remembered. I almost forgot." Annabelle gave him an unsteady grin.

"Annabelle." He swallowed, the pain in his eyes was torture to her. "I'm so sorry."

She wanted to reach for him. To tell him that she didn't care about his past or his mistakes or why he didn't tell her. But he took a step back and shoved his hands in his pockets. He was still wearing the athletic shorts he'd worn when he'd come over earlier. How could she have not seen it?

"So you're a baseball player?"

"Yes." He looked down at the ground as if it was something to be ashamed of. "I was."

"A pitcher. For the Goliaths." She hadn't really paid attention to the team until Marco had shown up and she'd befriended Hunter. And it wasn't like she and Clayton discussed his business, either of them.

"Yes. Until they traded me for Santiago." His voice held a bitter note. She couldn't blame him for not being happy about the trade. It had worked out for the Goliaths, and that must have made it even harder.

"You were that good?"

He looked up in time to see her smile.

"I was hurt." He didn't return her grin. "I was hurt and too stubborn to admit it. Just like I was too stubborn to tell you why you should've stayed away from me."

The bus pulled up, and Annabelle sighed, knowing she'd have to finish this conversation later.

Sophie and Olivia bounded off the bus. They raced over to Cooper and started chattering about their day. They each took one of his hands and dragged him down the street. Her girls loved him. And judging by the smile on his face, Cooper loved them too.

As for their feelings for each other, that would take some more investigation.

When they approached her front porch, Annabelle tried to get her daughters' attention.

"Guess who came to visit us today?" She kept her voice upbeat. "Auntie Hunter and Uncle Marco."

"Really?" Olivia let go of Cooper's hand, but the smile on her face remained.

"They're not really our aunt and uncle, you know." Sophie put her hands on her hips. She was so...so sure of herself that Annabelle was just a little bit envious of her daughter. "But they're like family."

"That's great." Cooper tried to match the girls' enthusiasm. "Sometimes friends who are like family can be just as good as real family."

Annabelle's heart did a funny little flip. Fell right out of her chest. Because, that was how she felt about Cooper. He was her friend, but it wouldn't be hard to imagine him becoming part of her family.

"Why don't you two run on in and say hello to our company." Annabelle needed a few minutes alone with Cooper.

* * * *

He watched Sophie and Olivia dash off to see Annabelle's friends, the ones who were like family, and realized that Annabelle and her daughters were the family he'd never known he wanted. He'd had a taste of something special. Only he knew it was temporary. Like a fairy godmother's spell, it wouldn't last.

It killed him to think about how disillusioned the girls would be when they found out what he'd done. He'd cheated. How could he look into their eyes? Sing to them? Hold their hands when they crossed the street?

And Annabelle? He'd blown it with Annabelle. Big time.

"I'll let you get back to your company." He couldn't look at her. Couldn't bear to see the disappointment in her eyes.

"Cooper, wait," she pleaded.

"You don't need me." He turned and walked toward the beach, praying she wouldn't follow. Even if a part of him wished she would.

When he reached the water, he stood looking out over the Pacific. He'd grown up on the beaches of Southern California. He'd learned how to surf before he played ball. But he hadn't been on a board since he'd signed his first contract. Hadn't wanted to risk a stupid injury. Like a shark bite or jellyfish sting to put him on the DL. He hadn't wanted to put any strain on his shoulder. A lot of good staying out of the water had done him.

He flopped down on the sand, feeling sorry for himself. Picking up a handful, he watched the grains slide through his fingers. Like the rest of his life. His career, his integrity, and his chance with Annabelle.

Oh, God. Annabelle. He could still taste her. Still hear her moans of pleasure. Could still feel her.

He closed his eyes as lyrics filled his head.

Your name on my lips
Is like a song in my heart.

The smile on your face
Is like a rare work of art.

Oh sweet, sweet Annabelle,
You've got me under your spell.

The words came to him fast and furious. He itched for his guitar and his notebook. Instead, he pulled out his phone to jot down the lyrics. The tune would stay in his head until he could get back home.

He jumped up, encouraged. Maybe he'd blown it with Annabelle, and with baseball, but he still had his music. And that was something.

He picked up the pace, breaking into a jog back to his place, only to run into Marco in front of Annabelle's house.

"Hey." The other man stood in front of a classic Mustang. "What's the deal with you and Annabelle?"

"You her big brother?" Cooper didn't need to answer to this guy. The guy who'd taken his roster spot.

"We're friends." Marco removed his sunglasses and eyed Cooper carefully. "We go way back."

"Oh really? And does your wife know how far back you go with Annabelle?" He had a fifty-fifty shot at Marco having been more than friends with Annabelle. He took a chance.

"I don't keep secrets from my wife." Marco stared him down.

Okay, he got it. Marco was the bigger man. But that still didn't give him the right to have a pissing contest over a woman he claimed was just a friend. Not when he was married to another woman. A woman that Cooper had nothing but respect for, once he'd gotten over the fact that she'd traded his sorry ass.

"Well, good for you." He still didn't think he needed to defend his relationship with Annabelle, not that he had a relationship with her. "I'm glad your wife doesn't have a problem with you getting all worked up over an old *friend*."

"Annabelle is Hunter's friend, too." He changed his tone into more of a friendly *I'm just trying to do the right thing* vibe. "She's been through a lot in the last year."

"She's been through a lot this last week." Cooper inched forward. He wanted to protect Annabelle just as much as anyone. "I was here through it all. And I can tell you, she's a hell of a lot stronger than anyone gives her credit for."

"She's still vulnerable." Marco crossed his arms over his chest. "I don't want her to get hurt."

"I don't want her to get hurt, either." Cooper took another step toward the man. "You can count on that."

"Can I?" Marco asked.

"Yes. I know I let a lot of people down." Cooper raked a hand through his hair. "But I won't let Annabelle or her girls down. I'll make sure they're taken care of."

Even if it meant keeping his feelings, and his hands, to himself.

Chapter 14

After dinner, Annabelle put on a short movie for the twins. They'd finished their homework and were a little too wound up to go to bed. So they made popcorn and settled in for a special treat.

"Hunter tells me you two are thinking of starting a family." Annabelle wasn't surprised to find Marco helping load the dishwasher while Hunter wiped down the table.

"Yeah. Maybe." He looked over at his wife with absolute love and pride and eagerness. "We kind of figured we should get started now, so that I'll be ready to retire by the time our kids are old enough to play ball."

"What he's really saying is that he wants to make sure he misses most of the diapers and midnight feedings." Hunter snapped a towel against his backside.

"Hey. You know I'll be willing to do my part when I can." He came up to her and grabbed her wrists, pulling her arms around him. "I'll do anything for you."

"Marco, please." Hunter giggled as he dropped little kisses along her neck.

Annabelle cleared her throat.

"Sorry." She grinned at the loving couple. "Maybe you two wouldn't mind practicing. I mean, the parenting part. Not the baby-making part. I have a feeling you've got that down."

Hunter turned around, facing Annabelle, but with Marco's arms still wrapped around her.

"Would you mind babysitting?" Annabelle asked. "I have some things I need to take care of, and I'm not sure how long it will take."

"Sure. Do you need one of us to drive you somewhere?" Marco asked.

"No. It's just next door." Annabelle felt warmth creep up her cheeks.

Hunter smiled, as she realized where Annabelle needed to go. "No problem. Take as long as you need."

"Thank you." Annabelle hoped she wasn't making a mistake. She trusted them with her girls, but she didn't know if Cooper would let her in. To his house, sure, but his life? "The girls can skip their bath tonight. Just make sure they brush their teeth and are in bed by eight."

"We can do that," Hunter said.

"And do make yourselves at home," Annabelle offered. "I may be out late."

"I certainly hope so." Hunter winked at her. When Marco started to butt in, she shook her head and gave her husband a look that meant *none of your business*.

With that out of the way, Annabelle kissed her daughters on the tops of their heads and went upstairs for a wardrobe change.

She had far too many clothes to choose from. Her designer gowns were too formal and her workout wear too casual. Besides, she'd mostly lived in yoga pants these past several days. If she hadn't been in such a hurry, the outfit she'd worn to the doctor would be wearable, but she'd shoved it into a laundry basket. As if she'd just throw the silk blouse into the washer with the girls' school clothes.

She tried to think. How did she want Cooper to see her? Not as the invalid he'd been taking care of. Nor as the former trophy wife.

Of course. She approached the hope chest at the foot of her bed. She pulled out the red swimsuit she'd packed away years ago. The one she'd worn for her first swimsuit cover. The cover hanging in Cooper's weight room.

She carefully unwrapped it from the tissue paper and held it up. Then she wriggled out of her clothes and slipped on the bikini bottoms. Annabelle let out a sigh of relief that it still fit. Turning toward the mirror, she tied the top around her neck and then did a neat little bow in the back.

Not bad. Not bad at all. Her curves were a little more pronounced, but she wasn't nineteen anymore. There was still a slight bruise on her left side, but if things went as planned, it would be dark. Her breasts weren't quite as firm as they'd been, but they still filled out the suit nicely.

Still, she couldn't just march next door wearing nothing but an itsy-bitsy, teeny-weeny, red-hot bikini. Returning to her closet, she searched for a simple, yet sexy cover-up. Finally, she settled on a multicolored sarong, which she tied around her waist, and a soft ivory cashmere sweater that she slipped on over the bikini top.

She didn't even bother with shoes and slipped out the back door while Sophie and Olivia were watching their movie and Hunter and Marco were watching each other.

With her heart pounding, Annabelle stood at Cooper's door. She could hear the soft sounds of his guitar coming through the open window. Taking a deep breath, she rang the doorbell and waited.

The door opened and he stood there with a pained expression on his face. A mixture of emotion played with his features. Regret. Longing. Lust.

"Can I borrow a cup of sugar?" She gave him an innocent smile.

"I don't have any." He heaved a sigh as if just seeing her was painful. "I'm sorry."

"Well, then, I'll just have to find some other way to satisfy my craving." She pushed her way past him into the house.

"Annabelle…" His voice did that funny little thing when he said her name.

"Tell me the truth." She needed to get this out of the way. "Is this your big secret? The steroids? The suspension? Is that what you've been hiding behind all this time?"

"Yes." He hung his head.

"And did you take them because you were hurt?"

"Yes."

"Were you taking them your whole career?"

"No." He lifted his gaze. "It wasn't until my shoulder started acting up that I even considered it."

"How did you get involved with FITNatural?"

"You've got a lot of questions."

When she simply nodded, Cooper reached for her hand and led her to the sofa. She had a feeling it was going to be a long story. But she had all night.

"We were in Miami for the last series in August. My shoulder was flaring up just as the division race was heating up." Raking his hands through his hair, he leaned back against the sofa. "We were so close. We could feel it."

He closed his eyes and Annabelle waited for him to continue.

"And then there were the rumors about Henry Collins." He leaned forward, resting his elbows on his knees. "He was dying. And none of us wanted to be the reason we didn't make it to the playoffs."

"So you did whatever it took." She reached for his hand, but he pulled it back as if he felt like he was contaminated.

"I asked around, and found this company that had 'all-natural' products." His voice took on an edge of bitterness. "So I bought this cream. And it helped. Enough to get me through the series."

"So what was in this cream?"

"At first, it was legitimate. They assured me all the ingredients were safe and legal." He rubbed his hands together. "But then it stopped working, so they suggested something stronger. And when that stopped working, they offered…alternatives."

Pushing off the couch, he stood and walked across the room. With his back to her, he looked out the window.

"And that got you through the season?" Annabelle walked over to him and put her hand on his shoulder.

"Yeah. But we still came up short." He didn't pull away, but she could feel his tension in his shoulder.

"So how did you get caught?"

"I'm such an idiot." He turned to face her. To look her straight in the eye. "I panicked. I was supposed to do this charity thing. A clinic for underprivileged kids before we reported to spring training. I was worried I'd screw up my shoulder tossing the ball underhand or something stupid like that. I didn't want to take any chances. I figured I had two weeks for the stuff to get out of my system. But…"

"But they tested you sooner."

"Yeah. As we were getting ready for Fan Fest, they pulled a couple of us aside for random preseason drug testing." He let out a big, frustrated sigh. "I knew I was screwed, but in a way, it was a relief. I didn't have to keep looking over my shoulder. It was over."

Annabelle wrapped her arms around him and leaned against his chest. She could hear the steady beat of his heart. Could feel him trembling beneath her touch. He was so strong, yet he'd given in in a moment of weakness.

"I just have one more question for you." She lifted her face and smiled. "Where's your bedroom?"

He looked confused.

"I hear you have quite the magazine collection. I'd like to see them."

The corners of his lips twitched in a half-smile.

"Really?"

"Yes. We have some unfinished business." She grabbed his hand and started tugging him toward the stairs.

"Annabelle…"

She stopped. Turned around and reached up to touch his jaw.

"You sing my name." Her heart swelled, filling her chest. "You don't say it, you sing it. Every time."

* * * *

She was right. Her name was a song. A song he never wanted to stop singing.

"Annabelle." He pulled her closer and lowered his mouth over hers. He drank her in, kissing her with everything he had, marveling at the fact that she was here, in his house, in his arms.

"Your bedroom?" She pulled away, urging him upstairs.

With trembling hands, he led her to his room. She didn't waste any time in tugging off her soft sweater and wrap skirt then striking a pose in a red bikini. *The red bikini.*

"So do you have that magazine?" She asked with a mischievous grin on her face. "I can't quite remember the pose."

His feet froze, his mouth dried up, and his dick got instantly hard. She was going to act out his ultimate fantasy. Right there in his bedroom. Just moments after he'd confessed to steroid use that had possibly ruined his career.

Slowly, he made his way to the bedside table. He pulled open the drawer that held her magazines and an unopened box of condoms. Guess it wasn't just wishful thinking when he'd picked them up on his way home from his workout.

He reached for the magazine and held it up for her to see.

"Oh that's right." She arched her back, pressed her breasts forward, and drew her hand through her long golden hair. Her lips parted seductively and she gave him that half smile that had fueled his fantasies for years.

"Oh, Annabelle." He dropped the magazine and stood there with his jaw just inches from the floor. "Do you have any idea what you do to me?"

"I hope it's the same as what you do to me." She inched closer to his bed. "Let's finish what we started."

"Are you sure?" He hesitated. "I mean, after what I've done?"

"We all make mistakes." She fell onto the mattress. "But I think our biggest regrets are for the things we don't do."

Well, he wasn't going to regret not living out his fantasy. Not now. Not when she was right here. Wanting him. Even though he didn't deserve her.

He reached for her, his hands shaking as he pulled on the tie of her bikini top.

"Wait."

Oh no. She'd changed her mind.

"Let's get you undressed." She tugged on his T-shirt. "It's only fair."

"Yeah. Sure." He wriggled out of his shorts and stood over her, feeling as eager as a teenager. Yet, he now had enough sense to savor this moment. To drink in her beauty and appreciate the gift she was about to give him.

"Come closer." She leaned back wearing nothing but the tiny triangle of red between her thighs. "What are you waiting for?"

"Trying to decide which one of my fantasies I should act out." Yeah, that did sound even dumber out loud than it had in his head.

She laughed. "We've got all night. Why not try them all?"

He went for fantasy number seven. His favorite. In which he slowly, meticulously slid that red bikini down her thighs, dropping kisses on her exquisite skin along the way. And just like in his dreams, she was hot, wet, and ready for him. He slipped one finger inside her—perfect—and stroked her carefully, listening to her moans, watching her eyes flutter shut as he pleasured her. When her breathing got frantic and her hips thrust against his hand, he knew she was close.

"Cooper," she breathed. "Please. Now."

He reached for the box of condoms. Damn, why hadn't he opened it yet? Had one ready? He tore open the box, and grabbed the little square packet. His fingers trembled as he tore open the package and quickly covered himself.

"Now where were we?" he asked as he positioned himself over her.

Chapter 15

Annabelle, at least, was right at the edge of paradise. Only she didn't speak the words out loud. She couldn't speak as he plunged inside her. This was supposed to be his fantasy, but she was the one living a dream. Her body hummed with pleasure.

"Annabelle." He sang her name as he thrust again and again. Hard and fast at first, then he slowed down, almost as if he wanted to savor every moment, every slip of his skin against hers.

She arched up against him, drawing him deeper, and feeling more and more connected until she no longer felt a part of this earth. A flash of color burst before her eyes and she cried out as the most intense climax she'd ever known washed over her.

He stilled, both of them frozen in time, and then he started moving again. Slowly, building higher and faster until finally he made one final thrust, letting out a groan before collapsing on top of her.

Cooper rolled over, bringing her with him, and held her on top of him, stroking her hair and smiling.

"You are so beautiful. Words can't—" He closed his eyes and started humming. It was a familiar tune. The one he'd been playing the other night. When he'd been singing about her.

"So did I live up to the fantasy?"

"Annabelle..." He wrapped his arms around her. "You're a dream come true."

"You might sing a different tune once you find out I hog the covers." She nuzzled against him, content to lie in his strong embrace.

"Does that mean you're going to spend the night?" he murmured. "Or do you have to get back to the girls?"

"I have overnight babysitters." She lifted her head. "That is, unless you want me to leave."

"Stay, Annabelle. Please stay."

* * * *

The sun was barely peeking through the window when Cooper awoke to the movement of Annabelle getting out of bed. She wrapped the skirt around her waist and pulled her sweater over her head.

"I should get back before the twins wake up." She offered an apologetic smile. "It's a school day."

"Yeah." Trying to remember the last time he'd slept so well, he rubbed his hands over his face. "Let me know if you need anything."

"You can count on it." She bent down to place a kiss on the top of his head.

"Annabelle." He wrapped his arms around her. "Thank you."

"My pleasure. Really."

"No, I mean, thank you for asking the questions you asked last night." He held her, wishing the sun wasn't quite up yet. "I needed to talk about it. I wanted to tell you, but I was afraid."

"I thought maybe you already had, and I'd forgotten." She tried to make light of the whole thing, bless her heart.

"I didn't want to hurt you."

"Of course not." She shrugged. "But I'm a big girl. I can handle the truth. Look, I'm not perfect."

She reached up and touched the side of her face. Maybe it was a subconscious thing, or maybe she was making a point.

"You're an amazing woman." He brushed the hair off her cheek.

She pulled away. "I really do have to go. But I left you a little something to remember me by."

"Besides the memory of an incredible night?"

"Call it a souvenir." She pulled the nightstand drawer open to reveal a flash of red.

"The swimsuit?" Damn if his dick didn't grow rock hard in an instant. She smiled and backed out of the doorway.

He flopped back on the bed.

He'd spent the night with Annabelle Jones. She was amazing. Incredible. Sexier than he'd imagined in his wildest fantasies.

And she'd left him with her swimsuit. The one she'd worn on the cover of the magazine that had first caught his eye back when he was a rookie fighting for a roster spot.

She'd left him with the will to fight his way back onto a major league team.

* * * *

Annabelle tiptoed through the back door. She'd hoped no one was up yet, but she bumped into Marco in her kitchen.

"I hope you don't mind me starting the coffee." He filled the pot and poured it into the coffeemaker. "You did say to make ourselves at home."

"No. That's fine." She crossed her arms over her chest, a little self-conscious about wearing nothing at all under her sweater. "I hope everything went okay last night."

"Yeah. Your kids are really sweet."

"They are." She couldn't help but smile. "I'm so blessed to have them."

"So, everything went okay for you?" He avoided her gaze and started opening cupboard doors, apparently looking for the coffee mugs.

"Yes. Yes it did. Thank you for helping me with that." Her cheeks flamed. "I mean, by watching the girls and…"

"I hope everything works out for you. Really, Annabelle, you deserve someone who can make you happy."

"Thank you." She reached for one of the mugs he set on the counter. "I have a pretty good feeling about us."

"Good. I'm happy for you." He stared at the coffee dripping into the pot. "For both of you."

"So tell me, what will it be like when he goes back?" She grabbed some cinnamon and the half and half. "Will there be a lot of hard feelings from his teammates? Suspicion?"

"I don't know. I guess it depends on what kind of clubhouse he ends up in." Marco shrugged. "It probably helps that he didn't try to deny it. He took the suspension without question. And he cooperated with the initial investigation. That's something."

"But I suppose there will always be some who think it's unforgivable."

"Yeah. There will be guys who'll resent him. But then there are the ones who think 'if you aren't cheating, you aren't trying.' I suppose he'll get the most grief from guys who had a hard time getting to the majors. They might think he took a spot from someone else. Someone who deserved it more."

"But he didn't take someone's spot. He was just trying to keep the place he'd earned."

"Maybe. But the thing is, people will question him for the rest of his career." Marco poured coffee into her mug before filling his own. "If he has a poor performance, it'll be because he was juiced before. If he has a really good outing, people will wonder if he's using again."

"That sucks."

"Yeah, the whole thing sucks. But it's part of the game. It's not going anywhere." Marco took a sip of coffee. "Not with the pressure on players to perform. Not with the amount of money thrown at them."

"Did you ever?"

"No. And I can't imagine ever being in a situation where I'd even consider it." He exhaled. "I've got too much to lose. Hunter has too much to lose."

"But she's not involved with the team anymore."

"Not officially. But come on, she's the heart and soul of the Goliaths. She always has been. She'll get back into the game, I'm sure of it."

He smiled as if he knew a secret. Or maybe he was just smiling because he was happy. Why wouldn't he be? He had everything he could ever want. A World Series championship, a long-term contract, and the love of his life by his side.

"Wow." Annabelle sighed. "You really admire her, don't you? I mean, I know you love her, but..."

Annabelle's throat got all tight on her. It wasn't jealousy, exactly. But she wondered what it would be like to be absolutely worshiped by a man.

"Hunter is my world. But baseball is a close second." Marco flashed his dimples and went back to drinking his coffee.

"Is there anything I can do to help him? I mean with baseball?"

"I don't know. How is he, physically?"

"Stunning." The word slipped out of her mouth before she could filter. "I mean, he's in great shape. He's definitely very strong."

"That's part of it." Marco shifted, a little uncomfortable with the topic of discussion perhaps. "But for a pitcher especially, there's a lot more than just strength. Mechanics, for one. And then there's the whole mental aspect. He'll have to be able to keep his head in the game, even with the inevitable backlash. It could be even harder for him to keep his focus."

"So, am I an unwanted distraction?" Annabelle asked. "Or could I help him with his focus?"

"That depends."

"On what?"

"Oh, hell, I don't know." Marco set his mug on the counter. "I'm hardly an expert. I just know from my own experience. I know I've become a better ballplayer because of Hunter. The right woman can definitely help a guy's career."

"But the wrong woman could send it the other direction?" She wondered what kind of woman she could be for Cooper.

"I don't know. I don't think you're the wrong kind of woman. I mean, you're not...well..."

"I'm not a groupie or a gold digger?"

"Yeah, you're neither of those types of women."

"But?"

"You're the kind of woman that a guy starts asking himself if he wants to get serious."

"And if the answer is no, then he'll take off running?"

He shrugged, their shared past hanging between them.

Footsteps on the stairs prevented them from venturing any further down memory lane.

"Good morning." Hunter gave Annabelle a slight smile before turning to her husband with a megawatt grin. "Is that coffee I smell?"

Marco moved to pour her a cup.

"So did you have a good night?" Hunter took the mug from Marco and sat down at the table.

"Yes. It was just what I needed. Thank you." Annabelle sat across the table from her friend. "And I hope everything went well here. The girls didn't give you any trouble?"

"They were a little disappointed when Marco didn't know any bedtime songs, but he read them a story and they settled down."

"Cooper is a talented musician." Annabelle couldn't help but sigh. "He's been suckered into singing to the girls at bedtime."

"How sweet."

"So tell me more about his baseball talent." Annabelle wanted to know everything. "Does he have a shot at making it back to the majors?"

"He was one of the best, when he was healthy." Hunter's voice took on an eager tone with the discussion turned to baseball. "And a left-handed pitcher is always in demand."

"So you think he could find a team who'll be interested in signing him?"

Hunter bit her lip, as if she knew something she didn't want to share. "I heard he's turned down at least one of the offers that came his way."

"Why would he do that?"

"Either he didn't feel it was good enough"—Hunter glanced at Marco—"or maybe he's thinking he's not good enough. If he's not one hundred percent, he might not trust his stuff. It's always tough on an athlete coming back from an injury."

"Either way, I suppose the closer we get to spring training, the less likely he'll make a team?" Annabelle worried for him.

"Possibly. But there's still a chance. Deals could fall through. Players might not pass their physicals." Hunter's speech became more animated. "There are always one or two last minute signings that make for an exciting camp."

"I knew it." Marco laughed, pouring himself another cup of coffee. "You have baseball in your blood. I don't think you'll make it to the All-star break before finding some way to get back into the game."

"I made my choice." Hunter crossed her arms over her chest. "I don't regret anything."

"Oh baby…" Marco came up behind his wife. Putting his arms around her, he kissed the top of her head. "I still can't believe what you gave up for me."

"It's just baseball." Hunter tried to brush off his statement. "It's a business."

She wriggled out of his embrace and turned to Annabelle. "If Cooper's healthy, he'll make it back. There are plenty of teams who need another lefty in the bullpen. I think Philly or Baltimore are still looking for a guy like him."

Philadelphia. Baltimore. Both east coast teams. Her heart did a crazy little lurch at the thought of him packing up and leaving for the other side of the country.

"Oh my, look at the time." Annabelle didn't want her friends to see her cry. "I'd better get in the shower and get the girls up for school."

She hurried upstairs, blinking back the tears that stung her eyes. She was going to lose Cooper. He'd tried to warn her. Only her stupid heart had ignored him. She'd gone and fallen in love with him anyway.

Love. How was it possible? She'd only really known the man a week. Sure, she'd listened to him play his guitar every night after she put the girls to bed. She'd kept her bedroom window open, unless it was raining, and she couldn't help but overhear his soulful voice, the loneliness that resonated with her. She'd recognized the longing in his music.

So they may not have spent that much time together but they had connected. On a much deeper level than she'd connected with anyone. And that was even before she'd let him act out his fantasies with her in the red bikini.

* * * *

After Annabelle left, Cooper took a quick shower, downed a high-protein smoothie, and took off for a run down the beach. He had a lot on his mind and there were only two ways he knew of to get out of his own head, through physical activity or through music.

He needed to run. A few chords on his guitar weren't nearly enough to unravel his thoughts. Annabelle was at the forefront of his mind. She was something. No, she was everything he'd ever dreamed of. Her beauty was just the beginning. She was sexy and sweet. Nurturing and needy. No, not needy, she just had certain needs. The kind that he had been more than willing and able to fulfill.

Holy shit. He'd made love to Annabelle Jones. Yeah, he'd *made love* to her. He didn't bang her, nail her, or screw her. No, this was something else entirely. Sex on a whole other level.

Yeah, right. He was officially losing it. He just hadn't had sex in so long that he'd gone overboard. He'd built it up in his head so that it seemed better than it actually was. Just like he'd built Annabelle up in his head.

No. In his wildest dreams, Annabelle hadn't been nearly as incredible as she was in real life.

Real life. For the past several months, that's exactly what he'd been avoiding. He'd screwed up. Then he'd gotten hurt. For the first time in his life, things hadn't come easy for him.

So what'd he do? He'd given up. Buried his feelings deep in the back of his closet along with his glove. He hadn't faced the music at all. He'd taken his suspension, but he hadn't taken responsibility for his actions. He hid behind his shame and his scars.

But his scars were nothing compared to Annabelle's. Yet she still put on a brave face. She was so brave and so strong. She wasn't afraid to ask for what she wanted.

She wanted him. Even after she found out who he was and what he'd done. Maybe it was just sex, but he didn't think so.

The question was, what was he going to do about it?

He reached the end of his run, downed a bottle of water, and stretched. Then he pulled out his phone and made a call he'd put off for too long.

When his agent didn't pick up, Cooper left a message explaining how he was ready to get back to work. He was one hundred percent healthy and would give even more than that to any team willing to give him the chance. He added that he'd prefer a West Coast team before hanging up.

Yeah. Like he had any say in the matter. But he didn't like the thought of leaving Annabelle behind. The only thing worse would be to have nothing to offer her.

He had two options. Getting back in the game or giving back to the game.

He returned home, grabbed his gear, and headed over to Sanders Baseball Academy. They weren't open to the public until after school hours, but he knew Sanders would be in his office. Cooper was ready to test his arm. To see if he really had what it took. And if he didn't, he'd decided to find out more about what Plan B would entail.

"Hey, Coop. What brings you here this fine morning?" Sanders ushered him into his office. "It's a little early for a throwing session."

"Yeah, I hadn't thought of that." He dropped his bag on the extra chair. "But while I'm here I thought I'd find out a little more about what kind of program you've got here."

"I know you don't have any boys to enroll, so does that mean you're interested in joining the coaching staff?"

"Maybe." Cooper sat across from his friend, his thighs twitching with nervous energy. "I need to know what my options are. Can a guy actually make a living coaching kids?"

"It depends on what you mean by 'make a living.' If you want to make the kind of money you're used to, the answer is not even close."

"I mean the kind of money that can support a family." And yeah, the image of Annabelle and her daughters stood forefront in his mind.

"Does this have anything to do with the car seats in the back of your Escalade?" Sanders leveled his gaze at him. "With Annabelle Jones?"

"Yeah, like I'm going to get Annabelle Jones to marry me." Until he said it, he hadn't realized that's exactly where his fantasies were headed. "Shit."

Sanders threw his head back and laughed. "Man, you're in deep. Real deep. Annabelle freaking Jones."

"Hey, that's my…my neighbor you're talking about."

"You really want to coach or do you want to look like a good guy to try and impress the lady?"

"Somehow, I've already impressed her." He should stop talking. He didn't need to hash out the details of his night with Annabelle. It was private, something between the two of them. "Look, money isn't really an issue. At least it won't be for the next five, maybe ten years. But a man's got to have some pride. A man's got to have a job."

"You are serious." Sanders nodded. He got it. "Good. We'd love to have you on board."

Cooper wiped his hands on his athletic shorts. Damn, he was sweating like a kid on his first date.

"Wait a minute." Sanders leaned back in his office chair. "You're not giving up on playing are you?"

"No. I just want to have a backup plan."

"So, I'm a last resort? Like that time you were the emergency catcher?"

"No. That's not it. I just want to cover my bases."

"Don't give me that cliché crap." Sanders always could smell bullshit a mile away. Or at least sixty feet, six inches away. "What do you really want?"

"Until this morning, I didn't have a fucking clue."

"What happened this morning?"

"None of your damn business." Cooper leaned forward. "But let's just say I had a moment of clarity. It's not just about me. Not anymore."

"You still want to play?"

"Yes."

"And do you think you still have it in you?"

He stretched, reaching his arms back over his shoulders. When he didn't hear a pop, didn't feel a twinge, he nodded.

"I think I need to try." He leaned back in the chair, closing his eyes. He tried to visualize himself on the mound, with the grass so green and the sky so blue and the crowd buzzing in the background. He could see the target, the smooth, round leather of the catcher's mitt. He could picture himself winding up, letting go, and firing one in. Right on target. Except instead of Roberto Luis's ugly mug behind the plate, he pictured Annabelle standing up and tossing the mask, smiling as she threw the ball back to him.

"Tell you what…" Sanders had picked up a pen shaped like a miniature baseball bat and was tapping it on his thigh. "If you're not on a spring training roster, then plan on a trial run as one of my pitching coaches. We run three clinics a week during the season. We have six camps over the summer. Three week-long sessions, two two-week sessions, and an intensive month-long camp for the elite players who actually have a shot."

"All right." Cooper extended his hand to shake on it. "If I don't have any offers by the last official reporting day, I'll be here."

"Good." Sanders stood. "I hope you can join us. But I hope you have to put it off another year or two or even more."

"Me too."

Chapter 16

Even though she'd invited him for dinner and he'd agreed, Annabelle was surprised to see Cooper at her front door. He was dressed in dark designer jeans that fit him like nobody's business. His tailored shirt was a silvery green, the color of eucalyptus leaves. Longing stirred inside her. For the man, yes, but she also longed for home.

She leaned in and gave him a quick hug.

"Your cologne smells like eucalyptus. It reminds me of San Francisco."

"It's the lotion." He smiled. "Are you still using the stuff I gave you?"

"The one made by the little old lady from Mendocino?" She'd been using it religiously. And it really did help with the stiffness. "Are you hurting? Is your shoulder okay?"

"The shoulder's fine. I still use it out of habit, I guess." He reached up and rubbed his shoulder. Also out of habit? "Plus, it smells good."

"It does." She stepped aside to let him in. "How long did you live in San Francisco?"

"Nearly six seasons." He held a bottle of wine in his left hand.

"Do you miss it?"

"Sometimes. It's a great city." He transferred the wine to his other hand. "I always kept my place down here, though. I guess I knew I wouldn't stay in San Francisco forever."

"You don't want to be here, do you?" Annabelle noticed he stood stiffly, like a kid forced to wear a starched suit. "Is it me or my friends?"

"Annabelle." He still sung her name. "I do want to be here. With you."

To prove it, he set the wine down on the hall table and kissed her, his whiskers tickling her lips. He'd trimmed his beard, and she liked the way it looked. She really liked the way it felt. Her body sang with his touch.

"Good. I worried that maybe since we…" She took a deep breath.

"You thought that since we slept together, I'd, what? Lose interest?" He shook his head. "I don't know what kind of guys you've been with before, but…"

"You've met my ex-husband." She didn't want to talk about the other guys she'd been with. Especially not that disaster that happened in New Zealand. And she didn't think he wanted to hear about her relationship with the guy he'd been traded for. "But that doesn't matter. I don't want things to be weird between us."

"I don't want things to be weird between us, either." He reached down and brushed her hair off her forehead. Then he placed a gentle kiss on her scar. The tenderness moved her in a deep way.

"But you don't want to have dinner with my friends, do you?"

"It's not that." He let out a sigh. "They're part of the baseball world. I disgraced the game, and I don't know if I'll be a part of that world anymore."

"Maybe it's time you find out." She led him back to the kitchen.

* * * *

Cooper set the wine on the counter. He reached into the drawer where Annabelle kept her wine opener, but then he thought maybe he was making himself too much at home.

"Do you want me to open this now or save it for dinner?"

"I'll have a glass." Annabelle smiled at him hopefully. "Hunter?"

"Sure. Then we'll get started on the salad." Hunter headed for the sink to wash up.

"I was going to have a beer." Marco acknowledged Cooper with a slight nod. "You want to join me? We can get the grill going."

Cooper took a deep breath. This was important to Annabelle. She wanted him to fit in with her friends. "Sure. Grab me a cold one."

He'd given up drinking, women, and baseball. He'd basically given up on living, too. Time to step back into life.

Cooper uncorked the wine, poured two glasses for the ladies, and followed Marco out onto the deck. He accepted an IPA and debated whether he should allow the other man to take charge of the barbecue or if he should be the one to act as man of the house.

Marco must have been wondering the same thing. They both stood there, beers in hand, staring at the stainless steel gas barbecue. After what felt like several awkward moments, Marco raised his bottle and gave a nod before taking a long swallow.

Cooper repeated the motion. Sometimes he appreciated not having to say anything.

"You use this grill before?" Marco asked.

"No. But I'm sure I could get it started." Cooper approached the grill. He flipped the knob and the gas lit.

They both stood there, staring at the blue flame. Avoiding conversation like only a couple of guys could do. Cooper imagined the girls were inside chatting away, probably talking about the two of them.

"So, I hear you got a pretty good contract with the Goliaths." Cooper decided to get the conversation started.

"Yeah. I know Hunter is behind the deal, but don't tell anyone." A proud grin lit Marco's face. "She's under the delusion that she's out of the game."

"What do you mean, 'out of the game'?"

"She sold her share of the Goliaths immediately after we won the World Series." Marco's grin widened. "So technically, she had nothing to do with my re-signing."

"So, is Barry still a part of things?" As in, Annabelle's ex.

"No. He sold out before the whole FITNatural story broke."

"I guess I've been out of the loop." Hiding out, in other words.

"How's the shoulder?"

"Feels good. I've been building strength." But he hadn't tested it.

"Great. That's good news."

Before they could get any further into the discussion, Annabelle came out with the marinated steaks. She looked amazing. Her jeans hugged her body as if they had been invented just for her. She wore a white tank top under a pale blue sweater that wrapped around her waist, hugged her shoulders, and did amazing things for her breasts.

Unable to help himself, he brushed a kiss across her left cheek. He tucked her hair behind her ear. "There, now I can see your pretty face."

She tried to shake her hair loose, to cover the scars.

"You're beautiful." He shouldn't have to remind her.

"Thanks." She gave him an insecure smile that killed him. "I'd better get back and help Hunter with the salad. I bought a big bunch of kale, so I need to trim the thick stems."

She turned away from him, and swept her hair over her scars before going back inside.

Cooper grabbed the grill brush and started scraping with a little more force than needed.

"Need any help with that?" Marco asked.

"I'm good." Cooper had almost forgotten the other man was there.

Marco leaned against the deck railing, taking a long drink of beer. He eyed Cooper carefully, almost suspiciously.

Santiago was the kind of hitter who would stare down a pitcher, daring him to throw his best pitch. It felt as if he was daring Cooper to make a mistake. But instead of challenging him on the field, he was challenging him over Annabelle.

"Look, you don't have to tell me how special Annabelle is." Cooper couldn't help but be a little defensive.

"No, I don't." Marco gave a slight shake of his head.

Cooper started throwing the steaks on the grill. He felt like he was on trial here. It was almost like when he'd given his testimony to the league during the preliminary hearings in the FITNatural investigation. He'd given his answers as honestly and completely as possible and it still felt like they didn't believe him.

"I certainly don't want her to get hurt." It was too soon to turn the steaks, but Cooper felt like he should be doing something. Anything to take the pressure off.

"You care about her," Marco acknowledged.

"Yes. And her daughters, too." Cooper smiled, thinking of how special Sophie and Olivia were. How attached he'd become in such a short time.

"They're sweet." Marco took a step towards him. "But can you tell them apart?"

"Yeah. Actually I can." Cooper turned to face the other man. "First of all, Olivia is usually in pink. She's a little more girly. And Sophie is more… Outgoing. Confident. She's like Annabelle in some ways."

"Yeah?"

"But even though Olivia is a little more hesitant, she's very loyal." Cooper's heart swelled a little knowing she'd accepted him.

"Also like her mother." Marco gave a little nod.

"How well do you know Annabelle?" Cooper wasn't crazy about the idea that she'd been with Marco.

"We dated about eight years ago." At the height of her career.

Cooper just gave a nod.

"She was beautiful and sweet," Marco said. "But she was pretty insecure, especially for someone who'd been on the cover of *Sports Illustrated*. But then I guess we were all pretty insecure at twenty."

"Yeah. Insecure and cocky at the same time. Not a good combination." Cooper remembered what he'd been like at that age. No good for anyone.

"I guess I started thinking she couldn't handle the lifestyle." Marco was now the one sounding defensive. Like he had to explain himself to the other man. "Would she need constant reassurance when I was on the road? The last thing you want to think about when you're trying to get your career off the ground is having to calm your girlfriend down before every road trip."

"Guess you don't have to worry about that with Hunter?"

"No. She's got faith in me." Marco's face lit in a goofy grin. He was one hundred percent in love with his wife. "It's pretty amazing when you think about it. To have someone who believes in you even when you don't believe in yourself. Especially when you don't believe in yourself."

Cooper turned back to the grill. He was starting to feel like he knew what Marco was talking about. Annabelle believed in him even after she learned about his steroid use. She still wanted him. It wasn't anything like Hunter giving up her team for Marco, but it was something. Something he could build on.

"Hey, you need another beer?" Marco asked.

"No. I'm good." For the first time in a long time, he really was.

Marco disappeared into the house and returned with another beer for himself. "I think the ladies are talking about us in there. They got real quiet when I went into the kitchen."

"I'm sure they are."

"I almost get the feeling Annabelle is worried about us out here." Marco tilted the bottle and took a quick sip. "Maybe she's just used to the way her ex acted when any other men dared even look at her. The guy was a real jerk."

"Yeah. I always got that feeling about him." Cooper didn't really want to think about the man Annabelle was technically still married to, let alone talk about him. "But there must have been something appealing about him. She did marry him. He gave her two wonderful children."

"The guy doesn't deserve them." Marco had a lot of contempt for the man. "When I think of how he could have brought down the Goliaths… He could have ruined Hunter."

"Yeah, well he wasn't the only one who put the Goliaths in a bad position." The sick feeling returned to Cooper's stomach. "Your wife was smart to get rid of me."

"Yeah. I almost forgot you were involved."

"I can never forget." Cooper downed the last half of his now warm beer. "And I'm sure there are a lot of people that will make sure I don't ever forget my mistake."

Marco made a grunting noise. It wasn't a comfortable topic of conversation. But Marco wouldn't have to keep having the conversation for the rest of his life.

"Are you looking forward to going down to spring training in a few weeks?" Cooper was more than a little envious. "This year's going to be a lot different coming off a World Series win."

"Yeah." Marco sounded less than enthusiastic. "I mean, I'm ready to get back to work. I have a lot to prove with the new contract. And defending the title is going to be tough. But we've got a solid team. We only lost a few guys. I just hope we can replace Scottsdale."

"I can't believe he retired. Man, that guy is a legend." Cooper just shook his head, wishing he hadn't screwed up and would have had the chance to go through the season with the man. "But I guess if anyone deserved to go out like he did, it would be The Monk."

"He is going out at the top of his game. He's got nothing left to prove. The man's got two Cy Young Awards, a perfect game, and as soon as they're back from the designer, he'll have his World Series ring." The conversation was starting to flow, now that they were talking about baseball.

"You'll have that ring, too." Envy gnawed at Cooper. He should have been a part of that team. And it was his own damn fault he hadn't been.

"Oh, I've already got the most important ring there is." Marco glanced down at his left hand. The he looked at his beer and shook his head. "Oh man, listen to me. You're gonna have to call the league. Have them come take my man card."

"Nah." It wasn't just missing out on the World Series that made him jealous of Marco. "But it's not like the league would listen to me anyway."

"You think you're the first guy to make a mistake?" Marco took a long drink. "And sad to say, but you won't be the last. If you hadn't gotten hurt, you'd be counting the days until you have to report."

"If I hadn't gotten hurt..." Cooper let out a frustrated breath. "I wouldn't have your contract, but I'd be in pretty good shape."

"You're still in your prime." Marco said. "You've got a lot of baseball left in you."

"That's what I thought. I figured I'd be one of those guys they'd have to pry the ball out of my cold, dead hand."

"There's nothing worse than a guy who should've quit a long time ago but doesn't see it."

"Yeah. It's almost painful."

"Then there are the guys who quit too soon." Marco shook his head again. "I mean, is Johnny Scottsdale going to wake up in a few years and wonder if he still had it in him?"

"Probably." Cooper had asked himself that same question many times in the last few months.

"See, that's the thing." Marco sat down in one of the patio chairs. "I worry about Hunter. I don't think walking away from the game is going to be any easier on her than it is for us players."

"Yeah, but she can always come back."

"True. She doesn't have to worry about her age catching up with her." Marco stretched out his legs. "She'll be back. By the time I've got to be dragged out of the game, she'll be ready to step back in. I just hope..."

Marco shifted in his chair. He was restless. "I just hope she doesn't resent me for taking her away from her work. Maybe it would be easier if we had kids."

Cooper didn't know what to say. He barely knew the guy, yet he was sharing some personal stuff. Maybe a little too personal.

"These steaks are about done." Cooper removed the steaks one by one, placing them on the clean platter Annabelle had provided for him.

"Let's eat." Marco stood, grabbed his beer bottle and the empties, and followed Cooper into the house.

Chapter 17

Dinner was going along smoothly when Sophie picked up a green bean, bit it in half, and turned to Cooper. "So are you my mom's boyfriend?"

He carefully set his fork down, swallowed, and gave Annabelle a look that was a cross between a plea for help and a question of his own.

"What makes you ask that, sweetheart?" Annabelle wondered how much her daughters had seen, heard, or imagined about her relationship with Cooper.

"I don't know?" She popped the other half of her green bean into her mouth, chewed, and swallowed. "It just seems like he should be your boyfriend."

Annabelle snuck a peek at his face. He was smiling. Maybe he agreed with Sophie's assessment.

"He's your friend. And he's a boy." Olivia joined in the conversation. "He should be your boyfriend."

"He is my friend." Annabelle felt her cheeks grow warm. "But we can talk about this later. We have company."

"Daddy has a girlfriend," Sophie informed them. "So I guess you should have a boyfriend. And we like Cooper."

"Yeah. We like Cooper," Olivia confirmed.

"I like you, too." Cooper gave each girl a warm smile. "All three of you."

He gave Annabelle a different kind of smile. The kind that suggested he would be more than happy to discuss this later. Much later.

"So tell me about your new school." Hunter, bless her heart, steered the conversation in a different direction.

The girls quickly switched gears, filling them in on Miss Ramirez, the hundredth day of school play they were working on, and a list of all the activities going on in Kindergarten.

Finally, dinner was over.

"I'll take care of the dishes," Cooper offered. "While you get the girls cleaned up."

It had become routine, but with the girls' comments about whether or not he was Annabelle's boyfriend, she wondered if she shouldn't tell him he didn't have to help clean up. But she knew he'd do it anyway.

"Can Cooper sing to us when we have our jammies on?" Sophie asked.

"Yeah, can he?" Olivia made the request unanimous.

"Sure. I'll run next door and get my guitar." His smile told Annabelle he wasn't in any way frightened off by the girls' inquiry.

Annabelle herded her daughters upstairs to the bathroom. She turned on the bathwater while the girls undressed.

"So is he your boyfriend?" Sophie stood there half undressed, with her hands on her hips, demanding an answer.

"I don't know if 'boyfriend' is the right word." Annabelle's cheeks flushed. "We haven't known each other long enough to get too worried about that kind of thing."

"But you do like him?" Olivia stepped cautiously into the tub.

"Yeah, like, *like him*, like him?" Sophie followed her sister, but with a splash.

"Yes. I like him." Annabelle felt her blush spread from her cheeks to the rest of her body. "I really like him."

"Maybe you'll marry him and he can be our new Daddy," Olivia suggested.

"Oh, I don't think that's going to happen." How did they get to this point so quickly? "I don't want to get married any time soon."

"Why not?" Sophie reached for the shampoo.

"First of all, it's not a good idea to get married right after getting divorced." It wasn't a good idea to get involved with someone when she wasn't even divorced yet. "And you already have a Daddy. No one will ever replace him."

"Yeah, but we can have two daddies." Sophie made it sound so simple. "Lots of kids do."

"Yeah, there are all kinds of families." Olivia chimed in. "Some have a mommy and a daddy that live in the same house. Some have just a mommy or just a daddy. Some have two houses. Some even have two mommies or two daddies that live in the same house."

What were they teaching them at school? Tolerance, sure, but the puzzled look on Olivia's face told Annabelle she couldn't quite figure out what it all meant.

"Well, the important thing to remember about families is that they love each other." Annabelle tried to soothe her daughter's concerns. She wasn't sure if they were feeling a little insecure about their family situation. Maybe that's why they were pushing for a romantic union between her and Cooper.

"We love Cooper," Sophie said and then she dunked her head under the water to rinse.

"Yeah. We love Cooper." Olivia looked at Annabelle with big, hopeful eyes.

"Let's finish your bath, get your pajamas on, and get your teeth brushed." Annabelle worried that her daughters would be crushed when Cooper was no longer a part of their lives.

"Okay." Sophie was far too cooperative.

"Then we can have our bedtime song." And Olivia was far too attached.

They all were.

* * * *

Sure enough, Cooper returned with his guitar just in time for bed. He sang silly songs, eliciting giggles and applause from the twins. He sang a mix of classic rock ballads and a few songs from the girls favorite princess movies. And then he plucked a now familiar melody, but he left out the words. Because she'd told him not to sing about her. Or maybe because he didn't want the girls to get too excited about him singing a song just for her.

Finally, both girls were barely able to keep their eyes open.

"Goodnight, Cooper." Sophie smiled at him, melting Annabelle's heart.

"Goodnight, Sophie." His smile liquefied more than her heart.

"'Night." Olivia jumped out of bed and flung her arms around him.

"Goodnight, Olivia." He returned her hug and Annabelle had a feeling they were all setting themselves up for a huge fall when this cozy little arrangement fell apart.

Cooper stood outside the door while she said her own goodnights. He pulled her into his arms the minute she stepped into the hallway and kissed her. Soft. Sweet. So damn sexy.

"Cooper." She tried to push him away, but they both had been waiting all night for this. For more. Her body was already anticipating taking a few more steps down the hall until they reached her bedroom, guitar and clothing optional. Well, the guitar was optional, clothing was definitely not necessary.

But her brain kicked into gear. It was a sharp and painful blow.

"Wait. We can't…" Every nerve ending screamed in protest.

"Right. You've got company." He gave her a wicked grin. "Maybe they'll be turning in soon."

"No. That's not the problem." Now her heart started to scream in objection.

"Annabelle, what's wrong?" His voice held a note of concern that made this conversation even harder.

"I just think that maybe we shouldn't have gotten involved on a physical level." Even as she said the words, she knew she didn't mean them.

"I see." He took a step back and shoved his hands in his pockets. "You regret what happened last night?"

"No. That's not it." She hated the look on his face. She'd hurt him. "I just didn't think things through. I didn't realize how much our actions would affect my daughters."

"The whole boyfriend conversation?" He tried to sound like he wasn't hurt. "I didn't say anything because I wasn't sure how you'd want to handle it."

"I think we should handle it by backing off." Was it possible to have her heart ripped out of her chest and still be able to breathe? Apparently. She sucked in a breath and, to her surprise, it filled her lungs. "They've gotten too attached to you. Not to mention this crazy idea of theirs that we're all going to be one big happy family."

"Annabelle." His voice had less of a singing quality as he said her name, but it was still there. That little melodic sound that tugged her heartstrings "Look at me."

She lifted her gaze to meet his eyes.

"I'm not going anywhere." He cupped her cheek. "If you don't want to sleep with me again, that's fine."

She could hear the pain in his voice, but she couldn't take the words back. Nor could she defend her decision.

"Okay then. I'll stay out of your bed. But I won't stay out of your lives." He raked a hand through his hair. "If you think not sleeping with me will keep things simpler, then fine. Just remember, I'm right next door. I'll be around. Day after day. Night after night."

"Until you get a contract and have to leave for spring training." She hated the sound of disappointment in her voice. "And then who knows where you'll end up."

"So you think it will be easier if we stay away from each other?" He reached up to brush her hair back away from her face. He was always doing that. Making her feel so exposed. And so cherished. "I'm through looking for the easy way out."

Her resolve started to crumble.

"Annabelle." He caressed her cheek, lightly touching her scars. But instead of recoiling in disgust, he closed his eyes in reverence. "You are so beautiful. So damned beautiful. But you're so much more than just a pretty face."

"Please, don't say things like that. You're not my boyfriend." She took a deep breath. "And you're not going to be their new daddy."

He looked like she'd just slapped him. He nodded slowly, finally getting what was happening here. "I'll go. I'll just walk out of your lives. I'll keep my curtains closed. Only play my guitar when you're not home. I'll make sure we don't cross paths at the mailbox. Is that what you want?"

"No." That's not at all what she wanted. "You don't have to hide from us. We can still be neighbors. You know, in case you need to borrow a cup of sugar."

"I don't eat sugar." He picked up his guitar and walked away.

* * * *

Three days later Cooper took his early morning run down the beach. He'd done as Annabelle asked and stayed away. He wasn't going away, just giving her space. Her friends were still there so he didn't have to worry about her running out of milk. But damn. He missed her. Missed the girls, too.

He was nearing the halfway point when a man came up alongside him. Marco Santiago.

"Annabelle said I might find you out here. Guess she knows your routine."

"Yeah. I guess she does."

"Look, I need a favor"

"Is Annabelle okay? The girls?"

"They're fine." Marco's face twisted into a grin. "It's my wife..."

"What's the matter with your wife?"

"She's dying of curiosity." Marco sounded like someone asking a huge favor. "She wants to know about your arm. If you can still pitch. She sent me to, um, scout you."

"To scout me?"

"Yeah, she wants me to find a park where we could play a little catch." He sounded like he was almost embarrassed to ask.

"You got your glove?" Cooper asked. He couldn't believe he was going to play catch with the man who'd taken his roster spot with the Goliaths.

"Always." They both slowed their pace. "So you okay with this? I mean, I could tell my wife…"

"Yeah, right." Cooper laughed. "I have a feeling the only thing you'll be telling your wife is 'yes, dear.'"

"What are you suggesting? That I'm whipped?" Marco came to a dead stop. "Because I'm not. I only go along with her when she's right. She just happens to be right most of the time."

"Sure. Whatever, man." Cooper took advantage of the pause to roll his shoulders. It was one thing to play catch with a kid. But an All-star, World Series champion?

"Hey, I'm not a pitcher, but I do know you won't be satisfied until you've given it your all."

"A philosopher, too? You're quite the well-rounded guy."

"I guess I'll tell Hunter you're not ready. That there's a reason you turned down the offers that came your way." Marco tossed that out there as if it was no big deal. "I'm sure she won't say anything to Annabelle."

Cooper knew he was screwed.

"Let's grab our gloves and head out to my buddy's training facility." Might as well get this over with.

"I knew you'd come through." Marco smiled at him with genuine solidarity.

They took Cooper's Escalade. Bruce Sanders was waiting for them with a big grin on his face. When Cooper introduced Marco, Sanders took a long look at Marco's right hand.

"Where's the ring?"

Marco held up his left hand, a shiny gold band graced his finger.

"Not that one. The World Series ring." Sanders extended his hand.

"Don't have it yet. Won't get it until the first home stand." Marco shook hands with the man.

"Oh man, I was hoping to see one up close." Sanders gave a hearty chuckle.

"I guess you'll just have to come up to San Francisco in a couple of months." Marco gave a little shrug.

"Yeah, this guy's never going to bring me the bling." He clapped Cooper on the shoulder. "Especially when he won't really push himself."

"That's what we're here for." Cooper had had enough of the small talk. *Get on with it already.*

"Good. Let's get you in a bullpen to warm up and then you can throw some batting practice." Sanders led them into the facility. "Bet you're itching to take a few swings, huh?"

"Spring training will be here before we know it." Marco followed Sanders, with Cooper bringing up the rear.

Batting practice? He hadn't thrown a pitch in almost six months. And he was going to throw batting practice? He could refuse. But then they would know he was scared. And it would get back to Hunter. It would get back to Annabelle. Oh, and the rest of the league, too.

Cooper did his warm up stretches, rotating his shoulders, rolling his neck from side to side, and taking a few calming breaths.

They started with a few warm-up tosses, getting into the rhythm of two ballplayers playing catch. Forget that one of them was sitting on the top of his game and the other one had fallen about as low as he could fall. Forget that one of them had a fat new contract, a pretty new wife, and a World Series ring on the way. And Cooper was without a contract, without his pride, and without the woman of his dreams.

Once they were both warm, Marco strapped on the catcher's gear and crouched behind the plate.

"Hey, maybe I can fill in as emergency catcher," Marco joked as he tried to get his long limbs into a squat. "I'll let Javier know I've got experience."

Juan Javier was the Goliaths' manager. Someone else Cooper had failed.

Sanders stood on the sidelines, chuckling to himself as if this was just the most fun he'd had in a long time.

"Hey Coop, wasn't he the guy they traded you for?"

"Yeah." Was Sanders trying to get his goat? Get him all worked up so he would throw harder? Back in the minors, sometimes a little pregame trash talk helped him get his velocity up. Getting a little bit pissed off helped him channel all that energy into his pitching.

Cooper had to shake off the thought that he could have gone a lot farther if he'd had his battery mate in the big leagues.

He stepped up to the pitching mound, toed the rubber, and hoped like hell he wouldn't make a fool of himself.

His first pitch was a little high and outside. But at least Marco grabbed it before it went to the backstop.

Ball one.

His next two pitches were right over the plate. Sophie or Olivia could have crushed either pitch. But at least he didn't bounce it two feet in front of the plate.

Which he did on his next throw.

He was in his head. Thinking too much. He stepped off, picked up the rosin bag, and took a few deep breaths to regain his focus.

Chapter 18

"So do you think I was wrong to break things off with Cooper?" Annabelle was nervous about going back to the doctor. What if she didn't pass the cognitive test? Would they take her license? She felt better each day. More aware, alert, and the only confusion she had was about Cooper.

"Do you think you were wrong?" Hunter slipped behind the wheel of Marco's classic Mustang and pulled her hair back into a quick ponytail. "Because it doesn't really matter what I think."

"I don't know." Annabelle tied a scarf around her hair. She tucked the loose strands beneath the silk fabric. "I think we rushed into things too quickly. And the girls have this fantasy that we'll end up one big happy family."

"They're six." Hunter reminded her. "They believe that first comes love, then comes marriage, not to mention the baby in the carriage."

"I know. They watch way too many princess movies." Annabelle wondered if she'd overreacted. "They think that it's perfectly reasonable to fall in love at first sight and live happily ever after, after only a few days."

"It's kind of scary when it happens that way." Hunter turned to Annabelle. "You try to convince yourself you must be crazy. That there is no way you can meet someone and just *know*, you know?"

"Is that how it happened between you and Marco?" Annabelle wondered. "Was it love at first sight?"

"In a way. I knew the moment he stepped into that limo, everything would change. I wanted to believe it was only about the team. But there was definitely something happening between the two of us. Something beyond all logic." Hunter's face lit up as she described their first meeting. "I didn't want to call it love, though. Way too scary."

"Yeah. Way too scary." Annabelle just knew that the moment Cooper had walked into her hospital room, she'd felt a click. Like it was a moment that should be captured for all time. Only since that moment, her world had been turned upside down.

"What if I blew it?" Annabelle wondered aloud. "What if he decides I'm just crazy? I threw myself at him, even when he didn't want to get involved because I'm technically still married. Then after he finally gives in, I kick him out of my life?"

Yeah, she was definitely crazy.

"I wish I knew what to tell you. I only know that you have to decide for yourself if he's worth fighting for."

"It would be a whole lot easier if it was just me who had to deal with the consequences." Annabelle pulled the seatbelt across her lap. "But I can't let Sophie and Olivia get hurt."

"They adore him."

"Yeah. I know. And they miss him." Annabelle missed him, too. "They think it's somehow their fault he hasn't been around these last few days."

"Would you still be seeing him if you weren't worried about them?"

"That's not a fair question." Especially since the answer would be a definite yes.

"Whoever told you all is fair in love and war hasn't experienced either." Hunter jabbed the key into the ignition and started the engine.

They drove to the doctor's office and Annabelle tried to concentrate on the road. She focused on how she would navigate the streets if she were cleared to drive. She mentally weaved her way through traffic, watching for distractions, obstructions, and frustrations.

She wanted to get back on the road. To get back to freedom. She didn't want to have to go crawling back to Cooper when she needed a ride somewhere.

If she was going to go crawling back to him, she wanted it to be for something much more satisfying than a gallon of milk.

When she got to the doctor's office, she tried to avoid the magazines, but front and center was the latest on the FITNatural scandal. The magazine promised the most in-depth coverage from the first suspensions to the current hearings.

Annabelle and Hunter exchanged a look as they both reached for the magazine.

Tears clouded Annabelle's vision. She handed the magazine to Hunter. The scandal had touched both their lives. Maybe if Annabelle hadn't been so wrapped up in her own little world, pretending to be too busy with the twins to pay attention to her husband's affairs, she might have seen it coming. Or maybe she would have been able to warn Hunter.

But she hadn't even really paid attention to Hunter until Marco joined the team. What an odd way to start a friendship.

"Here." Hunter reached across the table and picked up a second copy of the magazine. "It's not like either of us can *not* read it."

Annabelle took a deep breath, and opened the cover. She scanned the table of contents and found the page where Nathan Cooper's early suspension was detailed. Seeing him in uniform sent a jolt of pride through her, mixed with sorrow for what he'd had and lost. He looked amazing in the Goliaths' uniform. So handsome and strong. With an intimidating gaze coming from under his cap. So this was Nathan Cooper the baseball player. A left-handed pitcher who had once been one of the top relievers before injury had driven him to seek the aid of banned substances. The author of the article had made it clear that he was especially disappointed in Cooper since he'd been one of the "so-called good guys." He gave to charity, signed autographs with a smile, and always had a quote for the media.

Annabelle had only known Cooper, the man. The guitar-playing, lullaby-singing, pancake-making neighbor who had stolen her heart and the hearts of her daughters.

"Annabelle Jones." The nurse called her name and Annabelle tossed the magazine on the table before standing and following her back to the exam room.

They took her blood pressure and weight, although she wasn't sure what either of those two things had to do with her ability to drive.

The nurse left and the doctor administering the test returned.

"I see you've taken this exam once before." She made it sound like it was no big deal to be deemed unfit to drive a car in California. "And it looks like you passed all but one part. So you'll only have to re-take the section you didn't pass."

"That's good." She hoped she could pass so she wouldn't have to submit to the humiliation again.

The doctor went over the testing procedure again and Annabelle tried to be patient. She couldn't rush through the test, but she also couldn't go too slow. She had to concentrate and focus. Two things that were difficult in her current state of distress. She'd pushed a good man away. She'd hurt him with her indecision, her insecurity, and her inability to stand up for what she really wanted.

She wanted Nathan Cooper. She wanted to be strong enough to fight for him. To fight with him in his return to baseball.

The first test question popped onto the screen.

* * * *

Cooper stood on the mound, the protective screen in front of him, a bucket of balls at his feet. Sixty feet, six inches away stood Marco Santiago. The worthy opponent. If he could face this batter, he could face anyone. All he had to do was come set, windup, and throw. If he could do this, then maybe he could return to baseball.

But if he returned to baseball, he could lose Annabelle.

He stepped off the rubber. Picked up the rosin bag, and shook his head. Hell, he'd already lost Annabelle. Baseball was all he had left. If he even had that.

Stepping back onto the mound, he brought his hands together, looked in for the sign, even though the catcher was only there to provide a target, not work with him on the strategy of getting hitters out.

Deep breath. Shoulders relaxed. Eye on the target.

He threw a fastball right down the middle. Santiago stroked it just past his right shoulder. If they had been on a real field it would have easily been a double. Instead, it hit the net and dropped to the artificial turf.

The next pitch was also over the plate, and it, too, was crushed. Several more pitches were hit hard. Either Santiago was really dialed in, or Cooper had lost his touch.

Screw that. Cooper reached back, and threw a cutter. The pitch had a little more movement, and even though Santiago made hard contact, he fouled it straight back. It was a definite improvement and it did wonders for Cooper's confidence. He wasn't ready to throw his slider yet. That would be foolish. He hadn't thrown it in almost six months. And although it was a pitch that put more stress on the elbow than the shoulder, he wasn't ready to risk it. Not yet.

He settled in and started challenging the hitter. Little changes in location, dropping the arm slot, and taking a little off the fastball made a difference. Santiago was still getting contact on the ball, but he was fouling off just as many pitches as he hit straight.

It was a good sign. A very good sign. For the first time in a long time, he felt that itch. To get on the mound. In a game. With the crowd all around him, the real battle was man to man. Pitcher against batter. His arm against the best bats in the world.

He missed the game. Missed it more than he wanted to admit. Finally, he was ready to get back to what he was meant to do. To get back to baseball.

"Hey, thanks man." Cooper dropped the ball he was holding into the bucket. He didn't have to prove anything more. "I needed that. I needed that in the worst way."

"No problem." Marco shouldered his bat and gave a nod. "I needed it, too."

"You're going to have a great year."

"Hope so. I've got a lot to prove."

"Don't we all?"

They cleaned up and Cooper waited for the pain in his shoulder. He couldn't remember the last time he'd thrown that many pitches without the fire that invariably came afterward.

He rolled his shoulders. Nothing. No shooting pain. Not even tightness. Just that feeling of having worked hard and pushed himself.

He'd know more after a couple of hours. Would the pain return after his muscles cooled down? Would he be stiff in the morning? For the first time in a long time, he looked forward to finding out how his body would respond after a throwing session.

He started running pitch sequences through his mind. Thinking about location. Speed. Movement. He'd thrown all fastballs this first time out. Played it safe. But at least he knew he could still get the ball over the plate. Worst case scenario, he'd be able to hire himself out to throw batting practice. Or maybe Santiago was just that good.

"So how long are you and Hunter planning on staying?"

"I guess it depends on how Annabelle's test goes today," Marco replied. "If she's not cleared to drive, we'll stick around a few more days. But I have to say, I'm ready to go home. Be alone with my wife until I have to get back on the road."

"She went back to the doctor?"

"Yeah, Hunter took her."

"I hope she gets some good news." He was a little hurt she hadn't told him. But he wasn't surprised. She'd told him to hit the showers. He never did like being pulled out of a game early. If he came in to pitch an inning, he wanted to finish it. He knew his role. He wasn't the closer, so he was okay with not pitching the last inning. But he wasn't okay with getting knocked out before he had a chance to finish the job.

He wasn't real happy about not getting to finish things with Annabelle, either. And it wasn't because it was the first time he'd been dumped since high school. No, he wasn't finished with her. Not by a long shot.

He was ready to take another shot at baseball. Maybe he could figure out a way to take another shot with Annabelle.

* * * *

"You passed." The doctor smiled when she delivered the good news to Annabelle. "A big improvement."

"That's a huge relief." Annabelle felt her shoulders relax. "I hate having to rely on my friends for the simplest things, like picking up a gallon of milk."

"Actually, I'm surprised you came back in." The doctor turned to face her. "Most people wait until they feel like they're back to normal and just start driving again. Your license wasn't revoked at the scene."

"I have two young children. I wouldn't even consider getting behind the wheel if…" Her throat got tight at the thought of putting her children in danger. "I know there is always a risk, but I'm not about to take an unnecessary one."

"Well, I'm glad you came in." A warm smile spread over the doctor's face. "There's a lot of attention on concussions and sports these days, but there isn't as much research on how a head injury affects non-athletes."

"So, I'm like a guinea pig?"

"No, but having the data does help." The doctor became a little more animated. "In fact, if you would be interested in completing a questionnaire, it would be extremely helpful. There's a lot more data on brain injury among athletes and soldiers returning from combat."

"But not so much on brain injuries in supermodels." Annabelle could laugh at herself, even if it was only to keep from crying.

"That's where I know you from. You're a swimsuit model."

"I *was*." She swallowed the lump in her throat. "But, now I'm just a mom."

Was it her imagination or did the scars on her face start to throb? It must be her imagination. The nerve endings were damaged. She couldn't possibly feel anything. It was like the phantom pains amputees felt in missing limbs.

"And you'll be back in the carpool, now."

"Yeah. Carpool. Except my car is totaled." Annabelle pasted on a smile. "So, yeah, I'll have time for a questionnaire."

"Great." The doctor turned her attention to the computer. She printed out a single piece of paper. "Here is the website for the survey. A username and password has been created for you. Just login and answer the questions as truthfully and specifically as you can."

"Sure." Annabelle looked forward to feeling useful, even if it was only in taking a survey. "And thank you."

"Good luck to you." The doctor stood, signaling the exam was over and she needed to attend to other patients.

Annabelle rose to her feet, ready to get on with her life. She was cleared to drive. She was even going to contribute to the medical community with her survey answers. So why did she feel like such an idiot?

Two words.

Nathan Cooper.

Chapter 19

Did Annabelle have more company? When he pulled up in front of his house, Cooper noticed a Mercedes SUV parked in Annabelle's driveway. Right behind it stood a sleek, black classic Mustang.

"Looks like the girls are back." Marco gave a nod toward the house. "I still can't believe I found a woman who could handle my Mustang."

"The car's what, fifteen years older than you are?"

"It was once my most precious possession," Marco said with a kind of reverence in his voice. "The first car I ever bought. Fixed her up myself."

Cooper looked down at his leased Escalade. He would have traded it in at the end of the season, like he usually did, but this year nothing had gone as planned.

"Had that beauty since I was twenty-one."

"Yeah?" The only thing Cooper had had since he was twenty-one was his crush on Annabelle.

"But the beauty driving it? She's a keeper." Marco let out a breath. "Yeah, I know, I sound like a damn fool."

"No." A damn fool was one who'd been halfway in love with a woman for ten years only to let her walk away.

"Hey, thanks for helping me start gearing up for the season." Marco changed the subject, and Cooper was grateful.

"You keep hitting like that, you'll be MVP." Cooper knew he hadn't challenged him much, but the guy was dialed in. Especially for a guy who'd been on his honeymoon for a couple of months.

"You went easy on me today." Marco played the humility card very well. "How's the arm?"

"Feels good. Real good." And he wasn't even bullshitting.

"Glad to hear it." Marco turned to him and smiled. "You know, I'll be reporting the details to my wife. Word could get out."

"What, that I'm available to throw batting practice?"

"No. That you're healthy." Marco gave him a serious look. "You'll get a call before spring training."

"Hope so." An awkward silence fell between the two men. Neither wanted to talk about the suspension. It was one thing to come back from injury. But he had the stigma of being a cheater to get past as well.

Marco opened the passenger door. "I'll see you around."

"Yeah." Cooper slid out from behind the wheel.

"So what about you and Annabelle?" Marco held his glove loosely in his throwing hand. "You haven't been around."

"She wanted some space. I gave it to her." Cooper missed her. Terribly. "But I'm not going anywhere."

Marco tightened his grip on his glove. He eyed Cooper carefully, sizing him up, and finally nodded his approval.

"Well, I'm going to hit the shower." Cooper dismissed Marco with a lift of his chin.

He was surprised Marco hadn't left him with one last warning about not hurting Annabelle. Maybe it just didn't need to be spoken.

Dropping his equipment bag at the bottom of the stairs, Cooper felt the relief of no longer needing to hide it in the back of his closet. Annabelle was a big reason for that. Even if things didn't work out between them, he would be forever grateful she'd given him a reason to get back into the game.

Cooper stood under the shower, letting the water run off him. Rolling his shoulders, the muscles in his back and neck began to relax. He felt good. Really good. The tiny scar on his left shoulder was barely even visible anymore.

Would Annabelle's scars fade, too? She was still beautiful, but it killed him to see how self-conscious she was about them.

As he was toweling off, the doorbell rang. He threw on a pair of shorts and headed downstairs.

Hunter stood on his doorstep. "Marco told me about your practice session this morning."

"Yeah?" He'd been hoping for Annabelle.

"We're planning on leaving tomorrow." She gave him an assessing look. "But I wondered if I could get some film before we head north."

"Film?"

"I'm not with the Goliaths anymore, but I still know a few people in the game." She tucked a strand of hair behind her ear. "If you've got the kind of stuff Marco says you've got, they'll want to know about it."

"You dropped me like I was a disease." Cooper wasn't sure why she wanted to scout him now.

"I wanted Marco." She narrowed her gaze. Intimidating. He almost felt sorry for anyone who crossed her. "I did what it took to get him."

Then she smiled. "It was just a business decision. And it worked out pretty well for the Goliaths."

"Yeah. Congratulations." He couldn't be jealous about not being a part of it. Not when it had been his own damn fault he wasn't.

"You're healthy now?" She crossed her arms over her chest. "One hundred percent?"

"Yeah. I feel better than I've felt in a long time."

"How long?"

"Too long." He hated to admit that he could have saved them both a lot of trouble if he'd just been honest from the beginning.

"How did you keep it from the trainers?"

"It's not like the old days, when they were the ones injecting the stuff." Damn, he didn't want to have this conversation.

"Not the steroids." Hunter shook her head in disgust. "The injury. Why didn't you say something? We've got the best staff in the league. If you'd gone to them at the beginning of your injury…"

They both knew why he hadn't. A combination of pride, denial, and not wanting to upset the clubhouse during a difficult time. His shoulder pain started getting to the point of concern about the same time news of her father's cancer became public. Everyone had felt an added pressure to make every inning count.

"I screwed up." He might as well have the words tattooed on his forehead.

"Yeah. You did." Her disappointment was displayed clearly on her face. "I still want to see what you've got."

"I'll set something up. Tomorrow morning?" He was going to have to start paying Sanders for rental of his facility.

"Sounds good." Hunter gave a quick nod. He couldn't quite figure her out. She'd made it clear that she no longer worked for the Goliaths, yet here she was in essence setting up a scouting session. She still had baseball in her blood.

Did he?

* * * *

Hunter was waiting for him right on time. She seemed almost giddy at the prospect of watching him pitch.

"Where's Marco?" he asked as he grabbed his once again well-used gear bag. "Isn't he coming?"

"No he's helping Annabelle with some caulk."

"Excuse me?"

"Replacing the *caulk…*" she enunciated the last word carefully. "In her bathroom."

"Oh. I guess I didn't hear you right." The fact that his mind drifted to a completely different place disturbed him. "You know they used to date."

"Yeah. I know." She chuckled and shook her head.

"It doesn't bother you that they're together? Alone?" He unlocked the door of his Escalade.

"No." She let him hold the door open for her and climbed in. "I do have to admit I was a little jealous at first. When Marco and I were still getting a feel for each other."

He nodded before heading around to the driver's side.

"I trust them both." Hunter clicked her seatbelt into place. "Marco is an honorable man. And Annabelle doesn't have a deceitful bone in her body."

"Yet she's committed adultery." He tried to keep that comment to himself but it slipped out.

"And that bothers you." Hunter not only heard his statement, she read the underlying feelings.

"Yeah. A little. Technically, she's still married." Not that he wanted to jet off to Vegas and tie the knot anytime soon. But maybe he'd like to have the option. "Believe it or not, I'm not the kind of guy who likes to break the rules."

"Not unless you're desperate?" Hunter guessed. "I think I understand why you violated the league's drug use policy. I wish you hadn't, but I do understand it."

"It was stupid and selfish." His gut churned even now. "I wish I had done things differently. I wish I had just gone to the trainer like I should have."

"I still would have traded you for Marco," Hunter said with a smile. "So why Annabelle? Why did you break the rules for her?"

"She's everything I've ever wanted." It was true. "The first time I saw her picture, I knew. She's the one. Every woman I've ever gone out with has been unfairly compared to her."

"That is pretty unfair." Hunter agreed.

"Yeah, I know she's stunning. But it wasn't just her looks. There was always something about her…" He'd never been able to explain his obsession with Annabelle. Not even to himself. "And now that I know her… She's more than just a pretty face. She's warm, and funny. And smart, too. She's a great mother. A good friend…"

"Sounds like the perfect woman."

"Except for one thing." Cooper admitted. "She's still married."

"She filed for divorce before she even met you." Hunter reminded him. "She moved down here to make a fresh start."

"Yeah. I know." But they couldn't move past the beginning. Not until her marriage ended. "And then she got into an accident. And her independence was shattered."

"She got the all clear to drive."

"Good. Then she doesn't need me."

"Yes she does." Hunter reached across the center console to pat his hand. "Just make sure she doesn't feel like she needs you."

"Easier said than done."

"Yeah, but if you pull it off, you could retire and make billions off the self-help book."

"Maybe I'm not ready to retire."

"Isn't that what we're going to find out?"

Chapter 20

"I really appreciate you taking the time to help with this." Annabelle stood in her downstairs bathroom watching Marco squeeze caulking along the edge of her bathtub. "I'm just not very handy with this kind of thing."

"You could have asked Cooper." Marco wielded the caulk gun with the same confidence he wielded at bat.

"Maybe." She shook her head. "I don't know. I think I dropped the ball with him."

"How?"

"I pushed him away."

"He hasn't gone far."

"A guy like him..." She blinked back the tears stinging her eyes. Swallowed the massive lump in her throat. "He's got plenty of options. Even without a baseball contract—with his looks, his voice... You know why musicians get even more girls than ballplayers, don't you?"

"No smelly jock straps?" There was that charm of his. But she didn't feel that little flutter of attraction. Maybe it was because he was married to her friend. Or maybe it was because there was someone else who sent her heart racing.

"Come on, women would line up to wash yours," Annabelle teased. She still liked him, and would always appreciate his friendship.

"The clubhouse attendant takes care of the laundry." Marco pretended he didn't know what she meant. "Besides, I'm a married man. Happily married."

"I know. Hunter is perfect for you."

"She is." He looked up at her with a goofy, happy grin on his face. But then he got all serious on her. "Look, I don't know if Cooper's right for you. You'll have to figure that out on your own."

Marco smoothed the last bit of caulk with his finger and wiped his hands on an old towel.

"Do you think he'll pitch this year?" She watched him clean up the supplies.

"I would be really surprised if he didn't."

"So he could only be around for another month or so?"

"Teams start reporting to spring training in mid-February."

"So I guess I need to decide if it's worth getting involved in what can only be a temporary relationship?" Annabelle asked.

"I moved around a lot as a kid." Marco stood and looked her straight in the eye. "I know what it's like to leave people you've grown to care about. But I never regretted making friends, even when I knew there was a good chance I'd never see them after I moved again."

"Did you ever have a close relationship with any of your mom's boyfriends?"

"My mom didn't have boyfriends." He crossed his arms over his chest. "I guess maybe she did, but none she ever brought home. The only man I've ever met that she's been involved with is my father."

He reached up and rubbed the back of his neck. "I'm sorry. I can't help you with how your dating Cooper will affect your daughters. I know they like him."

"I just don't want them to get their hopes up."

"Too late." Marco leaned against the tile wall. "I was there at dinner. Of course they have fantasies about you marrying again. They play with dolls, watch fairy tales, and still need to believe in a happily-ever-after."

"Maybe I should have them play with toy cars or Legos instead."

"They'd drive the cars to pretend dates. Build dream houses out of the Legos." He shook his head. "I always wanted my mom to find someone and get married. Do you have any idea of how many coaches I tried to set her up with?"

"You were looking for a dad?"

"No. Well, maybe. But mostly I wanted her to be happy." He smiled. "And your girls want you to be happy."

"Even if it is only temporary?"

"Don't deny yourself some happiness because you worry it won't be forever." Marco leaned forward. "Not every relationship is meant to be permanent. And sometimes friendships can endure even when you don't see each other every day."

"Like we've remained friends?" Annabelle asked. "I still owe you for helping investigate Clayton. And I'm not talking about the money you spent on the private investigator."

"You don't owe me anything." He shifted uncomfortably. "But let me ask you something. You filed for divorce after finding out about Clayton's involvement in FITNatural. The same company that provided the steroids Cooper took."

"So what's your question?"

"Why did you divorce your husband?"

"I think I was ready to divorce him when I asked you to help me investigate him. His investment in FITNatural was just the final straw." She really didn't want to get into it, but she needed to explain how she could forgive a man she'd just met while giving up on the man who'd been her husband for almost seven years. "He'd betrayed me in so many ways. He never loved me. Sure, he loved the idea of having me as his wife. *The beautiful Annabelle Jones.* But he never loved me. He never even…"

No. She wasn't going to discuss her marital woes with Marco. No matter how sympathetic and well-meaning he was.

"I know it seems kind of hypocritical of me to divorce Clayton in the midst of the scandal, only to fall into bed with the man who was also involved. But I'm convinced Cooper only did it because he was hurt. He just wanted to help the team. Clayton was only after the money."

"Some will say it was greed that drove Cooper, too. If he hadn't been caught, he could have signed for a ridiculous amount of money."

"But now he's just hoping to find a team who'll invite him to camp." Her heart ached for Cooper. "And he'll have to work twice as hard to prove he belongs there."

"Probably. But he belongs there. The man can pitch."

"And that makes up for everything?"

"No. But as much as we'd like to believe all is fair in love and baseball, certain truths remain. A talented player is going to get away with more than a less talented one. Especially in a game that brings in nine billion a year."

"But that's not why you play. It's not why either of you play the game."

"No. But it's part of it. I mean, yeah, the money's nice. You know, feeling like I can take care of my family. I wanted to be able to give my mother everything she never had. I wouldn't be able to do that in any other job." He ran his hands through his hair. "I do love the game. And yeah, the thought of not playing anymore can be terrifying. Can make a guy take desperate measures."

"So he'll do anything to get back in the game?"

"I don't know him well enough to say for sure, but for most of us, leaving the game before we're ready…" His face twisted into goofy, love-struck grin. "God, I'm such a lucky bastard."

"Yes. You are."

"Hunter wouldn't let me give up baseball. I would have, for her. But she knew me so well, she gave up her team so I could stay in the game."

What would Annabelle give up for Cooper? She didn't have much to sacrifice. Her career was over. Her fortune would only last so long. About the only thing she had left was her independence, but she'd never really had that in the first place.

* * * *

Cooper stood on the practice mound. He'd warmed up and was getting ready to pitch in front of his former owner. The woman he'd hurt the most by his suspension.

He was baffled by her request to videotape him throwing a bullpen session. Forty to fifty pitches should be enough to give her an idea of what he had left in his throwing arm. But why? She had nothing to gain by seeing if he was ready to return to the game.

Marco had hinted that she was bored. According to him, she'd been the real force behind the Goliaths' success for the past several years. Now she was relegated to the status of a player's wife. She'd gone from the front office to the background.

"Whenever you're ready." She held her camera steady, just waiting for him to show off his stuff. The radar gun was already set up. Brandon was in the squat behind the plate.

Cooper tried to empty his mind. He didn't want to think about how much slower his fastball was. Or what would happen if he didn't make it back. Hell, he didn't even want to think about what would happen if he did.

He just needed to think about throwing the ball sixty feet, six inches. The rest would fall into place after that.

He picked up a ball. Held it in his left hand like an old friend. With a nod to his catcher, he stepped up to the rubber. Digging his toe in the dirt, he tried to find just the right feel. Once he was comfortable in his footing, he brought the ball and his glove to his chest.

Thump-thump. Thump-thump. Thump-thump went his heart. Throwing a baseball was as natural to him as breathing. He'd performed in front of sold-out home crowds, hostile opposing team fans, and die-hard hold-outs who'd stuck around for five extra innings of scoreless baseball hoping he wasn't going to be the one to blow it and send them all home disappointed.

It took him three pitches to stop thinking. He settled into the rhythm of pitching. The ball was going where he wanted it. The pop of the catcher's mitt sounded like he was throwing at least ninety. Not as hard as he used to throw, but hopefully hard enough.

After about forty-five pitches, Hunter put down her camera. "I've seen enough."

She had a hopeful grin on her face.

Cooper rolled his shoulders, tilted his neck from side to side, and tried to contain the excitement he felt from knowing he'd done his best. It wasn't quite like being in a real game, facing professional hitters, but after being out of it for so long, it was something.

"So what are you planning on doing with the video?"

"Sell it to the highest bidder." Hunter was almost giddy, but he wasn't sure if it was from his performance, or simply because she was back in the game herself.

Like so many things in his life, he'd only come to appreciate all the work she'd done for the Goliaths after he'd been let go. They were a family. And he'd been the spoiled kid who hadn't realized how good he'd had it.

He knew the chances of him being welcomed back were pretty slim. But the fact that Hunter had enough faith in him to even take a look was something. Or maybe she was just doing it for Annabelle's sake. The two women were good friends.

But if he signed with any team other than L.A., Anaheim, or even San Diego, his relationship with Annabelle would be seriously challenged. A minimum of eight months away would not make it easy on her. Or her daughters. It's not like he could ask them to go with him, wherever he ended up.

Getting back to baseball could mean losing Annabelle. But if he didn't have baseball, he'd have nothing to give her.

Chapter 21

Annabelle stood on his porch with a measuring cup in her hand. "Can I borrow a cup of forgiveness?"

"I don't know." He stepped back to let her in. "Are you sure you need it?"

"I pushed you away." Remorse flickered in her eyes.

"I told you I wasn't going anywhere." His heart thumped in his chest. She'd come to him. He'd been afraid he'd lost her, but she'd come back. "I've been here the whole time."

A smile lit her face. God, she was beautiful. So beautiful it hurt.

"Did your friends leave?" When he'd returned with Hunter, Marco had the car already packed and ready to go.

"Yes. They've got, what, a month before Marco goes back to work?"

"About that." Position players reported a few days after pitchers and catchers.

"So, am I forgiven?"

He answered by pressing her against the door and covering her mouth with his. Kissing her, tasting her, needing her.

The measuring cup slipped from her hand and hit the wood floor with a thud.

He pushed her hair back away from her face. He looked into her eyes, shining with the same desire he felt.

"Annabelle." She was right, he did sing her name. "You're so beautiful. You probably get tired of hearing that, but it's true."

"I like hearing it from you," she said. "It means something coming from you."

He reached up to stroke her face. Her beauty was breathtaking. But there was more to her than just her looks.

"You're amazing, Annabelle." He didn't know how to really explain the way she made him feel. He wanted to take care of her. He wanted to be taken care of. He wanted...

Pulling her closer, he kissed her again.

"The school bus will be here in about fifteen minutes." Annabelle pushed him away. "But you can come to dinner."

"So does that mean we're friends?"

"Yes."

"Just friends?"

She shook her head, her cheeks still flushed from all the kissing.

"With benefits?"

A sly smile accompanied her nod.

"We can work out the details after we pick up the girls." She reached for the door handle and tilted her head indicating she wanted him to follow.

They walked side by side to the bus stop. He wasn't going to push his luck by taking her hand. For now, he was satisfied with being invited back into her life.

"Cooper!" Both girls came rushing toward him.

"Where have you been?" Sophie demanded, with her little hands on her jean-clad hips.

Olivia crashed into him with a hug around his knees. "We missed you."

"I missed you girls, too." He tried to keep the emotion from choking off his voice. "But you had company. I didn't want to get in the way."

"You won't get in the way," Sophie insisted. "You're practically family."

Something bloomed in his chest. Hope. Longing for something more than what he and Annabelle shared in the bedroom.

"Yeah, and that means you can come to our Hundredth Day play." Olivia looked up at him, hope shining in his eyes.

"I wouldn't miss it." He stuck out his hand, and Olivia eagerly took it.

"Yeah, we get to go on stage and everything." Sophie grabbed his other hand and practically dragged him up the street. "We have a special song, and there's even dancing."

"Dancing?"

They chattered on about the plot of the play, basically finding all the different ways and various items they could count to one hundred. The girls were as excited as if they were performing *Cats*.

They reached Annabelle's house. The girls rushed inside, eager for their afternoon snack.

"I'm not sure how we'll work this out." Annabelle hesitated at the door. "But I'm sure we'll think of something."

"I'm sure we will."

He wanted to pull her into his arms. Wanted to devour her, but it was three-thirty in the afternoon and her daughters were just inside.

"So dinner? Around six?"

"Sounds good. Can I bring anything?"

"Just your appetite." She started to turn the doorknob. "Oh, and your guitar."

"My guitar? What, you think I'll just perform for you on command?" He gave her a teasing grin. "I thought I was your friend. Or am I your boyfriend?"

"Friend, neighbor, and..." She took a deep breath. "Yeah, I guess you're my boyfriend. If you want to be."

He stepped closer. He could feel the heat coming off her. Could smell her shampoo. And he'd swear he could hear her heart beating as rapidly as his own.

"I want to be with you, Annabelle." Closing the last few inches between them, he reached for her. Her eyes fluttered shut when he stroked her cheek. She no longer recoiled when he touched the left side of her face.

He placed a soft, almost tentative kiss on her lips.

She threw her arms around him and pulled him in for a hotter, bolder kiss. She moaned as he slid his tongue between her lips. Hungrily, she opened for him. And she gave as good as she got.

* * * *

Annabelle closed the door behind her. She'd invited Cooper back into her life. Into their lives. Both girls looked up at her expectantly.

"So is he coming to our play tonight?" Sophie asked.

"Yeah, is he?" Olivia chimed in.

"The play is tonight?" She'd been distracted by her feelings for Cooper and she hadn't been listening to their conversation. She remembered reading about it in the class newsletter, but hadn't quite fixed the date in her mind.

"Yeah. Tonight. At six o'clock." Sophie gave her a look that was almost, but not quite an eye roll.

"Yeah, but we have to be there at five-thirty to get our costumes on and go to the bathroom *before* we go on stage," Olivia demanded.

"Okay. I'll let him know we'll have to leave early and see if he wants to join us." She pulled out her phone to send him a quick text. "Maybe we can all go out for pizza afterward."

"Yeah. Cool." Sophie's eyes lit up at the idea. They hadn't been out since before the accident.

Both girls finished their snacks and raced upstairs to start getting ready.

Annabelle cleaned up the kitchen, and put the teakettle on. She sent Cooper a text and he texted back, letting her know he'd be happy to join them for the girls' school play. He even offered to drive, and even though she'd been waiting for clearance to drive herself, she was relieved she wouldn't have to. Her nerves were a jangled mess. She'd made the decision to let Cooper into their lives, and she was scared of how neatly he fit.

She was even more afraid of the hole he'd leave behind when he signed with a new team.

"Wow, you two are ready already?" Annabelle had just sat down with a cup of tea when the girls bounded down the stairs. "We won't leave for another hour."

"We're just super excited." As if Sophie's bouncing didn't make that obvious.

"And Cooper's coming." Olivia was only slightly more restrained than her sister. "He'll get to meet Miss Ramirez and everything."

"Well now, let's not get too excited." She needed to explain a few things to her daughters. "Have a seat girls."

They took up their regular places around the kitchen table.

"Cooper is our neighbor. He's my friend." She felt a little guilty about not telling the whole truth about her relationship with Cooper. "He's not going to be your stepfather. Are we clear on that?"

They both nodded, but they shared a look with each other that had her worried they had other plans. They wanted a fairy tale ending. Nathan Cooper was Prince Charming, and their mother was the queen. They would be little princesses and they'd all live happily ever after.

"Your father will always be a part of your lives." She worried how frequently or consistently they'd see him, but that wasn't the main point of this conversation. "He loves you both very much. And even though he and I aren't married anymore, we still care about each other. We're still your parents."

"We know." Sophie looked at her as if she couldn't figure out why she was telling them this all again. "But Daddy would want you to get married again so he wouldn't have to pay abalone."

"Where on earth would you get an idea like that?"

"Um, Uncle Leonard." Olivia looked almost scared to out him. "He and Daddy were talking at Christmas. He said if you married someone else he wouldn't have to worry about you making him bleed."

"Did he say 'bleed him dry' or something like that?"

"Yeah. That. Why would getting married to someone else keep Daddy from getting cut?" Olivia took everything she heard literally.

"Oh honey, it's an expression. I think he meant that if I were to remarry, and I'm not saying I will, then he wouldn't have to pay me money for being his ex-wife." She wasn't going to explain that he'd already given her a payout instead of alimony. The only money he'd have to pay would be child support, and that wouldn't change if she remarried.

"He doesn't have to pay you because you're a model. Isn't that a job?" Sophie was trying to figure out the complicated lives of adults.

"I did have a job, but I'm not going to be a model anymore."

"Why not?"

"People don't want to look at pictures of great big scars." She brushed her hair off her face, to remind herself as well as her daughters that she was flawed. "I'll just have to find another job."

"You could work at our school," Olivia suggested.

"I don't think so." Annabelle knew that she wasn't qualified. "I didn't go to college, and they only let really smart people work with kids."

"Why didn't you go to college?" Sophie asked. "Is it because you got married?"

"No. I just never really thought about going." She'd never been encouraged, either. "When I graduated from high school all I wanted to do was get out and see the world. I did that as a model. I got to go to New Zealand, Costa Rica, and even South Africa."

"But then you married Daddy, so you didn't need to go to college?" Olivia was trying to piece the story together.

"I married your father, and I stopped modeling so I could stay home with my beautiful babies."

Both girls smiled.

"But now we're big, right? And you can get a job if you want?" Olivia questioned.

"Or you could even go to college," suggested Sophie.

"I could go to college. Sure." She'd never thought about it, but why not?

"We're going to go to college," Sophie announced with pride.

"Yes, you are." She just hoped she wasn't putting too much pressure on her girls. They'd barely begun to read, and here they were discussing college. She wanted to encourage them, sure, but maybe they needed to be little girls a little longer.

"I'm going to be a teacher." Olivia had decided that on her first day of school.

"I'm going to be a singer." Sophie's aspirations changed quite frequently. But Annabelle had little doubt where this latest career choice had come from. "Do singers make more money than baseball players?"

A knock on the door prevented Annabelle from even trying to answer that question.

"Cooper!" Both girls rushed to the door and dragged him inside.

"Do you make money as a singer?" Sophie barely let him get a foot in the door before she blurted out her question.

"Um, I sing mostly for fun." He gave Annabelle an amused grin. "I have played a couple of times for charity events, so whatever they paid me, I just donated back to the cause."

"Oh. So are you rich from being a baseball player?" Sophie didn't know that these kinds of questions were rude.

"I made pretty good money as a baseball player." He rubbed his chin. "And I managed to save a lot of that money for when I'm done playing."

"Are you done playing?"

"Sophie. Please, enough with the third degree." Annabelle was a little embarrassed by her daughter's relentless questioning.

"What's the third degree? We've been learning about weather. I know there's an F on one side of the thermometer and a C on the other." Sophie was too much sometimes.

"So, are my little actresses ready for their performance?" Cooper knelt down to give the girls his full attention.

They nearly knocked him over when they rushed to give him hugs. He took one girl in each arm and lifted them up.

Annabelle couldn't breathe. It was getting harder to think she could just keep this casual, enjoy his companionship until he left for whatever team he ended up with. Not with the way her girls had fallen head over heels for him. And she wasn't very far behind.

They piled into his SUV and drove to the school. As soon as the girls saw their teacher, they almost forgot about her and Cooper. Almost.

The girls checked in with Miss Ramirez and then dragged Cooper over to meet her.

"This is Miss Ramirez." Olivia's voice was filled with awe.

"And this is our neighbor, Cooper." Sophie finished the introduction.

"It's very nice to meet you." Miss Ramirez passed a look between Cooper and Annabelle, but she didn't question their relationship. "Okay girls, let's get into your costumes."

They scampered off, and Cooper turned to Annabelle.

"I'll be right back. I have a little surprise for the girls."

* * * *

As soon as Annabelle texted to tell him the play was tonight, Cooper had dashed off to the florist. He'd picked up a dozen roses, split into two mini bouquets. He planned to present them to Sophie and Olivia after the performance.

"Oh, Cooper, that's so…" Annabelle held her hand over her mouth, hiding a smile.

"Too much?" He wondered now if it would draw too much attention from the rest of the parents. Maybe the other kids would feel bad if they didn't get roses.

"No. It's sweet." She reached for him, but dropped her hand at the last second. "Besides, they're already completely smitten with you."

He wanted to know how their mother felt about him, but that would have to wait. For now, he was just happy to be there with them.

"They're great kids. And I thought it would be nice to celebrate their stage debut." But then he didn't really know if it was their first time in a play.

"Thank you." She offered him a grateful smile.

The audience settled and the teacher stepped up to the microphone. She welcomed the families and introduced "One Hundred Days, The Musical."

They started with a choral piece, the whole class singing about how they were "one hundred days smarter." Then a group of ten students stepped forward to sing about counting by tens. They were followed by a group of five kids, and then Sophie and Olivia stepped up to the microphone.

They were dressed in matching camouflage jackets and hats, looking like twin soldiers.

"Two, four, six, eight, counting by twos is really great." they sang and marched.

"Ten, twelve, fourteen, sixteen, eighteen, counting in pairs won't keep us waiting."

The song went on like that until they got to "ninety-six, ninety-eight, one hundred. After all that counting we're really tired." They ended with a dramatic sweep of their hands across their foreheads.

For the finale, the whole class counted to one hundred and ended with "We are one hundred days smarter."

The audience cheered, and when Sophie and Olivia came off the stage, Cooper presented them with their flowers. They were thrilled.

"Look Mommy, we got flowers." Olivia buried her face in the blooms and inhaled.

"Just like real actresses," Sophie exclaimed.

"Or princesses," Olivia added.

They ran off to show their teacher and their friends. The auditorium was a buzz of excitement. Twenty-seven five- and six-year-olds were running around, singing the songs, and munching on cookies and cider.

Just as he'd feared, one little girl was unhappy about not getting flowers. When tempting her with a second cookie didn't satisfy her, the father approached Cooper.

"How dare you show up here?" Red-faced, the man balled his fists.

"I guess I should have brought flowers for everyone." Cooper might have been able to divide up the flowers for each girl in the class, if he'd thought of it in time.

"I'm not talking about the flowers, asshole." The man leaned closer, his voice raised in fury. "You're a fraud. A cheater. A disgrace to the game and this country."

Cooper could feel everyone's attention turning toward them as the man continued to inch his way forward.

"Maybe we should discuss this outside." Cooper tried to keep his cool, like he did on the mound, when instead of coming in and shutting the opposition down, he'd been lit up like Opening Night fireworks. "There are children here."

"Oh, now you give a damn about the kids?" The man's voice got even louder. "You sure as hell weren't thinking about the kids when you stuck a needle in your arm."

He knew he couldn't win an argument with this man. He turned to Annabelle and said, "I am so sorry. I'll wait for you at the car."

Half hoping the man would follow him, he turned and left the school auditorium.

The coward stayed behind.

Even so, he didn't walk directly to his vehicle. Even though it was a well-lit parking lot, the thought of an ambush played in the back of his head.

What had he been thinking in coming to the play? He'd ruined it for everyone. How was he going to explain to Sophie and Olivia why their classmate's father had felt the need to verbally attack him? How was he going to explain what he'd done?

Pacing in front of the school, he tried to ignore the suspicious glances cast by the parents as they ushered their performers to their cars.

He'd paid for his sin. Fifty games, plus the trade. But it would never be enough. There would always be some guy somewhere who would feel the need to point out his mistake. Loudly and publicly.

Chapter 22

Annabelle gave her thanks and congratulations to the teacher and then she gathered up her daughters. The wife of the man who'd confronted Cooper gave her an apologetic glance, but Annabelle couldn't help but feel like every eye was on her and her girls.

What had been a wonderful evening had degraded into something else. Sophie and Olivia looked shocked and confused that their classmate's father would start yelling at Cooper. They too thought it had something to do with their flowers, and they weren't quite sure what to do with the thoughtful bouquets.

They found Cooper pacing in front of his SUV. She could tell by the way he moved that he was agitated. He looked like a man who wanted to hit something. Or someone.

But as soon as he saw the three of them, he stopped pacing. His face broke into a wide grin and he crouched down to the twins' level.

"You two were fantastic." He held his arms open and both girls crashed into his embrace. "I'm so proud of you both."

"Thank you." They remembered their manners at least.

"That was the best hundredth day of school play I've ever seen." He continued the praise like the two of them were the only things that mattered. "Probably the best anyone has ever seen."

"Did you really like it?" Olivia asked, eyes wide.

"I did." And he sounded like he meant it.

Cooper unlocked the doors of his SUV, helped Olivia climb into the backseat, and buckled her in. Sophie scrambled up the other side, and he reached over to make sure her seatbelt was fastened before walking around to get behind the wheel.

He shot Annabelle a quick glance before starting the vehicle. Despite his brave face for the girls, he was rattled. Her heart ached knowing how hard he was trying to keep from showing his frustration. How hard he was trying to keep the mood light and focused on the reason they were there tonight.

"Are we still up for pizza?" He asked as he pulled out of the school parking lot.

"Maybe some other time." Annabelle didn't want to put him under any more pressure.

"Well, we need to eat, don't we?" He had a point.

"True, but maybe we could get it to go?" she suggested.

"Sure. I forgot how superstars need their beauty sleep."

Giggles erupted from the back seat.

Cooper picked up a pizza and they took it back to her place. Annabelle got a couple of vases down for the girls' flowers while he dished up slices of pizza.

Sophie devoured two whole slices, but Olivia picked the pepperoni off her slice and nibbled as if she was being forced to eat overcooked vegetables.

"Why did that man yell at you?" She pushed her plate aside. "Was it because Skyler didn't get flowers, too?"

"It had nothing to do with the flowers." Cooper wiped his mouth with his napkin.

"He called you a big cheater." Sophie was still chewing. "Why would he call you a cheater when you're not?"

"Well." He pushed his chair back and set his napkin on the table next to his plate. "You see, I did cheat."

Both girls looked at him, wide eyed, with grave concern on their faces.

"See, I took some medicine—no, drugs—I wasn't supposed to." He looked like he was facing an executioner. "I knew they were against the rules, but I took them anyway. And I got into a lot of trouble for it."

"What kind of trouble?" Olivia asked.

"I got suspended for almost half the season," Cooper explained. "That means I couldn't play and my team had to find someone else to do my job."

"Oh."

"Why did you take the bad drugs?" Sophie wanted to know.

"Well, I was hurt. And I was afraid if I told the trainers, I'd have to miss some games." It couldn't be easy for him to admit his mistakes, especially to a couple of six-year-olds. "But I should have told the truth from the beginning. I should have talked to a doctor instead of trying to take care of it myself."

"Are you going to play baseball again?" Sophie asked.

"I hope so." Cooper shifted in his chair. "I had an operation on my shoulder and it's all better now. But some teams might not want me because of what I did."

"Because you cheated?" Olivia sounded like the word was hard to pronounce. "And cheaters never win."

"Right. Cheaters never win." He held his head high, but Annabelle could tell he wanted to get as far away from them as possible. Yet he was doing much better than he probably thought. "But I won't do it again."

"Promise?" Olivia asked.

"I promise." He nodded.

Olivia slid off her chair and went to him. She wrapped her arms around him and buried her head in his chest.

* * * *

Cooper could feel Olivia's little heart beating as she held on tight. He didn't deserve her affection. Or her sister's. He certainly didn't deserve Annabelle's.

When Olivia let out a loud yawn, Annabelle suggested they get ready for bed.

"How 'bout we skip the baths, tonight?" Annabelle made it sound like a special treat.

"Okay." Sophie yawned, too. "As long as we still get to hear a bedtime song."

"Please?" Olivia's wide-eyed plea was impossible to resist.

"Sure." He finished the last bite of his pizza. "I'll sing you a bedtime song."

"I'll take care of the cleanup while you run and get your guitar." Annabelle's smile went straight to his heart. He wanted this. Wanted it so much. But he couldn't risk putting them through another public embarrassment. He didn't want to have to worry about strangers coming up to him and laying into him about his steroid use. They didn't need to be exposed to that kind of scene again.

"Thanks." He patted Sophie on the top of the head and gave Olivia his best smile before slipping out the back door.

By the time he returned, the kitchen was clean, and the girls were already in bed, tucked in tight and waiting for him to sing.

He took his too-familiar place between them. He tried to think of something upbeat, but his fingers could only pick out sad songs.

But they seemed to do the trick. Both girls were soon fast asleep.

Annabelle stood in the doorway, with a sleepy, come-hither smile on her face.

He stood, carefully carrying his guitar to the hallway. "I should go."

"Or you could stay."

"I don't think that's a good idea." His heart twisted at the thought of disappointing her. But better to let go now, before it got that much harder to walk away.

"Why not?" She leaned against the wall, keeping her voice low.

"I'm really sorry about what happened at the play." He had to fight to keep his hands to himself. He wanted her. More than ever. But... "I hate that you and the girls had to hear that. I don't want to put you through that again."

"It was a little embarrassing. But I felt more sorry for that guy's daughter than for us." She pushed off the wall, leaning toward him.

"But it was my fault. Everything he said was because of what I'd done."

"You made a mistake." She put her hands on his shoulders. "You're human."

"But you shouldn't have to pay for that mistake."

"Maybe not, but you've already paid for it."

"Only officially."

"You think you're the only one who's screwed up?" She shook her head, frustrated with him. She dropped her hands to her sides. "You think you're the only one with regrets?"

"No."

"You want to know why I quit modeling?"

"Because you got married. Had babies."

"No. I'd walked away before I met Clayton."

She started down the hall, motioning for him to follow her to her bedroom.

"I quit because I made a fool of myself." Annabelle sat on the edge of her bed. He stood in the doorway, not trusting himself to come all the way in. "I got greedy. I wanted a third cover. I thought it would be my ticket. I would have done anything to get it. Including sleeping with the photographer."

"I guess I'm glad you didn't."

"I did. I slept with Alfonso. He'd promised to make me a star. He told me his camera would reveal the fire deep inside me." Her voice contained a note of regret. "He convinced me that I could be wild, unleashed, and uninhibited."

"That's just great." He really didn't want to hear about her sexual liberation at the hands of the famous artiste, Alfonso. A guy so famous he only needed one name.

"For the first time in my life, I felt like I didn't have to hold myself back." She crossed her arms over her chest, as if she were trying to hold back painful memories. "It was liberating. Until I found out he'd also been sleeping with two other models."

"I'm sorry." And he was, mostly. He didn't like that she'd been hurt. "That was a rotten thing to do."

"My reaction was pretty rotten, too." She rubbed her hands up and down her arms, as if she felt a sudden chill. "I was a total bitch, actually."

"He probably deserved it." The son of a bitch.

"I destroyed half his camera equipment." She didn't sound quite so justified. "Probably thousands of dollars' worth, but that wasn't the worst part."

He waited for her to go on.

"The worst part was how I lashed out at the other girls." She shuddered at the memory. "I would have made a reality show producer blush. I got into a hair-pulling, nail-clawing, face-slapping cat fight. I actually drew blood on Serena's face."

She closed her eyes and clenched her fists. Then she let out a huge sigh and drew her hand up to the left side of her face, where the scars were still fresh.

"Maybe this is my penance." She gave him a crooked smile, the left side of her mouth still not able to stretch into a full grimace. "My payback for being such a bitch."

"You don't deserve this." He moved from the doorway to her side, and reached up to stroke her cheek. "There is nothing you could have done to deserve this."

"I don't know." She lightly touched her scars. "I went on a bit of a self-destructive phase. After the Alfonso fiasco, I went a little crazy. Sowed my wild oats."

He didn't want to think about what that meant.

"Sometimes I miss the wild girl I used to be." She sighed. "But then I settled down to become this closed off, uptight woman who ended up *settling*. I don't think either of them are the real me"

"So who is the real you?"

"I think I'm somewhere in between. I'm not the wild child who slept her way through New Zealand and South Africa. But I'm not the empty shell of a woman who just smiled and pretended my world revolved around my husband. I think I'd like to be a woman who goes after what she wants." She gave him a wicked grin and reached for him. "I want you,

Nathan Cooper. I like who I am when I'm with you. I feel…alive. And safe. When I'm with you, I feel beautiful."

She touched her scar, but he grabbed her wrists, gently pushed her onto the bed, and covered her mouth with his. She tasted so good. So full of passion and hunger. Even a little bit wild.

He kissed her, slow and hot. Deep and wet. She made him feel everything. And for the first time he could remember, he welcomed the feelings. All of them.

"I like who I am when I'm with you, too." He came up for air and pulled his shirt over his head. "I feel like I can be a better man. I want to be a better man for you."

"You're a good man already." She helped him tug his shirt all the way off and moved toward his jeans. "A very good man."

"I'm trying to be." He shimmied out of his pants and went to work on her clothes. "I want to be the best you've ever had."

"Oh, you are." She arched her back as he slipped her blouse over her head. He unfastened her bra and watched with awe as her breasts spilled out of the lace cups.

"Annabelle," he sang. "You're so beautiful. So damned beautiful. I…"

He'd better shut up before he made a complete fool of himself. He took one luscious nipple into his mouth, savoring and sucking on her sweet flesh. His hand drifted below her waist and she squirmed, trying to get closer.

Slipping one finger between her folds, he felt her quiver. Heard her sigh. He picked up the pace, stroking and sliding his fingers along her most sensitive flesh. She felt so good. Too good to be true. But she was true. She was real. And she wanted him. Even after everything.

"Please Cooper," she moaned. "I need you."

Chapter 23

The next few days went by in a bliss-covered fog. Annabelle was happier than she'd ever been. Her daughters were delighted to have Cooper meet them at the bus stop each afternoon. He helped with their homework or made them dinner, and every night he sang to them.

And every night he sang to her. Then he made love to her as if he was playing the world's finest and rarest instrument.

She didn't worry about getting too close, because it was already too late. She was in love with Nathan Cooper. It seemed a little crazy at times, but there were those little moments where it made perfect sense. Like at dawn, before the world intruded upon them. Before he had to slip out of her bed, put on his clothes, and tiptoe out the door.

"I hate sneaking out like this." The sun was barely up, the light filtering through her sheer curtains as he pulled on his pants.

"We've been through this." Annabelle reached for the pajamas she'd left on the floor next to her bed. She slept better in the nude, once she got past the fear that one of the girls would wake up and discover her and Cooper naked together in her bed. Thank goodness for door locks.

"I know. I just don't like it." He gave her a quick kiss on the top of her head. "I wish…"

He sighed and grabbed his shirt.

"You can come by for breakfast."

"Sure." He'd already stocked her fridge with his favorite foods. Lots of leafy green vegetables, fresh fruits, organic eggs, and hormone-free, uncured bacon.

"I'll have the coffee ready." She got the feeling he wanted more. But they didn't talk about it. They didn't talk about how she was still a married woman. They didn't talk about him leaving in a few weeks if he got the call.

"I'll see you in a little while." He didn't bother taking his guitar with him. He spent more time here than at his own place. He came over for breakfast, left for his workouts during the day, and returned for dinner each night.

It was almost perfect.

After he left, Annabelle took a quick shower, dressed, and got the girls up to get ready for school. She made sure they were dressed and had their teeth brushed before they went downstairs to start breakfast.

She was just starting the coffee when she heard a familiar knock on the back door.

"Cooper!" Sophie and Olivia both jumped up to let him in.

"Good morning." His smile lit up the whole kitchen. "How are my three favorite girls this morning?"

"Good." Olivia wrapped her arms around his waist.

"Did you come for breakfus?" Sophie asked.

"You don't want me eating all your food, do you?" His smile was teasing and the girls just ate it up.

"Don't be silly." Sophie cocked her head to the side, making her curls bounce. "We have lots."

"Yeah. Lots." Olivia looked up at him with such admiration it hurt. Just a little.

"Okay, if you insist." He ruffled her hair and made his way across the kitchen. Pulling eggs, bacon, kale, and a hunk of parmesan out of the fridge, he started prepping to make omelets.

"Make yourself at home." Annabelle had gotten used to him taking over in the kitchen. He was much more willing to give and take in the bedroom.

She turned away from her daughters, hoping they wouldn't catch the blush on her face.

He let Olivia and Sophie crack the eggs and rinse the produce.

While Olivia whisked the eggs together, he got to work chopping the kale and the bacon to add to the mixture.

"I'll make toast." Sophie scooted over to the bread box and popped two slices of bread into the toaster.

Annabelle poured coffee for herself and Cooper. She stirred half and half into her cup and sprinkled cinnamon on top. She handed him a cup of black coffee and was rewarded with a warm smile.

It was almost as if they were one big happy family.

Almost.

After cleaning up the breakfast dishes and getting the girls' backpacks packed, the four of them walked to the bus stop. Olivia hugged Cooper before getting on the bus, and Sophie gave him a kiss on the cheek before charging up the bus steps.

He grinned and waved as the bus pulled away, and Annabelle couldn't help but think he was just as smitten with the girls as they were with him.

"So what have you got planned for today?" He waited until the bus rounded the corner before pulling her close. "I've got to get my workout in this morning, but after that…"

"I guess I should return my agent's calls." Annabelle sighed. "He's been trying to get ahold of me the last couple of days."

"He's probably worried about you." He ran his hands up and down her back. "You should give him a call."

"I know, it's just…" She pulled away and started walking toward the beach. She had a feeling it had something to do with the anniversary show and wasn't sure how she felt about not showing up. But she couldn't imagine they'd still want her.

"Call him. Get it over with." Cooper took her hand, and walked with her. "I know it's hard, believe me, I know. But the more you avoid him, the harder it's going to be."

"I guess I do need closure." She looked up at him and saw encouragement and unconditional support in his eyes. "Would you mind?"

She pulled her phone out of her pocket and scrolled through her contacts. Cooper took a few steps toward the water to give her some privacy.

She fully expected to get Victor's voicemail, but he picked up on the second ring.

"Annabelle, darling!" He sounded happy to hear from her. "I was starting to think you'd fled the country."

"Sorry. I've been busy with the kids and getting back into my everyday routine." There was a slight breeze and she had to brush her hair away from her face. "But everything is fine. I'm doing much better. I'm even able to drive."

"Good. That's great." The change in his tone told her small talk time was over. "Listen, I need an answer on the Fiftieth Anniversary party. It's a week from Sunday."

"You think they'll still want me?" She wasn't sure what would be worse, showing her face on primetime or showing her face to the model she'd been so bitchy to.

"Annabelle, honey, of course they want you." He sounded like he was losing his patience with her. "You were the third best-selling cover of all time. They want you there."

"That sounds wonderful, but..." She wasn't sure if she was strong enough. "I'll need to find a babysitter and..."

"Let me know as soon as possible. And Annabelle?"

"Yes." Her hands were so sweaty, she almost dropped her phone.

"You can do this, kid. I know you can."

"Thank you." She blinked back the sudden stinging in her eyes. "I'll be in touch."

She hung up the phone and turned to look for Cooper. She already knew what he'd say, but she wanted to run it by him anyway.

"Well?" he asked. "What did your agent have to say?"

"He wants me to go to the fiftieth anniversary party for *Sports Illustrated Swimsuit Edition*."

"That's wonderful. When are you going?"

"I'm not sure that I am."

"Of course you are." He wasn't being bossy or overbearing, it was one hundred percent support that made him ignore her hesitation. "When is it?"

"Why, so you can rent a tux?" She smiled, just thinking of how hot he would look.

"You don't want me to go with you?" Now he was the one with reservations.

"I'm certainly not going without you."

"But what if...?"

"I guess I'll call Victor back and tell him I can't do it." She reached for her phone, but he grabbed her hands.

"You really want me to go with you?"

"Of course. I need you to be there. I can't do this on my own." She sighed. "I need your strength. Your support. Just the thought of being on camera, like this..."

She brushed her fingertips over her scars. Something she realized she did far too often.

"Annabelle, you're beautiful."

"You can say that because you look beneath the surface." God, she loved this man. "You see me as more than just my face, my body... That's not what this is about. It's all about the outside. What can be captured on camera."

"Hey, I first fell for your pretty face." He stroked the side of her face that was scarred. "You captivated me with your smile. Your brilliant blue eyes. You still have that smile. That sparkle."

"Oh please. I hardly sparkle anymore."

"I have seen you glow." He gave her a naughty grin. "But that's private."

"Yes, it is. And I'm not sure if I can go onstage and publicly display my wounds."

"Why not?"

"The whole idea is to celebrate beauty. Perfection." She was afraid. Afraid people would recoil in horror at the way she looked now. Especially when compared to the way she used to look. "I'm as far from perfect as you can get."

"You can't hide forever, you know."

"It's too soon. My scars are too raw." They were still red and raised. "I don't think I can cover them enough for television."

"So expose them," he suggested. "Show the world what happens when people don't stop to think about their actions. One lousy text and you're afraid to celebrate one of your biggest accomplishments."

"You're saying I should stand up there and tell the audience, 'Don't text and drive or you'll end up looking like me'?"

"Sure. Why not?"

"Because. That's not what I'm there for. It's supposed to be a celebration."

"So celebrate."

"Will you accept your ring?"

"What ring?"

"You were on the Goliaths' roster until the trade." She'd discussed the matter with Hunter. The way the rules were set up, he'd be issued a ring along with his teammates.

"But I'd only appeared in two games before they traded me."

"But you were a part of the team. You'll get a ring."

"I can't accept it." He almost sounded afraid of the idea. "I didn't earn it."

"The Goliaths won the two games you played in." She'd looked up his stats. "They might not have won the division without those two games."

"Look, this isn't about me," he said. "This is about you attending the anniversary celebration. You should go. You don't have to go up on stage. Just sit in the audience and support the other models."

"What if they hate me?"

"Why would they?"

"I told you, I wasn't very ladylike on that last shoot. I got into a fight with another model."

"I'm sure she's over it."

"What if she's not?"

"Then you'll have a chance to apologize. Make it right." He reached up and tilted her chin, offering a warm smile. "I know you'll regret not going."

"You have to come with me, please."

"As if I could ever deny you anything, Annabelle." He dropped a kiss on her temple, somehow making her think that it was a good idea to go, maybe even speak in front of the live television audience about her experience.

* * * *

"Tell me it isn't true," Cooper was on the phone with his agent as soon as he got home. "Tell me they're not seriously going to give me a ring."

"It's in the contract. I'm sure they can mail it to you if you don't want to accept it in person."

"I don't want to accept it at all. I don't deserve it."

"There have been other guys who've accepted their rings gladly after serving a suspension or being traded."

"I don't want a ring unless I earn it."

"So are you ready to get back to work? Earn the next one?"

"Yeah. I'm ready." Cooper ran his hands through his hair. "I'm more than ready to get back on the mound. I feel great. Stronger than ever."

"Are you sure you're ready?"

"I just told you I was."

"It sounds to me like there's something holding you back. Is it guilt over the ring?"

"No. I'll take the damned thing. I'll put it on my bathroom sink and let it remind me every day what I could have had."

"So what aren't you telling me?"

What, was he supposed to tell his agent he was in love? That he didn't want to have to deal with a long-distance relationship on top of carrying around his 220 pounds of guilt every time he looked in the mirror?

"I guess I'm just a little nervous about going to a new team. The Goliaths were like family and I let them down." He didn't know how else to describe the difference in the two clubhouses. "I had a hard time adjusting in St. Louis. I felt like everyone was waiting for me to disappoint them. And then I did."

"Look. I'm not going to lie to you," his agent said. "You're not going to find another organization like the Goliaths. But then, they're going through some changes right now with the ownership shakeup. It's going to be hard for them to repeat their championship season."

"They've got their core group of guys. If anyone can do it, they can."

"Are you looking for a team that's going to contend?"

"That's always one consideration." Damn. He'd hoped to avoid the whole free agency thing. His goal had been to sign a long-term deal with San Francisco before he became a free agent. Hadn't exactly worked out that way.

"Most of the top teams have already got their lineups in place. There's always a chance someone gets hurt."

"So what have we got in the middle of the pack? A team on their way up, maybe someone who'll have a chance to sneak in on a wild card or get hot at the right time."

"I'll ask around."

"Great. I'll keep working out. I've been throwing some bullpen sessions. Even threw some batting practice. And the arm feels good. It really does."

"That's good news." His agent's words were encouraging but Cooper could hear an underlying *but*. "How would you feel about overseas clubs? I know of at least one Japanese club who's very interested in what you have to offer."

And leave Annabelle and the girls? No way.

"I'll think about it."

Chapter 24

"What the hell happened to your face?" Clayton Barry barged right in when Annabelle opened the front door.

"It's nice to see you, too." Annabelle stepped aside so she didn't get knocked over. "I had no idea you were coming for a visit."

"So where are the girls?" He looked around as if he was going to make himself at home.

"In school."

"Oh, right. They're in school now." He walked over to the bookcase and picked up Sophie's school photo. The one taken in San Francisco in the fall.

"I was in a car accident." She saved him from having to ask again what was wrong with her face. "I'm fine by the way. I couldn't drive for about a week. But I'm doing much better."

"I'm sorry. I had no idea." He almost sounded as if he meant it.

"Well, you've had plenty of other things to deal with." She led him to the sofa, inviting him to sit down. "Have you wrapped up the hearings in Florida?"

"Yes." He flopped down on the couch, stretching his legs out and resting them on her coffee table. "What a nightmare. You'd think I was stealing old ladies' pensions or selling drugs to kids."

"You were selling drugs. And some of those players were kids," she reminded him.

"I wasn't the one selling the drugs. I wasn't the one injecting the players." The whine in his voice grated on her nerves.

"No. You were just profiting from it." Annabelle had looked the other way too long. "You didn't care what was sold or to whom, as long as you were making a profit."

"The business plan I was presented with was completely legitimate," he complained. "I had no idea it was a front."

"But you spent an awful lot of time in Florida," She'd thought he was having an affair. "What were you doing there? Counting your money?"

"You never complained about spending my money."

"No. And I never questioned where it came from." She was ashamed of how much she'd let slide. How much she'd ignored the little feeling in her gut that something wasn't right with her marriage. The obvious thought was that he'd been cheating on her. Why else would he spend more time in Florida than with his family—his children?

"You never worried about where it went, either," he said, bitterly. "I see you've got a shiny new Mercedes sitting in the driveway. How much did that set me back?"

"The reason I have a new vehicle is because the old one was totaled." He used to encourage her to buy new things. No, he'd pressured her to always have the best. "And I've been careful with my money."

"Your money?"

"Yes. The money I saved from the sale of the house, the money we agreed on instead of alimony, and the money I earned from my last job."

"You've never had a real job."

"Modeling is a job. And I was good at it."

Was.

"How much do you have left?"

"That's none of your business."

"Let's not fight over money." He changed his tone abruptly. "We never used to fight. I can't tell you how shocked I was when you filed for divorce. I mean, we always got along."

"No, I always went along." She brushed her hair off her face, exposing her scars, but she didn't care. Let Clayton see her at her worst.

"Can you get that fixed?"

"Get what fixed?"

"Your face." He couldn't look at the scars. "Could you have some work done, and go back to modeling?"

"No. I don't think they can fix this." She traced the largest scar from her temple to her jaw. "It's permanent. But that's okay. I don't need to be perfect. Not anymore."

"What about modeling? Can you get work that doesn't require them to see your face?"

"You mean like underwear ads?"

"I don't know, something." He shrugged.

"I think my modeling days are behind me." And over the last couple of weeks, she'd been fine with it. "I was actually thinking of going to college."

"College?" Clayton couldn't have looked more shocked if she'd suggested she take up prostitution or space exploration.

"Yes. I want to show our daughters that it's never too late to follow a dream." She had no idea where that dream would lead her, only that she needed to start dreaming. "Besides, I know the money I've saved won't last forever."

"I don't know if college is right for you."

"You don't think I'm smart enough?" Sure, her grades hadn't been the best in high school. But that was mostly because she hadn't worked as hard as she could have. She did enough to not get hassled by her cheerleading coach, but no one really pushed her into taking more challenging courses or preparing for anything beyond finding herself a husband.

"What about the girls? Who will watch them while you're in class? Or studying?"

"I'll take classes while they're in school. And we can do homework together." She'd really only been toying with the idea of going back to school. But the more Clayton doubted her, the more determined she was to make it work.

"I just don't know…" He stood up and walked over to the window. His shoulders were slumped and he let out a big sigh. "I can't take any more financial pressure right now."

"What do you mean, 'financial pressure'?"

"Look, babe. This FITNatural thing has cleaned me out." He turned around, and with an apologetic smile he moved toward her. "Maybe we should take some time and re-think our future. Maybe even hold off on the divorce."

"What?" She slipped away before he could reach up and brush her hair off her shoulder. "You're kidding, right?"

"No, babe." He tried to move closer, but she dodged him again. "I'm sorry. I should have stayed away from that company. I should have at least gotten out when I found out what they were into. But baby, I only did it to keep you happy."

"You thought I was happy?"

"Yes. You had everything you ever wanted. Money, fame, the glamorous life. Do you have any idea how much it cost to give you the best of everything?"

"So you're saying it's my fault you invested in that company?" Unbelievable.

"Oh come on, babe..."

"Don't call me 'babe.'" She was getting a headache over her left eye. "Please. Just don't."

"Look, Annabelle, sweetheart..." He really didn't get it. "Give me another chance. We'll start fresh. You and me and... Sophie and Olivia."

The way he'd hesitated it was almost as if he couldn't remember the names of his own daughters. But that was crazy. Of course he remembered. He was just upset. And apparently broke.

"I think you should leave."

"No. I have a right to see my wife. My daughters."

"I'm your *ex*-wife. It's over between us." He didn't really think he could come back here and give her this sob story about how he'd spent all his money and he wanted a second chance?

"I want to spend time with my daughters." His tone changed, no more hey-baby-let's-start-over. "I know my rights."

"Sure. You can see the girls. When they get home from school." She didn't want to make this any more difficult on them. They were doing so well, she didn't want them to get caught in the middle of a battle between their parents. "You can even stay for dinner."

She'd have to get word to Cooper that she had company. And she'd have to ask him to stay away until Clayton left.

"Could I stay longer than that?" he asked. "I have nowhere else to go."

"What do you mean you have nowhere else to go?"

"I had to sell my condo." He hung his head in shame. "Between the lawyers in Florida, and the divorce lawyers... I'm sure they'll come after the car next."

"Can't you sell the Ferrari?" Surely he could get a tidy sum for it. "What about your share of the money from selling the Goliaths?"

"It's gone. And as for the car..." He shook his head. "I haven't kept up the payments. They're going to take it back. I just need a place to stay for a few days until I can figure something out. At best, I think I can hold off for a few more months. But I'm probably going to have to file for bankruptcy."

"No. You can't do that." She was furious now. They were still married. It would affect her credit, too. "Not until the divorce is final."

"Come on babe, you're not going to make me go through with the divorce. I need you."

"How much do you need?"

"How much did you make modeling?" He eyed her suspiciously.

"Not much. But I can give you a loan." The last thing she wanted to do was touch the money she'd put away for her daughters' future. But she didn't want to be dragged into bankruptcy on top of everything else. "I can get you enough to stay afloat until the divorce is final. And hopefully by then you'll have something figured out."

"Sure, except for the child support."

"We don't need your child support." She would contact her own lawyer and see what kind of arrangement could be made without delaying the divorce any longer.

"Yeah, right. What are you going to do? You're sure as hell not going to model." He grabbed her face, stroking her scar in an unpleasant way. "No one would pay to see this."

He was trying to hurt her. And even just a few months ago, his words would have cut her to the bone. But she was stronger now. She'd been through a horrifying accident, and she'd survived. She could survive a few days of her ex-husband.

* * * *

There was a red Ferrari parked in front of Annabelle's house. Not that unusual of a car in this part of the state, but the only person he knew of who drove one was his former owner, Annabelle's ex-husband. Things had been going too good lately for it to be a coincidence. A quick text to Annabelle confirmed his fears. Clayton Barry was in town. She wasn't sure how long he'd be staying.

Well, shit. So much for topping off a great workout with an even better one.

He hopped into the shower and tried to ease the tension that had returned to his muscles the minute he saw that damned Ferrari. Was his shoulder tightening up? His gut sure was. He didn't want to think about the man who'd married his Annabelle. Who'd given her children. The man who'd slept in the same bed with her and didn't have to sneak out in the morning.

Cooper didn't want to think about the man who had provided the capital to get FITNatural up and running. If it hadn't been for his investment, who knows? Maybe Cooper wouldn't have tried the cream that sent him down the slippery slope from therapeutic remedies to banned substances.

Yeah, and if he was low enough to blame the other man for his transgressions, he didn't deserve Annabelle.

He toweled off and went to find his guitar. His music had been a source of comfort for him since he was a kid. He needed that comfort now.

Too bad he'd left his guitar in Annabelle's bedroom.

Time for plan C. If he couldn't spend the evening with Annabelle and the twins, and he couldn't play his music, he'd have to go out and catch one of his favorite bands he'd jammed with a time or two. They were playing in Oceanside, about an hour away. Perfect. He'd take a drive. Have a beer—just one—and listen to some music. He could give Annabelle space to entertain her husband and...

He knew he was overreacting. Annabelle wanted him, not her soon-to-be-ex-husband. He just needed to chill. Hell, at some point, he'd even need to find a way to deal with the man face to face. If he was going to be a part of Annabelle's life, he was bound to have to deal with the ex. Sophie and Olivia would see their father on their birthdays, graduations, their weddings.

Whoa. Talk about getting ahead of himself. Cooper shook that thought off and headed for his Escalade. The sound of the girls' laughter stopped him in his tracks.

"Daddy, Daddy, let's play catch." Sophie had been hooked on the game since that day at the beach.

"No. Let's play dress up." Olivia loved her princess gowns. His chest tightened at the memory of her tossing the ball around while wearing a ball gown. God he loved that little girl. Both of them.

But they already had a father.

With a heavy heart, he climbed into his SUV and shut the door. He cranked the engine and turned up the stereo as loud as he dared without drawing attention to himself. The last thing he wanted was for his girls to have to choose between him and their father.

As he drove south on Highway 1, he thought about what was best for Annabelle and her daughters. If she had a chance to reconcile with the father of her children, shouldn't she take it? Especially since Cooper had nothing to offer her except great sex, good food, and a decent singing voice.

By the time he pulled into the club where Bryan and the Stowaways were playing, he'd made a decision to at least think about playing in Japan. That is, if his agent wasn't only dangling that out there to keep him from getting depressed about his chances.

He sent a text requesting the details. He'd need to know more about the offer, if there really was one, before he made a major decision like that.

He'd been watching the Hot Stove reports. He knew more than he wanted to about which free agents were in demand, and who had already signed. He knew which teams still needed a lefty in the bullpen, and there weren't that many. It had been a busy offseason for everyone but him.

Maybe Japan was his only shot. But he couldn't very well ask Annabelle to follow him overseas. Not with two young children who'd already been through a big move. He couldn't imagine leaving them behind, either. Not unless it was his only chance at playing baseball again.

The image of that Ferrari made him realize that Annabelle was used to the finer things. She'd grown up the daughter of a wealthy Texas businessman. She'd had a short-lived, yet successful career as one of the world's top models. And she was married to a man who'd owned a Major League Baseball team, among other things.

She was used to living large. He wasn't going to be able to impress her with an assistant pitching coach's salary.

He had to get back to the majors. And if he had to go through a foreign country to get there, he'd just have to suck it up. But he wouldn't sign a long-term deal. One year. That's all he'd give.

Unless Annabelle got back together with her husband. Then he didn't give a shit about where he went or for how long.

Chapter 25

Clayton lasted about an hour playing with the twins. He didn't want to play dress up and he didn't want to play catch. So they'd taken a walk down the beach. Clayton complained about getting sand in his expensive leather shoes, but he'd stuck with it long enough to build a sandcastle.

Annabelle had hung back, letting them have time together. Trying to remember that no matter how angry she was with Clayton, he was their father. No matter how much he'd hurt her, or disappointed her, he had given her the gift of her children and she would be forever grateful for that.

"I was thinking we could order takeout for dinner." Annabelle shooed the girls upstairs to change out of their sandy clothes. "It's a school night, and we've got to catch up on the homework they didn't get to while they were playing."

"Aren't they in kindergarten?" Clayton asked. "They shouldn't have homework."

"Yes, they are in kindergarten, and they actually look forward to their homework."

"So what do they do, practice their ABCs?"

"They're starting to read." Pride in her girls could be heard in her voice. "And they write in a journal. Simple sentences, but they're writing. And they can count to one hundred."

"Whatever happened to learning how to line up and not eat paste?"

"Times change. We learned how to cut and paste using scissors and glue. They do it on the computer."

"They're doing okay in school, then?" His voice sounded more relaxed, more like the Clayton she'd been able to have civilized conversations with. They might not have had a grand passion for each other, but they'd never been hostile toward each other, either. The only time they'd ever really fought was after they'd gone out for the evening and he was both proud of the way other men looked at her, and jealous of their attention.

His outburst at the Goliaths' barbecue when she'd embraced Marco Santiago was only slightly overblown. No, she shouldn't have hugged Marco, but she'd been feeling ignored for some time. Their lives had settled into a pattern of Clayton being gone more often than not, and Annabelle was busy shuttling the twins from one activity to another. Keeping busy had become a substitute for being happy.

"They're doing great." Annabelle had cut back on the activities, choosing to let the girls spend more time doing unstructured things. Like going to the beach, playing dress-up, and even watching a movie now and then. They'd have plenty of time to learn the piano, take gymnastics, or play soccer. "They love their teacher, and they're right where they should be academically. Sophie is as confident and outspoken as always. And even Olivia has come out of her shell. You should have seen them sing a duet in their class play."

"They sang a duet?"

"Yes. It was wonderful."

"So, they're happy?"

"I think so." She reached over to pat his hand. "They miss their father, of course. But they're doing well."

"And what about you?"

She wasn't going to tell him that she was involved with another man. Someday she would, but not now. Not when he was already feeling pretty down.

"I'm doing much better. Each day I feel a little stronger, a little clearer." She forgot he didn't know the extent of her injuries. "I had some memory loss, and I wasn't able to drive for a short period of time after the accident. I'm not getting headaches, and I'm sleeping much better these days."

"I had no idea, I mean, I can see the scars on your face." He gave her a half-hearted sympathetic smile. "Why didn't you tell me if it was so serious?"

"I didn't want to burden you. You've had enough to worry about lately."

"Thank you, Annabelle. I appreciate that." He sounded truly grateful. "I just wish... I wish I didn't have to go through all this alone. You're so strong. I don't think I ever realized how strong you were. Are you sure we can't give it another shot? For us? For our daughters?"

"I made an appointment with my lawyer." She'd been able to catch him before he left for the weekend. "I'll meet with him on Monday to see if we can restructure the settlement, and reduce or eliminate the child support payments."

"So there's no chance for us?"

"There never really was." And they both knew it. "You never would have married me if I hadn't gotten pregnant."

"You wouldn't have married me." he said. "I'm still not even sure why you went out with me in the first place."

"You were safe." She could admit that now. "Someone I could take home to show my family I was a real grown up. That those months I spent out of control were just a phase. I was just acting out after not getting my way for the first time in my life."

"Who wasn't a little wild when they were twenty-one?"

"I went too far." She shuddered at the memory. And the fact that she'd been almost desperate enough to take Alfonso up on his suggestion that she have a threesome with him and Serena. Almost.

"So you picked the most boring guy you could find?" He'd never been secure in his place in her heart. Maybe because he'd never really earned that place.

"You weren't boring..."

"But I wasn't nearly as exciting as a photographer. Or a baseball player." His jealousy was flattering at first, but it soon became tiresome.

"I wasn't looking for excitement. I wanted stability."

"What about now? Have you found someone who gives you excitement, yet keeps you safe?"

Annabelle felt heat creep across her cheeks. She had found just that in Nathan Cooper. But she couldn't share that with Clayton. Neither could she deny it, by the look on his face.

"You are seeing someone."

"It's nothing serious." she lied. "Besides, Sophie tells me you have a girlfriend."

"I had a date. My brother set me up. And how the hell did Sophie know that?"

"She's very observant. Too smart for her own good, sometimes."

"Yes. And she also doesn't know when to keep things to herself. So who is this Cooper she was talking about? I take it he's more than a neighbor, then?"

"Maybe. He was there for me after the accident. And while nothing will erase these scars..." She swept her hand over her face. "He helped me heal on the inside."

"No wonder you're in such a hurry to get rid of me."

"Clayton, we should have divorced a long time ago." She was losing patience with the conversation. "You hardly ever made love to me after the twins were born. I practically had to beg for any kind of affection."

He sat there, silent, for a long time.

"I thought I'd lost you," he said finally. "In the delivery room. There was so much blood. And the screaming. I thought you were going to die right there in front of me. I vowed right then that if you pulled through, I'd never put you in that position again."

"There's this new thing called birth control." She couldn't keep the sarcasm from her voice. "If you were that worried, you could have had a vasectomy. Or I would have been willing to get my tubes tied, rather than a boob job."

"I know it was irrational, my fear." He got up and started pacing. "I watched you with the girls, holding them, nursing them, loving them. The three of you were so perfect together. I felt like an outsider."

"You were afraid to touch them. Even more than you were afraid to touch me."

"I know. I was afraid."

"Maybe if we'd had this conversation five years ago…" She let her voice trail off. "Well, I guess it's too late for what-ifs. I'll go pick up some dinner. Original or extra crispy?"

"Surprise me."

* * * *

"Where are the vegetables?" Olivia complained when she looked at her plate piled high with fried chicken, coleslaw, and mashed potatoes and gravy.

"Is this organic, free-range chicken?" Sophie asked.

"Back in my day, kids ate what they were served." Clayton had seemed a little harried by the time Annabelle returned from picking up takeout. The girls had balked at letting him help with their homework, complaining he didn't know how to do it.

"Yes, please eat." Annabelle gave both girls a stern look. "This is a special treat. Try the coleslaw, cabbage is a vegetable."

"But it's not green," Olivia whined.

"What about the chicken?" Sophie demanded.

"The chicken gave up its life, so you'd better eat it." Annabelle wondered how they'd gone from only wanting to eat chicken nuggets if it came with the right toy, and avoiding anything green, to insisting on organic produce and humanely treated poultry.

"Okay." Sophie begrudgingly took a bite of her drumstick.

"Yes, Mommy." Olivia put a tiny portion of coleslaw on her fork and wrinkled her nose as she hesitantly put it in her mouth.

"Why don't you tell Daddy about the play you were in?" Annabelle tried to get the conversation flowing.

"Oh, we were the Doubles Girls." Sophie licked her fingers and turned toward her father to tell him about it. "We were dressed like twins, which was funny because, of course, we are twins. And then we sang the counting by twos song and everyone clapped and we got a standing vocation and then we got flowers."

"But then Skyler's dad yelled at Cooper and everyone else got all quiet and…" Olivia looked at Annabelle and must have noted the look of alarm on her mother's face. "I don't know why Skyler's dad was so mad. Maybe he thought it wasn't fair that we got flowers and Skyler didn't."

"So your boyfriend went to this play?" Clayton glared at her. "How nice."

"Cooper's not Mommy's boyfriend, right?" Sophie gave her sister a look like she wasn't supposed to say anything in front of their father. "He's just our neighbor and our friend and he helps us with our homework and singing and building sandcastles and playing catch and…"

She must have realized she'd gone too far.

"Well now, isn't that sweet?" Clayton's words dripped with resentment.

"Let's finish our dinner, then it's bath time. And Daddy will read you a story." Annabelle gave both girls a look that said they'd better not complain or ask for a song or mention Cooper in front of their father again.

"Okay. Thank you for the chicken. It was yummy." Sophie finished her dinner and drank the last of her milk.

"Yes. Thank you." Olivia ate everything but the coleslaw. She pushed the offending side dish around on her plate and looked up at Annabelle with pleading eyes.

"You don't have to clean your plate." She gave in. Olivia had tried so many new foods lately, she wasn't going to push.

She sent the girls upstairs to get undressed.

"I'll take care of the kitchen when they're done with their bath." Annabelle waited for Clayton to say *"Don't worry about it, I've got it."* But he didn't.

She shrugged and followed her daughters to the upstairs bathroom.

"Are we in trouble, Mommy?" Olivia's eyes were so wide, Annabelle worried they might fall right out of her head. "I tried to eat all my food but there was too much sauce on the coleslaw."

"It's okay, sweet pea." Annabelle ruffled her hair. "It's not the healthiest vegetable anyway."

"Daddy's mad at us, isn't he?" Sophie stood there in her socks and underwear, with her arms folded across her chest. "He's mad we didn't invite him to the play."

"No. I think he understands he's going to miss a lot of things, with him living in Florida." Or wherever he moved to next. "I think maybe he's sad he missed the play. And maybe it's hard for him to hear about how much fun we're having without him."

"And he doesn't want you to have a boyfriend or even a friend who's a boy." Sophie was indeed too smart for her own good sometimes.

"You know how you felt bad about getting flowers after your play when the other kids didn't?" She tried to explain it simply, so they could understand. "But that doesn't mean you didn't appreciate the flowers, or the person who gave them to you."

"We said, 'thank you,' remember?" Olivia looked horrified that they'd been less than grateful.

"I know you did. But you also didn't go to school the next day telling everyone how you got flowers and Skyler and the other girls didn't. That would have made her feel even worse, right?"

"Yeah." Olivia nodded.

"Uh-huh." Sophie dropped her arms to her sides.

"So, it might make Daddy feel even worse about missing out on things if you talk about how much fun you had with Cooper."

A look of understanding passed over Sophie's face.

Olivia blinked back tears. "I didn't mean to make Daddy sad."

"Of course you didn't." Annabelle pulled both girls into a hug. "Now get into the tub and get ready for a bedtime story from Daddy."

"Okay." Olivia climbed carefully into the bath.

"And we won't mention the bedtime songs that Cooper sings," Sophie said earnestly.

"That's probably a good idea." Annabelle held her hand out for Sophie to grab onto as she stepped into the tub with her sister.

"But who's he going to sing to?" Olivia asked.

Who, indeed? Annabelle had tried calling while she was waiting for the chicken. Cooper had picked up but there was loud music in the background and the connection was spotty. It sounded as if he was in a bar or club. She'd just barely made out something about him staying out of her hair for the next few days.

* * * *

The drive took longer than he'd remembered, but that was okay. The place was lively. Full of hot and horny college students, twenty-somethings, and older singles trying to fake their way into feeling like they still had the goods. At least the music was good. That was the real reason he'd come all this way.

Cooper ordered an IPA and took a seat near the stage. Bryan and the Stowaways played a good mix of classic rock, newer stuff, and some original ballads. He wouldn't be surprised if they broke out in the next couple of years. All they needed was one big break.

He nursed his beer, keeping time with the music, and trying not to sing along. When the band took its first break, Bryan, the lead singer, gave him a nod and made his way over to him.

"Hey man, what are you doing down here? We're a little bit out of your neighborhood. Shouldn't you be getting ready for spring training?" Bryan sat down next to him and flagged the waitress.

"I just felt the need for some good tunes. And you guys are the best." He patted his friend on the shoulder. "Besides, I don't have a team. Not yet, anyway."

"Oh man, that stinks. But hey, glad you're here. You wanna come jam with us?" Bryan asked.

"I don't have my guitar." No, he wasn't going to start worrying about whether he'd see his guitar again. Or Annabelle.

"No way, man. I've never seen you without your guitar." Bryan shook his head in disbelief. "It'd be like you not having your left arm."

"Well, there's this woman," Cooper started to explain.

"Enough said." Bryan punched him in the right arm. "You're coming up on stage. You can play mine. It's not as sweet as yours, but you can make it hum like no one I know."

"You're so full of shit." Cooper laughed.

"Come on. We'll play one of those sappy love songs, make all the ladies in the house quiver."

"I'll sing a few songs, but not to get the ladies." He finished his beer and followed his friend up on the stage.

They played another set, Cooper had another beer, and he declined several offers from the ladies for drinks, dances, or whatever he wanted. He switched to water but it didn't help the headache pounding behind his eyes. The club was too loud. Too crowded. Had he once enjoyed that kind of life?

The music still appealed to him, and he was grateful for that. But the rest of it? The late nights, the strobe lights, the women? No thanks.

Tequila shots with a couple of hot brunettes held no appeal compared to tea parties with two sweet blondes. He'd rather do the Cinderella waltz with a pair of six-year-olds in princess costumes than get out on the dance floor with scantily dressed twenty-somethings.

And Annabelle?

His chest tightened just thinking about how right she'd felt in his arms. How right she'd felt in his life. Part of him wanted to march over there, bang on the door, and demand that she let him in.

But she'd had a life before him. One that included her husband. The father of her children. The man who could give her anything she ever wanted. Cooper didn't have a job, and the only prospect he had was on the other side of the Pacific.

Maybe he'd been kidding himself. He'd never had the stuff to be a starting pitcher. Oh, sure, when he'd first been drafted he'd had visions of Cy Young Awards, twenty win seasons. He'd dreamed of being a left-handed Johnny Scottsdale.

But he'd been sent to the bullpen. They'd made him a specialist. He'd felt he was good enough to go against both right-handers and lefties, but he hadn't been given the chance. One batter, at the most two was all he'd faced in recent years. Sometimes it seemed he'd throw one pitch, and walk off the mound with two outs. He was that good. Bring him in when the team was in a jam, and he'd get out of it.

Maybe that's the way it was with Annabelle. He'd been a fill-in. Come in when she was at her lowest, build her confidence, and then step aside while she got back to her real life.

If that was the case, he'd be happy for her. He'd hate it, but he'd be happy if she was happy. He'd been infatuated with Annabelle Jones for ten years. Infatuated with the way she looked, the way she smiled, even the way she'd gone into seclusion after her last magazine shoot so her love life wasn't splashed all over the tabloids.

Now, he loved her. As a woman, a friend, and a lover. He wanted nothing but to see her smile, for real, not because she was being paid to do it. He'd made her smile, made her laugh, and he'd made her bury her face in his chest so she wouldn't scream and wake the children.

By the time he arrived home from Oceanside, Cooper noticed all the lights in Annabelle's house were off. The Ferrari was still in the driveway and it killed him to think of another man in her house. He couldn't let his mind wander in the direction of her bed. Was she alone? Missing him? Or was she... Nope. Couldn't do it. Couldn't picture her with another man. Even if that man was her husband.

Chapter 26

"I talked to my attorney." Annabelle had gone to her lawyer's office after taking the girls to the bus stop and she felt a little empty not having Cooper by her side. She hadn't seen him since Clayton had shown up unannounced on her doorstep. "He told me that in order to restructure the settlement, it would delay the divorce proceedings. So, I'm just going to write you a check." Or she could transfer the money electronically. "You're sure you can hold off your creditors for a couple more months?"

"Yes. I'm sure." The once proud man didn't bat an eye at being bought off like that. She'd pay off his debts in exchange for an unimpeded divorce. When the decree was finalized, he'd receive an additional sum, if he needed it, to get started in his next, hopefully completely legitimate, endeavor.

"Thank you." She'd also spent the morning shopping for a gown to wear for the anniversary party. She needed the dress, but more than that, she'd needed a few hours away from her ex. She couldn't wait for this visit to come to an end. It had been a trying couple of days. "I hope we'll be able to remain cordial to each other. For Sophie and Olivia's sake. And, well, for all of our sakes."

"You hope we can remain friends?" He was loading his suitcase into his car.

"No. I know that's too much to ask." Annabelle felt the last, freeing heartstrings come loose. "I know we'll never be one of those couples who can act like the best of friends for the sake of the children, but I'm glad we're able to rise above being so busy trying to hurt each other that we don't notice the damage we cause to everyone around us."

"I never wanted to hurt you, Annabelle."

"I know. And I never wanted to hurt you." She leaned over and gave him a hug. Right there in the driveway. As she pulled away, she noticed movement in the window of Cooper's house. Well, in a few more hours, she'd be able to talk to him, and let him know that her divorce was still on track and they wouldn't have to worry about Clayton making things difficult.

"So you don't mind if I wait until the girls get home from school before I take off?"

"They need to say goodbye to their father." She wrapped her arms around herself. "They'll always need their father."

"So about the custody arrangements…" He shoved his hands in his suit pockets. "I don't know where I'm going to be living, and I really don't know how you do what you do."

"We'll keep it simple, like we agreed on. A week during Christmas break. Two weeks in the summer, and visitations when both parties can agree. That part of it won't be set in stone. As circumstances change, so will the arrangements. We'll be flexible, right?"

"What if you remarry?"

"You're their father. You will always have a place in their lives."

"Wow." He smiled and reached out to touch her shoulder. "When did you become so steady? So strong?"

"When I almost died." She brushed his hand away. "I guess I realized what's really important in life. And how quickly it could be taken from me."

She shuddered to think of what would have happened to her girls if she hadn't survived. Or if Cooper hadn't been there for them.

A smile crept across her face. She'd missed him. Missed him terribly, but tonight he would be back in her arms. Back in her bed. She just had to get through the next two hours with Clayton in her house.

"You don't mind if I take care of a few things? I've got some laundry to catch up on." She'd planned on washing her sheets, putting on some makeup, and showing Cooper just how much she'd missed him these last few days.

Clayton parked himself on her couch, while she cleaned the house, put the clothes away, and did her yoga. He'd spent a lot of that time on the phone, calling or e-mailing what she hoped were business contacts.

She wasn't that worried about Clayton. He'd bounce back. Guys like him always did. He wouldn't survive living anything less than the high life. He wasn't going to trade his Ferrari for a Ford. He wouldn't be satisfied in a modest two-bedroom bungalow; he needed the penthouse. Yes, Clayton Barry would find his way back.

Just like she'd found her way back. She'd had a long conversation with her agent. He loved, *loved* the idea of her taking the stage and making a plea against texting and driving. He'd suggested she find a knockout dress, one that demanded attention.

Between Cooper's unwavering support and Victor's unbridled enthusiasm, she was convinced that she could actually do this. She could show her face, scars and all, and use her misfortune to help others. And if she could do that, she could do anything. College? Why not? Or maybe she could find work for a charitable organization. Even if she had to start out as a volunteer, she would like to do something that gave back.

"Did you want to come with me to meet the girls at the bus stop?" Annabelle asked after she'd changed the sheets on not just her bed, but the guest room and the twins' beds too. The house was spotless, fresh flowers brightened the kitchen, and she'd placed scented candles by her bedside. She just needed Clayton to say good bye to Sophie and Olivia and hit the road.

"Yeah, that would be great." He pocketed his phone and stood to follow her down the street.

"Daddy!" Sophie bounded off the bus. "Guess what! I lost a tooth. And I got to put my name on the lost tooth chart next to the calendar!"

She grinned to show off the gap on her lower jaw.

"Wow, that's exciting." Clayton looked so pleased to be there for at least one of her milestones. "I'm happy for you."

"Yeah, and I think I have a loose tooth too." Olivia opened her mouth and put her finger on her bottom tooth. "See?"

"Oh, I think I saw it move." He bent down and peered into her mouth to inspect the so-called loose tooth. "Yeah, I definitely saw it move."

"Will you come play with us?" Olivia asked. "We could build sandcastles on the beach."

"Yeah, okay. I can stay for a little while."

"Yay!" Both girls raced to the house to drop off their backpacks and grab their sand toys.

They ran down to the beach, laughter ringing out loud and clear.

"You don't mind if I stay a little longer?" Clayton asked hopefully. "I don't know when I'll get another chance to build a sandcastle with my girls."

"Sure." She just hoped he'd be gone by bedtime. She needed a lullaby in the worst way.

"Thank you. For everything."

* * * *

He should have started his run sooner. Or later. Or not at all. But his internal clock had been set to be coming home in time to meet the school bus at three-fifteen. So, without even trying, he came up on Annabelle and Sophie and Olivia. With their father. Just one big happy family.

They were building sandcastles on the beach. The girls looked so happy. Annabelle sat back, radiant, watching them play. She didn't even see him as he jogged around them. Clayton Barry had his designer suit pants and shirtsleeves rolled up while he frolicked with his children.

His children. Not Cooper's.

He picked up the pace and ran down the beach. But he could still hear the girls' laughter. It was a sound he would carry in his heart for the rest of his life.

When he'd gotten far enough away, he stopped to catch his breath.

So Annabelle had moved on. He needed to do the same.

He pulled out his phone and called his agent.

"Stan, the man. Tell me more about Japan." Like that would be far enough away to get over her. But since they didn't need a left-handed reliever on Uranus, it was the best he could do. "I'm interested."

"The team is in Nishinomiya, the Hanshin Tigers. They want a three year deal, but it's negotiable."

"I can't do three years." His hopes started to fade. That would put him past his prime. Make it that much harder to return. "I want to get back to the majors. I know I can still pitch, I don't want to waste my best years overseas. I can do one year. Maybe with some kind of option for the second year, if we both agree."

"I'll see what I can do." Stan sounded optimistic. But then, that was his job.

"Keep me posted." Cooper wasn't sure if this was the right move. He wasn't sure of anything except for the fact that he couldn't just stand by and watch his career go down the drain. And he couldn't stand in the way of Annabelle's chance of keeping her family together. He loved them enough to let them go.

"I will." But Stan paused. "So are you willing to look at similar offers stateside? Or would you only be interested in long-term deals from Major League clubs?"

"At this point, I just want to get some work." He hoped that statement didn't make him sound desperate. But he needed something, anything to keep him from giving up on baseball. "Look, I know I missed some chances. I turned down opportunities that were more than I deserved."

"Hey, I didn't exactly stress the importance of any of those deals." His agent tried to put the blame on himself.

"It was one deal. I passed. My fault. I thought I'd have more choices."
And he would have, if he hadn't been so stupid. "I won't make the same
mistake."

"But you don't want to rush into anything either." How much of a pay
cut would he be taking for his agent to start hesitating now?

"When do you need a decision?"

"Take a week. Let me know by next Monday."

"I'll be in touch."

Cooper pocketed his phone and headed toward home. He wondered
how much longer he was going to have to look out his window and stare
at that damned Ferrari. The longer it sat in Annabelle's driveway, the
more convinced he became that they were working things out.

By the time he got home, he was afraid to look. He just marched past
her house and was halfway up his porch when he heard his name.

"Cooper!" He turned to see Sophie bouncing up and down. She was
covered in sand and hair was slipping out of its ponytail. "We missed
you."

She raced up to him and threw her arms around his legs, nearly
knocking him down.

"I missed you, too, squirt." He reached down to untangle her arms.

"Guess what?" She looked up at him and grinned, proudly showing off
a missing tooth.

"You lost a tooth."

"I did." She stuck her tongue in the gap. "Sthee?"

"I do see." He ruffled her messy ponytail.

"I have a loose tooth too." Olivia was right behind her. She put her
finger in her mouth and pressed on her bottom teeth. "It was there before."

"I'm sure you'll lose a tooth soon," he reassured her.

"And when I do, I get to put my name on the chart," Olivia explained.

"I see you heard the news." Annabelle had followed the girls over.
"The tooth fairy will be in the neighborhood tonight."

She looked good. Too good. Her blonde hair fell in soft waves around
her shoulders. Her blue eyes twinkled in the late afternoon sunshine. And
her smile… Her smile was enough to bring him to his knees.

"I'll be sure to keep an eye out." For the first time, he dared look in
the direction of her driveway. Only her Mercedes stood in the driveway.

"We've missed you the last couple of days." Annabelle brushed her
hair off her face, tucking it behind her left ear.

"You had company."

"Yes, well, he's moved on." He couldn't tell by the tone of her voice how she'd felt about her husband being there.

"Did you girls have a nice visit with your dad?" He turned to Olivia and Sophie.

"Yeah," Sophie said.

"Uh-huh." Olivia nodded in agreement.

"Good. I'm glad."

"It's too bad you didn't get to meet Daddy." Olivia said innocently.

"Maybe next time." That was his way of asking when he'd be coming back.

"I don't know if he'll be back before summer." Annabelle put one hand on each girl's shoulder. "Or they may go visit him when he gets settled in his new house. Wherever that may be."

She'd answered his question before he could ask it.

"Why don't you girls run on in and get started on your homework." Annabelle shooed Sophie and Olivia toward her house. "I'll be right there."

"We'd like to have you join us for dinner." Annabelle gave him an irresistible smile. "We've missed you. I missed you."

She emphasized the last three words, and it went straight to his groin.

"What can I bring?"

"I'd tell you to bring your guitar, but you left it at my house."

"And what did your ex say about that?"

"He never saw it." She gave him a sly smile. "He didn't step foot in my bedroom. Hasn't in years."

"Are you sure there's no chance for the two of you to make things work?"

"Not a chance." She leaned closer, speaking in almost a whisper.

"You're sure?"

"Absolutely." She closed the space between them, wrapping her arms around him.

He breathed her in. God, he'd missed her. Missed her so much.

After dinner, Cooper helped clean up and then sang to the girls. He followed Annabelle into her bedroom and set his guitar down on the side chair, but she shook her head.

"Sing me a lullaby." She gave him a sly smile and pushed him into the chair.

"Sure, what would you like me to play?" He plucked out a few notes.

She walked over to the window and looked out toward his house. "I used to listen to you play at night. My favorites were the love songs, like 'Every Breath You Take,' and that song that goes 'you crush me...'"

"Dave Matthews Band." He smiled and started to play. "'Crush,' one of my favorites."

"Yeah, that's the one." She sighed. "You have no idea what that song did to me."

"Oh yeah?" His fingers slipped on the next note. "Don't tell me you used my music the way you accused me of using your magazine."

She blushed, telling him more than he needed to know.

"Oh really?" He wasn't going to be able to balance his guitar on his lap as he pictured her alone in her room, listening to him play, and touching herself.

"I used to wish you were stroking me instead of that guitar."

"Show me." His voice cracked a little, like he had a bad mic.

"I couldn't..." Her blush deepened.

"Show me." He began to play the song with as much emotion as he could express without being naked. "I want to know how I pleased you even before you knew me."

Annabelle leaned against the wall next to her window. She closed her eyes and began to sway to the music. As he continued to play, she hummed along, running her fingers through her hair.

"Touch yourself, Annabelle." He continued with just the music. "I want to see how you'd touch yourself."

She stopped, looking embarrassed she shook her head.

"Take off your jeans." he insisted. "Take them off and lie on the bed."

After what felt like the worlds' longest missed beat, she complied with his request. She stripped down to her bra and panties and arranged herself on her bed.

"Play it again." She leaned back against the pillows and let her hand fall to her hip. As he continued to stroke the strings on his guitar, she moved her hand down her thigh. She spread her legs and began to inch her way closer to her sweet spot.

He almost dropped his guitar when she slipped her delicate finger beneath the elastic of her panties. A soft moan escaped her lips and that was more than he could take. He let his guitar fall to the ground and his own jeans followed.

"Annabelle," he croaked as he lowered himself to the bed.

He covered her mouth with his, crushing her beneath him. But he couldn't help it. He couldn't stand to see anyone else touching his Annabelle. Not even her.

He yanked her panties out of the way and slid his hand into the spot she was gently playing for him. He wanted to play her, to make her sing out in ecstasy so he played her with his fingers, his mouth, and when he finally slid inside her, her cries of ecstasy were the sweetest song he'd ever heard.

His body still humming like a perfectly played note, Cooper pulled Annabelle into his arms.

"Wow." She sighed, snuggling closer to him. "That was incredible."

"Yeah. It was." He couldn't agree more.

Annabelle closed her eyes, and made satisfied little noises as she settled in for the night. Or at least until dawn when he'd have to slip away.

"There's something I feel like I should tell you." Yeah, that sounded like a man who knew what he wanted. "I talked to my agent today."

"Oh, that's great!" She lifted her head, a huge smile spread across her face. "Does that mean you have a team interested in signing you?"

"Yeah."

"So why don't you sound very excited?" She looked at him, worry taking the place of her happiness.

"It's in Japan."

"No." She sat straight up. "You told him 'no,' didn't you?"

He shook his head.

"Japan? But it's…" She slid off the bed, reaching for her robe. "It's on the other side of the Pacific. How will we— Oh."

She wrapped the robe around herself, tying the belt into a knot. "I see. We won't."

"It's not like I could ask you to come with me." He sat up, swung his feet over the edge of the bed, and raked his hands through his hair. "I just don't have any other options."

"But Japan?" She shuddered. "I'm sure it's lovely there, but it's so far away."

"It is. Look, when I told him I'd think about it, your husband had practically moved in with you." Like that was an excuse. He'd panicked. Afraid of losing baseball and losing Annabelle. He'd done the only thing he knew how to do, he'd picked baseball.

"You thought that Clayton and I were getting back together? Why would you think that?"

"Because I'm an idiot." He stood up, naked and afraid he'd blown it again.

"Is there any way you can get out of the contract?"

"I haven't signed it. Yet."

"But you're considering it?"

"I don't know, Annabelle." He picked up his shorts and pulled them on. "I haven't had any other offers. What am I supposed to do, try and support you with my rental income? I made seventy dollars in tips last night jamming with a band in Oceanside. Or I could try to put Olivia and Sophie through college with the money I make as an assistant pitching coach at Sanders Baseball Academy?"

"Why would you be worried about paying for the girls' college?"

"Because I love you, Annabelle. I love you, and I love Sophie and Olivia." He just couldn't make her understand how he needed to have a job.

"You love me?" She stood there, a stunned look on her face. "You love us?"

"Yes. I do. And I want to be able to take care of you. I want to be able to give you everything you're used to. I need to make as much money as I can for as long as I can. And if it means spending a year in Japan, and then coming back to the States, I'll do what I have to do."

"Even if it means leaving me?" She blinked back tears. "Even if it means leaving us?"

"Oh, Annabelle." He couldn't stop himself, he pulled her into his arms, and held her. Held her as hot tears rolled down his bare chest. "I love you so much."

"I love you, too." She tried to wipe her tears. "And I'll try to understand why you feel like your only option is to go to Japan."

Chapter 27

"Hunter, you've got to help me." Annabelle had lain awake most of the night. Cooper had slept next to her, but he'd left at dawn. He didn't even come back for breakfast. "I need you to find a spot for Cooper on the Goliaths. As soon as possible."

"I'm not part of the team, remember?" Hunter said. "I have no say over who they sign."

"Then why did you bother scouting him?" Annabelle, like Marco, didn't believe that Hunter was truly through with baseball as she'd claimed. "Why did you film him with the radar gun to gauge his velocity?"

"Curiosity?" Hunter sounded like she'd been caught trying to pull a fast one.

"Please, I'm begging you." Annabelle had no shame when it came to groveling. Not when it was get down on her knees or watch Cooper board a plane for Japan. "At least get them to take a look. To extend an invitation to camp."

"There's still time," Hunter tried to hedge.

"No. There isn't. He got an offer from a team in Japan." Annabelle was desperate. "Even if he doesn't make the Goliaths, if he thinks he's at least got a shot at making it, he'll stay. I know he will."

"I can make a phone call." Hunter finally agreed. "But it would be better coming from you."

"Yeah, right."

"Call Dempsey. He's always had a soft spot in his heart for you." Hunter laughed, as if this wasn't a serious matter. "I think he even had a little bit of a crush on you. But don't tell him I told you. He thinks it's a big secret. He thinks Helen doesn't even know."

"Why would he listen to me?"

"Because, he'll hear it in your voice that you believe in Nathan Cooper. He'll realize that if you believe in him, he can trust him, too."

"I do believe in him. I know he'd never let the team down. He'll work harder than anyone else on the team. Even Marco."

"I'm sure he will. And be sure to tell Dempsey everything you told me."

"Do you think it will convince him?"

"Maybe," Hunter said. "But I think what will convince him the most is that you're in love with Nathan Cooper."

"Why would that have anything to do with him signing Cooper?"

"Because, he thinks it's good luck. That one of the reasons we won the World Series was because of me and Marco. Johnny Scottsdale and Alice. He's got a romantic side to him, you know."

"No. I can't see that." Annabelle had always been cordial with Marvin Dempsey. But she'd never really known him all that well.

"Maybe it's his age. Or maybe it's superstition, but he seems to think that love is what brought the title to the Goliaths. And if he thinks it will get us back to the World Series, he'll do whatever it takes to get us there."

"Us?" Annabelle teased. She was feeling more optimistic. "I thought you weren't part of the Goliaths anymore."

"Habit."

"No. You're a Goliath. You were raised a Goliath, and you'll always be a Goliath."

"Just a Goliath's wife, now." Hunter had a wistful tone in her voice.

"Right, and I'll be up for an Emmy this year." Annabelle laughed out loud.

"I'll be watching for you on prime time."

"Actually, I will be on TV. Sunday night." Annabelle was still a little nervous about doing the show, but figured if Cooper was willing to move to the ends of the earth to keep his career alive, she could show her face on national television and maybe save a life.

"Oh, really? You're not doing *Dancing With The Stars* are you?"

"No. *Sports Illustrated* is hosting a celebration to honor the fiftieth anniversary of the swimsuit issue." Annabelle was actually more excited than nervous. At least at the moment. "I'm going to be part of it."

"That's wonderful." Hunter sighed. "You know, if I didn't love you, I think I'd hate you right now."

"Why would you say that?"

"Because you're beautiful. And you're going to dazzle them all, even with…"

"Even with my face carved up like a cutting board?"

"No, I was going to say, 'with all you've been through,' and you still manage to come out on top."

"I wouldn't say that. I could step onstage and make everyone cringe in horror."

"I'm sure that won't happen."

"I'm thinking of going onstage and telling people about the accident. You know, kind of like a testimonial. And a plea for people to put their phone down while they're driving."

"Oh, Annabelle, that's so brave of you."

"You think so? You don't think I'll sound whiny or self-righteous?"

"Not at all. I think you're very courageous to use your misfortune to help others see the light."

"It was Cooper's idea."

"It's a wonderful idea."

"I'm not sure if I can do it."

"You can. You can do anything, if you want it bad enough," Hunter assured her. "You can do a public service announcement live on TV and you can convince Marvin Dempsey to bring Cooper to spring training."

"You think so?"

"I know so." Hunter sounded like she meant it.

Annabelle and Hunter chatted for a few more minutes before Annabelle hung up the phone. She could call Marvin Dempsey. The worst he could do would be to turn her down. And then she'd be in the same place she was now. Preparing to say goodbye to the love of her life.

If he said yes, then she'd at least have him in the same state. They'd still have to have a long-distance relationship, but San Francisco was a hell of a lot closer than Nishinomiya, Japan.

It took her fifteen minutes to gather up the courage to make the phone call.

"Well, hello, Annabelle. I had a funny feeling I'd be hearing from you." Marvin Dempsey sounded almost jolly. "What can I do for you?"

"Well, I was thinking..." Now that she'd actually dialed, she was about to lose her nerve. "I know you're always looking for new talent. I mean, after having won the World Series, you probably need to have even more, um, scouts. You know, to help you find players who might otherwise be overlooked, or get snatched up by other teams."

"Well, I did lose my number one scout." He chuckled, as if he found her stammering amusing. "We're going to miss having Hunter Collins, or I guess I should say Hunter Collins-Santiago as our head of, well, everything."

"I'd like to offer my services as a scout." Annabelle stood tall in her kitchen. "I have a player who I think can make an impact. No. I know he will be an asset to the Goliaths."

"Oh really? Our roster's pretty much set." Was he just humoring her?

"But you can always use another lefty out of the bullpen."

"That's true. But all the good ones have been snatched up already."

"Not all of them. This player is coming off an injury. And some trouble off the field." She had to stay strong. To be convincing. "But he's one hundred percent healthy. And I can personally guarantee that his prior indiscretions will not be repeated."

"You can personally guarantee it?"

"Yes. Absolutely."

"And you know he's healthy?"

"His shoulder is stronger than ever."

"I don't know, shoulder injuries have a way of coming back."

"Cooper is in terrific shape. Believe me."

"Cooper? Nathan Cooper?"

"Yes. I know he let you down before, but believe me, he won't let it happen again."

"You're sure of this?"

"Yes. Please Mr. Dempsey, you have to at least give him a chance. He knows what he did was wrong, and he bears that burden of guilt every day. He's a good man. Deep down, he's a very good man."

"You trust him?"

"Completely. I trust him with my life. With my children."

"And with your heart?"

"Yes. Yes. I do."

After a short pause that felt like an eternity, he sighed. "I can't guarantee a spot on the forty man roster. But I can get him an invite to camp. If he's as healthy and strong as you say he is, he'll have a chance to earn a spot with the club."

"That's all I can ask for."

"He's a lucky man," Marvin Dempsey said. "He's a very lucky man."

* * * *

Cooper stared at the PDF copy of the contract with the Nishinomiya Hanshin Tigers. He couldn't turn down the only offer he'd received, yet he couldn't bring himself to print it out and sign it.

How could he spend a year away from Annabelle? And that far away? The money was decent, but not enough to justify buying three first-class tickets to see him when the girls got out of school for the summer.

Would they be able to maintain a long-distance relationship? They'd have nothing but emails, texts, and Skype to keep them connected. With a sixteen hour time difference, even the video chats would be a challenge.

Still, a man had to have something to give.

Maybe he could manage more properties. After several years of decline, the market was improving. He could expand from his three rental properties and maybe become a real estate tycoon.

Was he really ready to trade his uniform for a suit and tie? To put down his glove and pick up a cell phone?

Maybe a part of him wanted Annabelle to ask him to stay. To try to convince him that she'd rather live a more modest lifestyle than be apart. Or even tell him they could live off her alimony while he continued the life of a beach bum.

But the fact that she understood his need to earn his living made him love her even more.

He closed the document. He still had a few more days. And he didn't want anything to ruin Annabelle's big night. She had kissed him this morning and gone off to get her hair and makeup done. He was more than happy to pick up the twins from the bus. He would miss that daily ritual most of all. Well, it would be one of the million little things he'd miss about being a part of Annabelle's life.

Chapter 28

Cooper waited for Annabelle to come downstairs. He felt like a kid going to his first prom, all dressed up in a rented tuxedo. Only this time he didn't have to make small talk with his date's parents. He wondered why guys rented tuxedos that looked pretty much the same as any other, while women would spend hundreds, if not thousands of dollars on a dress they'd wear once.

When Annabelle appeared before him, he understood. That dress was once-in-a-lifetime gorgeous. No one else would dare wear it. And no one else would look as stunning as she did.

It was a red, floor length gown that wrapped around her waist, hugging her breasts and draping over her right shoulder. The skirt had a slit almost to her thigh, but not quite. Just enough to draw his attention to her long legs, but not so much that he had to worry about anyone else seeing anything he didn't want to share.

Her hair was carefully arranged so that a cascade of curls fell across her left eyebrow, effectively covering the worst of her scars. It framed the right side of her face, showing off her flawless perfection.

It was all he could do to place a gentle kiss on her cheek rather than pull her into his arms and kiss her like he wanted to. He wanted to claim her, to keep her for himself. He didn't want to share her with the world, but that's what tonight was all about. Showing her off one more time.

"You look amazing." He could barely breathe. "Almost as pretty as you did in that hospital room."

She gave him a puzzled look.

"When you first saw Sophie and Olivia." He wasn't sure he could explain, but he would try. "Your face lit up. I've never seen anyone so beautiful."

"Sure, with a bandage covering my face, and my hair all matted with blood."

"You were radiant. Shining with love."

"That is the corniest thing I've ever heard."

"Maybe. But it's true. I was halfway in love with you from the first time I saw your picture." He took her hand, pressing his lips to her palm. "But seeing you in that hospital room, all banged up, but so happy to see your daughters, I fell all the way."

"That's why you wouldn't leave us alone."

"Yeah." He laced his fingers through hers. "That and the fact that I'm secretly Prince Charming."

"Of course you are." Annabelle squeezed his hand. "Let's go get this party over with. Sophie and Olivia are spending the night with a friend from school, and I intend to take full advantage of having the house to ourselves."

"Yes. Let's make the most of tonight." His chest tightened at the thought of having to make a decision tomorrow.

He would have to walk away from the game, and always wonder if he still had something left. Or he'd have to leave Annabelle and her daughters. Sure, they'd try to make it work with an ocean between them, but he hated the thought of being so far away with nothing but her picture to keep him company.

Her picture had once been enough. But now that he'd held her in his arms, now that he'd tasted her and touched her and loved her, he didn't know how he was going to survive without her.

* * * *

The limo pulled up in front of the theater. It was almost like going to the Academy Awards, the red carpet was out, photographers and spectators lined up outside, trying to catch a glimpse of some of the most beautiful women in the world.

He was proud and in awe of the woman on his arm. She hadn't wanted to come at first. Ashamed of her disfigurement, and worried her past behavior would come back to haunt her. But here she was, not only in attendance, but wearing a standout, knockout red dress.

She was here to make an impact.

"I'm proud of you," he whispered as they got out of the car. "I just want you to know that."

"Thanks, but I might not be able to go through with getting onstage."

"Sure you will." he assured her. "I'll be right here for you."

His cell phone buzzed in his pocket, but he wasn't going to check it. Tonight was all about Annabelle. Unless... "Did you leave my number as a contact when you left the girls at their sleepover?"

"Tanya has my number, and don't worry, I checked a few minutes ago."

"If you're not worried, then I'm not going to."

Placing his hand on the small of her back, he guided her into the ballroom. He felt a flat, hard lump just above her right hip.

"Is that your phone?"

"You'll see."

* * * *

Annabelle sat through the host's welcome speech, the first musical act, and brief montage of the earliest covers. A few more speeches, another musical performance, and a video showing the models spending time together earlier in the week. Finally, Annabelle was called onstage.

"Wish me luck," she whispered.

"You'll be amazing," Cooper told her.

Annabelle made her way onstage. After her introduction, she thanked the host and then turned to face the audience. Taking a deep breath, she smiled, careful to keep her right side prominent.

"Thank you, thank you so much..." On cue, her phone buzzed. Reaching behind her back, she pulled it out of where she had it tucked in next to the microphone receiver. "Sorry, I've got to check this. Single mom, kids with a sitter."

Glancing at her phone with a concerned look on her face, she hoped she could pull this off. "Oh, nothing to worry about, it's just a really cute picture of a baby giraffe."

She held it up as if the audience could see the tiny picture. Then she pretended to retweet it.

"Sorry about that." She laughed as if she were just having coffee with friends and was distracted by her phone. "Now where was I? Oh, right. How has *Sports Illustrated* changed my life? Well, the swimsuit issue was my first job. I was nineteen years old and pretty naïve. I was sheltered, a little spoiled, and I didn't really have any big dreams in life. Then I found myself traveling the world, meeting people I never would have met, and making money of my own. It was mine, not my Daddy's, not my husband's. Mine."

She blinked back tears stinging her eyes.

"I was proud of my work, even though to some people, it didn't seem like work. Just stand there, or lie in the sand, and look pretty. But it was work. Long hours, delays due to weather or lighting or just not 'feeling it.' It was good work, though. Satisfying. And I did make friendships. Modeling was my first job. It's the only job I've ever had. I guess you can say I lived much of my life in front of the camera."

Her voice shook a little as she was coming to the end of her little speech. She pulled her phone out again, and holding it up she said, "I want to remember this night. Now let me take a selfie…"

She flipped her hair back off the left side of her face, and after hearing the gasp from the audience, said, "It just has to be from the right side."

She snapped a picture.

"I know we've all become too attached to our phones. We're afraid to be out of touch for even an instant. But it only takes an instant to go from this"—she showed the audience the right side of her face—"to this."

She could feel the heat of the stage lights on her scarred face. "I was struck by a distracted driver. The young man who hit me had received a text message."

She glanced down at her phone. "According to the police report, it said 'Hey man, what's up?' And his response to this urgent text?"

She swallowed back the tears, and continued. "His response was, 'not much, I'm dri—' The good news? His phone wasn't damaged. So they were able to retrieve the unsent message."

She put her phone away for the last time that evening.

"Being a part of *Sports Illustrated's* swimsuit edition changed my life. But a simple text changed it even more."

Annabelle pulled her hair back, twisting it into a simple knot on the top of her head. With a smile and a nod, she simply said, "Thank you." And she walked off with her head held high.

She couldn't see the crowd through the tears, but she could hear the applause. Flashes of light went off around her and she allowed the escort to help her off the stage. When her vision cleared enough for her to make her way back to her seat, she was surprised to find the crowd was giving her a standing ovation.

Her phone buzzed repeatedly, but she wasn't about to check it. She'd made her point. The last thing she wanted was to trip over her gown because she couldn't ignore her phone. And since the special ringtone she'd programmed for the babysitter hadn't sounded, she knew her daughters were fine.

The applause didn't stop until she reached Cooper and he took her hand to help her sit. Once he sat next to her, the rest of the audience followed suit.

The next musical act was introduced and the show went on. The program ended with an award for the top cover presented to Kathy Ireland for her first cover, the best-selling issue of all time.

More pictures were taken as they made their way to the exit after the final presentation. Cooper kept his hand on her back the whole time. She didn't know what she would have done without him there. Probably chickened out about going onstage. No, she wouldn't have even come tonight without his support.

"Ms. Jones." A reporter caught her just steps from the door. "Can you tell us more about the accident that ended your career? Or should I say, resurrected it?"

"Resurrected? I don't think so."

"Oh sure, you could do public service announcements. You could be the new spokesperson for the campaign against texting and driving."

"Thank you, but that's not why I said what I said."

"So why did you? It was pretty clear you planned the speech, with the phone as a prop. You must have had an agenda."

"I wasn't going to come tonight. I was going to pass up the celebration of one of the best things I've ever done, besides having my two children. I was afraid to let people see me like this. Afraid to admit that I'm not the beautiful girl I used to be." She gave her most confident smile for the cameras. "But then a friend helped me see this as an opportunity to not only face my fears, but to hopefully help others. If I can save even one life, then it will be worth it."

"Just one?"

"I would love to think that every single person who watched tonight will never pick up their phone while driving, but I'm not that naïve." Pressure was building behind her eyes from the incessant flashes from cameras coming from every direction. Just a few more minutes and then she could drop the mask. "But each person who at least thinks twice before succumbing to the beckoning call of a new message will be a start."

"The lovely Miss Annabelle Jones." The reporter turned to the camera to do her sign off.

Cooper whisked her into the waiting limo, but not before she heard cries of "Ms. Jones, Annabelle," and other claims on her attention.

"You okay?" He asked as she buckled her seatbelt.

"Yeah. I think I am."

"You were tremendous."

"Tremendous?"

"Amazing. Fantastic. Remarkable." He kissed her neck, nuzzling that delicate spot behind her ear. "Not to mention, lovely, stunning, and I know I've said it before, but you are the most beautiful woman I've ever known."

"You sir, are just trying to flatter me." She giggled, both at his words and the tickling kisses. "If I didn't know better, I'd think you were trying to get into my pants."

"You're not wearing pants." His voice was almost a growl. "Please tell me you're not wearing underwear, either."

"You'll just have to wait to find out." She scooted away from him and her phone fell from its spot tucked into her dress.

He picked it up, glancing at the display. "You've got quite a few messages."

She took the phone from him, scanning for anything that might need her immediate attention.

"It's just my agent. I swear the man never sleeps." She slipped her phone into her purse and leaned back against the leather seat. It had been a long night. She was exhausted and exhilarated at the same time.

Cooper's phone buzzed.

"You seem to be getting some messages, too."

"Nothing that can't wait." He put his arm around her and she relaxed against him.

"Wait." She sat up, remembering the conversation she'd had with Marvin Dempsey. What if they were going to make him an offer? "I did give Kelsey's mom your number. Just in case."

He whipped his phone out so fast the car shook.

"It's just my agent." He relaxed back into the seat. "Apparently he doesn't sleep either."

"Maybe you should check."

"Tomorrow." He started to put his phone back into his pocket, but she grabbed it.

"He left a voice mail. Mind if I check?"

"Annabelle," he sang her name, but with more sorrow than the saddest blues song. "I don't want anything to put a damper on this night. You were triumphant. Let's just celebrate."

"I don't want to bury my head in the sand. If you're leaving me, I'd rather know before we make love. So I can savor every moment even more." She pushed the button to play his voice mail and held it up to her ear.

"Coop, I have some news…" He grabbed the phone from her before she could hear any more.

He listened, his face unreadable. After what seemed like an eternity, he switched off the phone and turned toward her, a smile creeping across his face.

"So? What's the news?" Annabelle tried to contain her excitement. Just in case.

"It seems I have another offer." He let out a huge sigh. "For some reason, the Goliaths want to take another look at me."

"Oh, really?" It was hard for her to pretend she knew nothing about it. And to keep from squealing with joy.

"You wouldn't know anything about that would you?"

"Well, I do recall a bullpen session you threw for Hunter. I know she's not officially part of the team, but…"

"Cut the bull, Annabelle." For the first time, he didn't sing her name. "You put her up to this, didn't you?"

"I called, and asked her to help you find a job in the United States." She couldn't tell if he was mad at her or not. "But she said she no longer had any influence. She sent the video, but that was all."

"So this is legitimate? They really want me?"

"How could they not?" She figured she'd wait until he made the team before confessing to calling Marvin Dempsey.

"I screwed up." He couldn't quite let that go.

"But you won't do it again."

"No. I won't." He reached over and grabbed her hand. "Do you really think I can do this?"

"Of course you can." She gave him a loving squeeze. "If I could show my face in front of a live television audience, you can get back on the mound."

"But Goliaths' fans were betrayed by me once." He raked his hand through his hair. "I can't let them down again."

"You won't. I have faith in you." She leaned over and planted a kiss on his cheek. The whiskers of his carefully trimmed beard tickled her lips. "I love you, Nathan Cooper."

"For real?"

"Yes. You're my knight in shining armor. My Prince Charming." She wrapped her arms around him. "My hero."

"Annabelle." He pulled her onto his lap and whispered, "You're my hero. You helped me believe again. Gave me a reason to make a comeback. I can't do it without you."

"I'll be here." She patted his chest, feeling his heart pounding beneath her touch.

"If I make the team, we'll at least be in the same time zone."

"We will. And when the girls are out of school, we'll come up to San Francisco. We can stay with Hunter and Marco and come to your games."

"That would be great." He picked up her left hand, and brought it to his lips. He kissed her ring finger. "I'm going to want more. You know that, don't you? I'm going to want the fairy tale."

"You think we can just live happily ever after?" Her heart swelled, the idea of spending the rest of her life with this man seemed too good to be true.

"I do." He let go of her hand. "But I'm not going to pressure you. I've waited ten years to meet you. I think I can wait a few more months to make you mine forever."

"Forever?"

"Yeah. I know I don't deserve even one night, but I'm an arrogant ballplayer. I want it all."

"I want it all, too."

Epilogue

The clubhouse had emptied as the Goliaths took the field early for the ring presentation ceremony. Cooper stayed behind, hoping for a few minutes to gather his thoughts. He'd arranged to receive his ring privately. He would accept it graciously, but he wouldn't ever wear it.

"I had a feeling I'd find you here." Annabelle's voice was like a breath of fresh air. He wouldn't be here without her. Not a chance.

"I'm just trying to lay low until the game actually starts."

"You're not going to get your ring?"

"I don't need a ring." He turned to see her. Beautiful. As always. He'd missed her. They spoke on the phone every night. Sent texts to each other—never while driving—and she'd brought the girls to Arizona during their spring break. "Well, I don't need a ring I didn't earn. I will want a ring someday."

"You've got a good chance to repeat this year."

"I'm not talking about that ring." He stood and put his hands on her waist. "I want a ring from you. I know it's too soon. Your divorce isn't even final…"

"I signed the papers yesterday." She gave him a little half smile. "I just needed to take some time to, mourn, I guess."

"I'll give you some time." He stroked her left cheek. "You've had a lot of changes recently."

"Who would have thought my little speech would go viral?" She laughed, recalling how much attention her discourse on the dangers of texting while driving had garnered. "They even replayed it during the Super Bowl."

And her agent had made sure she profited from it. Her career wasn't quite over. She'd been asked to do a couple of public service announcements. The jarring contrast between her former cover girl perfection and the jagged scars from the accident was sure to make people stop and think before picking up their phone while in the fast lane.

"Have you decided about college?" He hoped she would continue with her plan to take a few classes, part-time, starting in the fall.

"I'm looking into a major in Fashion Merchandising at Long Beach, or Apparel Design at San Francisco State." Pride shone in her voice as she talked about her future plans. "I've applied to both, so we'll see."

"Long Beach or San Francisco?" He wondered what her preference was. "You'll do great either way."

"You think so?"

"Do you want me to help you make a decision?" He leaned closer, brushing her hair off her face. "Or do you just want assurance that I'll be here whatever you decide?"

"I lived in San Francisco for seven years. There are so many things I love about the city," she said. "But I've come to love Aurelia Beach, too."

"That's the beauty of this. We can live in both places." He drew his finger along her jaw. "I can keep an apartment in the city, and a house on the beach. Or if you want to live here full time, I can sell my place down there."

She smiled, her imperfect, crooked smile.

"Annabelle, I'm going to ask you to marry me someday." He pressed his lips to her forehead.

"And I will say 'yes,' someday." She sighed, wrapping her arms around him.

"I suppose tomorrow's too soon."

She nodded.

He gave a little shrug and then turned toward his locker to retrieve his guitar. He pulled a guitar pick from his pocket and dropping to one knee, he began to play. The song he'd been working on since he'd met her flowed from his heart.

Your name on my lips is like a song in my heart
The smile on your face, a priceless work of art.

Annabelle,
You've got me under your spell.
A spell I don't ever want broken.

When you needed me, I learned how to feel.
One touch from you, and I was able to heal.

Annabelle,
You've got me under your spell.
A spell I don't ever want broken.

Your faith in me helped me believe again.
The love you gave taught me how to win.

Oh Annabelle,
Your love's a magic spell
And your heart won't ever be broken.

He stood, leaving his guitar propped against his locker. With tears in his eyes, he pulled her into his arms and buried his face in her hair. "Annabelle, I love you. I will always love you. And as soon as you're ready, I want to become a family."

"We're already a family." She wrapped her arms around him. "And don't worry, we'll make it official soon. Very soon."

There was a time when he'd been too impatient to wait for what he wanted. Impatient and cocky and just foolish enough to believe he was entitled to everything he'd been given. But now he knew he didn't deserve half of the blessings he'd received. He didn't deserve Annabelle or the love she so freely gave him.

He didn't deserve her. He didn't deserve any of this. But he was going to make sure he didn't take anything for granted. He was going to give everything he had to show his appreciation to the league, the fans, and most of all to his sweet Annabelle.

Meet the Author

Kristina Mathews doesn't remember a time when she didn't have a book in her hand. Or in her head. But it wasn't until she turned forty that she confessed the reason the laundry never made it out of the dryer was because she was busy writing.

While she resigned from teaching with the arrival of her second son, she's remained an educator in some form. As a volunteer, parent club member or para educator, she finds the most satisfaction working with emergent and developing readers, helping foster confidence and a lifelong love of books.

Kristina lives in Northern California with her husband of more than twenty years, two sons and a black lab. A veteran road tripper, amateur renovator and sports fanatic. She hopes to one day travel all 3,073 miles of Highway 50 from Sacramento, CA to Ocean City, MD, replace her carpet with hardwood floors and serve as a "Ball Dudette" for the San Francisco Giants.

Turn the page for a special excerpt of Kristina Mathews's

Better Than Perfect

Johnny "The Monk" Scottsdale has won it all on the baseball diamond.
He's even pitched a perfect game. Known for his legendary control both
on and off the field, his pristine public image makes him the ideal person
to work with young players in a preseason minicamp. Except the camp
is run by the one woman he can't forget...the woman who made him a
"monk."
Alice Harrison once traded her dreams so that Johnny Scottsdale could
make it to the Majors—and then her dreams fell apart. Now here comes
Johnny back into her life, just when she's ready to finally go after her
dreams. This time she's not letting up. Even if she has to reveal what
she kept secret for too long from her son and Johnny. She can't be sure
how things will turn out, but she's not leaving until she swings for the
fences...

Visit us at www.kensingtonbooks.com

On sale now!

Chapter 1

"Pitchers and catchers report to spring training in thirteen days, twenty-one hours and seventeen minutes," Hall of Fame broadcaster Kip Michaels announced, and the crowd went wild. "Kicking off today's Fan Fest, I'd like to introduce one of our newest players. Two-time Cy Young Award winner, perennial All-Star, and the last man to pitch a perfect game. Give a warm San Francisco welcome to Johnny 'The Monk' Scottsdale."

Thirty thousand people were expected at the ballpark today. A great crowd—for a baseball game. But instead of working the count, Johnny would be working the crowd. Answering questions. Signing autographs. Putting himself out there in a way he wasn't entirely comfortable with. He was as nervous as the day he'd made his professional debut fourteen years ago. Butterflies? Try every seagull on the West Coast taking roost in his stomach.

Focus. Breathe. Let it go.

"Thank you. I'm thrilled to be here." He'd much rather face the 1927 Yankees than sit in front of a camera and a microphone talking about his game instead of playing it. "I hope I can help the team bring home a World Series Championship."

He tried to relax his shoulders. Tried to hide his nerves. The Goliaths could be his last team. His last shot at a ring. His final chance to prove himself and leave a legacy that went beyond the diamond.

After fielding a few questions about what he could bring to the team, and deflecting some praise about his success so far, Johnny was released to another part of the park to sign autographs. Little Leaguers approached with wide eyes and big league dreams. Tiny tots with painted faces squirmed with excitement about getting cotton candy while their parents shoved them forward to collect an autograph. A shy boy with a broken arm asked him to sign his cast. The look on his face was more than worth the discomfort of being in the spotlight for something other than his on-field performance.

Johnny had signed the big contract. The team paid him a lot of money to pitch every five games. They also paid him to interact with the fans, to be an ambassador for the game he'd loved for so long. The game that had saved him from a completely different kind of life.

He shared a table with another new player, shortstop Bryce Baxter. They were set up near the home bullpen along the third base line. Several other stations were set up around the park, giving fans a chance to get up close and personal with the players. Some tried to get a little too personal.

"So you're the hot new pitcher." A busty brunette leaned over the autograph table, wearing what appeared to be a toddler-sized tank top. The team logo sparkled in rhinestones and she was obviously well aware of the attention she drew. "I'd be more than happy to show you around."

"No thanks. I'm pretty familiar with the city." He held his pen ready, although she didn't seem to have anything to autograph. Nothing he was willing to sign, anyway.

"I could take you places you've never been." She leaned over even more.

Johnny kept his head down, trying to avoid gazing at what she had to offer. He reached for a stock photo, scrawled his signature across the bottom, and slid the picture forward, hoping she'd take the hint and leave.

"You forgot your number." She pouted.

"Sorry. I don't give that out." Johnny wished he could retreat to the locker room. Get away from her and the crowd that seemed to be growing. He never understood why people would wait in line to make small talk and take his picture. He gripped the black marker, needing something to do with his hands. If he only had a baseball, he could roll it around in his palm. Feel the smoothness of the leather, the rough contrast of the raised stitches. Find comfort in the weight and the symmetry of the one thing he could always control.

His teammate inserted himself into the conversation. "Do you know who this is? The one and only Johnny 'The Monk' Scottsdale."

"The Monk?" She drew her gaze over Bryce, then glanced at Johnny before settling on Bryce once more.

"He's a god." He flashed a grin indicating he was more than willing to play her game. "Me? I'm a mere mortal." Bryce leaned toward her, clearly enjoying the interaction.

"You're new, too." She scooted over to his side of the table, dismissing Johnny's rejection as strike one. She must think she had a better chance of scoring with Bryce.

"I am. I think I left my heart somewhere in the city. Could you help me find it?" He slid one of his photos across the table to her.

"I can help you find whatever you're looking for." She took the pen from him and wrote something on the inside of his forearm. Her number, most likely.

Bryce grinned as if he enjoyed having a stranger tattoo him with a permanent marker.

"Bring your friend, too. If he's up for a challenge."

"I'll see what I can do, sweetheart." Bryce tipped his cap and winked at the woman.

Johnny exhaled, realizing he'd been holding his breath during the entire conversation.

"Thanks man, I owe you one." Johnny shook his head, as relieved as if Bryce had just snagged a line drive with two outs and the bases loaded.

"So it really isn't an act." Baxter eyed him carefully. "You really do walk the walk."

"What walk?"

"The celibacy thing. It's for real." A lot of guys thought he was full of it. That it was just for show. A way to get attention, and women. But once they realized he was genuine, most of the other players accepted him. Some even respected him. "You really don't mess around."

"No. I don't. I'm not perfect, but I try to stay out of trouble." Johnny removed his cap and ran his fingers through his hair. Since they were both new to the team, their booth wasn't as crowded as some of the others. They had a chance to catch their breath. He was able to finally sit back and enjoy the perfect weather. It was one of those glorious Northern California days when the sun came out to tease, dropping hints of spring and the fever that came with it.

"You looked like you were a little uncomfortable there." Bryce, on the other hand, seemed to relish the attention.

"I know it's part of the job, but it's not the part I'm good at."

"You let your game speak for itself. That's cool." Bryce reclined in his chair, looking as relaxed as if he was sitting in his own back yard. "Some of us have to use our charm to make up for lack of talent."

Johnny laughed. Baxter had plenty of talent. And more than enough charm to go around.

"She was pretty fine, though." Bryce continued to check her out as she walked away, collecting ballplayer's numbers like kids collected baseball cards. "Exactly what I need to get me in shape for spring training."

"Is that so?" Johnny managed to avoid the whole groupie scene. His entire career had been about control, both on and off the field. The Monk kept his cool. The Monk never got rattled. And The Monk maintained a spotless reputation. He had to, considering where he'd come from.

"There he is. Come on, Mom." A kid, about twelve or thirteen, rushed up to the booth, practically dragging his mother by the arm.

Johnny slipped on his best fan-friendly smile.

"We're, like, your number one fans." The boy was practically bursting at the seams. "Right, Mom?"

The boy's mother stepped forward, taking Johnny's breath away.

He'd had several reasons to come to San Francisco. Eleven million obvious ones, and several others that he'd done his best to articulate to the fans. There was only one reason he should have stayed away.

"Alice." Just saying her name sent a line drive straight to his heart. Even fourteen years later.

"Congratulations on your new contract. I know you're going to have a great year." She sounded like any other fan, wishing him well. She just marched right up to his table to ask for an autograph. A freaking autograph? Like he meant nothing to her.

A slight breeze blew her hair around her face. She tried to smile as she tucked a loose strand behind her ear. Blond, straight, silky—and if he remembered correctly—oh-so-soft. She wore modestly cut jeans and a soft blue sweater that on anyone else would have looked plain and proper. He didn't need to glance at her left hand to know she was off limits. Yet, she still moved him like no other woman ever could. Made him long for what he'd had. What he'd lost. What he'd tried for years to forget.

"Wait." The boy gaped at her. "You guys know each other? For real?"

"Yes. Johnny was…" She held Johnny's gaze just long enough for him to catch a flicker of regret. She turned to her son, who was about an inch or two taller than her. "He was your dad's college roommate."

"You knew my dad?" The boy seemed more impressed by that than the fact that people waited in line for his autograph.

"Yes. I knew him." Johnny swallowed the lump in his throat. "Before he married your mom."

"Cool." The kid smiled and nodded his head, like it was no big deal. "I mean, I know you played for the Wolf Pack when they went to Nevada, but I had no idea you guys were, like, friends."

Sure. Friends.

"Zach." She placed her hand on his shoulder, ready to steer him away. "I'm sure Mr. Scottsdale is a busy man. Let's leave him alone."

They'd once been as close as two people could be. But now he was Mr. Scottsdale.

The boy shrugged, dismissing her and looking up to Johnny with admiration. "It's totally awesome to meet you."

Johnny nodded, giving his most sincere smile, even though seeing Alice, and her kid, hit him like a 97-mile-an-hour fastball.

They started to walk away.

"Give my best to Mel." As if he hadn't already done that.

Alice turned around.

"Mel died. Eight years ago." A pained expression flashed across her face.

"I'm sorry. For your loss." Johnny said the words. He wanted more than anything to mean them, but he'd carried that resentment around for so long, it had become as much a part of him as his right arm.

"Thank you." Alice gave him a sad little smile. It was forced. Polite. The kind of smile she'd give a stranger. "It was good seeing you. Really good."

"Yeah. Sure." He could say the same, but he'd be lying. Seeing her again only reminded him of everything he'd sacrificed.

* * * *

The minute she'd seen Johnny on the stage, Alice's heart had swelled big enough to fill the stadium. There he'd been, larger than life. Damn. The man looked good. Better than on TV. Better than she remembered. He'd gained some muscle. A lot of muscle. Even without the jersey, there'd be no doubt he was an athlete. He moved with the kind of confidence and grace that came with being totally in tune with his body. Like he'd once been totally in tune with hers. She ached at the memory, but shook it off, uncomfortable having such thoughts with her son sitting next to her. Like Johnny had clearly been uncomfortable onstage, addressing the media and the crowds. He never did like to talk about his game. He'd simply let his talent speak for itself.

Just as she'd predicted, women lined up at his booth. They all wanted his autograph. Some of them wanted a little more. She hadn't been able to handle it back then. And now? What he did was his business. Especially since she'd been the one to walk out on him.

"Mom. Are you okay?" Zach was protective of her. And a little too observant.

"I'm fine, Zach." She shook her head to clear the fog of memories that rolled over her. With only the briefest look into his eyes, she couldn't forget the three years they'd spent together, nearly inseparable. Studying. Hanging out. Making love. "I'm surprised to see him, that's all."

"But you knew he'd be here." Zach had that tone, the unspoken *duh*. They'd been coming to Fan Fest every year since Mel's death. She'd known Johnny would be here. She just wasn't prepared for the impact of seeing him again. She'd thought she'd put those feelings behind her. Packed them away with her college sweatshirts and student ID card. "You were so excited when you heard it on the radio. Your favorite player finally becoming a Goliath. Why didn't you tell me you guys were, like, friends?"

"I didn't want you to think it's a big deal." She tried to place her hand on his shoulder, but he squirmed to avoid the contact. That was new. Not unexpected, given his age, but she missed her little boy. The first time they'd come to Fan Fest, he'd held her hand. Until they'd gotten to the miniature version of the ballpark. He'd joined the t-ball game like he was born to play.

"It is a big deal." Zach looked at her like she was hopelessly out of touch. Something he did a lot these days. "Mom, you actually know Johnny Scottsdale."

There it was. The star-struck admiration bordering on worship.

"I *knew* him, Zach." Alice tried to keep her tone neutral. She couldn't betray her emotions. A wave of regret washed over her. The question of what might have been. "But that was a long time ago."

"Wouldn't it be cool if he came to the foundation's minicamp?" Zach couldn't know why it would be such a bad idea.

She'd hoped to avoid him. Avoid digging up the past. And the question that had plagued her more and more as Zach grew. "I already have a pitcher lined up. Nathan Cooper. He's done it for years."

Alice had worked for the Mel Harrison Jr. Foundation since its inception, a little more than a year after her husband's death. The initial donations were privately funded, set up to provide grants to community schools and youth organizations. As the foundation had grown, they were able to provide services for greater numbers of children, but the more successful they'd become, the less contact she had with the kids.

Until a few years ago, when the team had approached her about setting up a minicamp for youth players. It evolved from a Saturday demonstration and meet-and-greet to a weeklong afterschool program where the ballplayers worked directly with the kids, helping them learn fundamentals of the game while boosting their confidence with the attention and mentorship of the pro athletes.

"Cooper's alright." Zach sounded disappointed, bordering on whiny. "But he's not Johnny Scottsdale."

"Zach, we made a commitment to Nathan Cooper."

"And Harrisons always keep their commitments." Zach parroted the family motto. She could tell by the tone of his voice he had to restrain himself from rolling his eyes.

"Yes, Zach, Harrisons keep their commitments." No matter what. She'd made a commitment to Mel, to the Harrison family. She'd hoped her feelings for Johnny would eventually fade. She'd made her choice. A desperate one at the time, but once she'd committed to Mel, she wouldn't look back. She still couldn't. "Cooper's a good player. A good guy. We can't just tell him we don't want him anymore."

"Well, maybe they could both do the pitching clinic," Zach suggested. "Since Cooper's a lefty, maybe it would be better to have a right-handed pitcher too."

"Johnny's a busy man. He doesn't need us bugging him." And she didn't need to be reminded of what she'd given up.

"Yeah, but he probably doesn't know very many people here yet." Zach sounded hopeful. Like they'd be doing Johnny a favor. "It would be good for him to get involved in the community."

"Zach. He doesn't need us." She'd made sure of it.

"But..." Zach couldn't let it go.

"I think it's time for some lunch." Lately, food seemed to be the best distraction.

"I could eat." Zach shrugged. "You want to split some garlic fries?"

"You know I do." The ballpark's signature fries had become a tradition. But if she ate a full order herself, she'd be sorry later.

"Can I get two hot dogs, then? Or maybe some nachos?"

"You're that hungry?" Wasn't it only yesterday that she begged him to eat? Playing airplane with the spoon or bribing him with a toy to take three more bites.

"Yeah. I guess meeting Johnny Scottsdale increased my appetite." He grinned at her. For a second there, he reminded her of someone she used to know.

"Oh, Zach..." She sighed, her emotions getting the better of her. Seeing Johnny for even a few minutes had her all mixed up.

It had been easier when Johnny was on the other side of the country. When he'd been nothing more than a box score. An image on TV. She'd followed his entire career. From his earliest days in the minor leagues, to his first start in Kansas City, to when he was traded to Tampa Bay. She'd watched him. Cheered for him. Wished him nothing but success.

"Oh please, Mom. Don't go there." She was embarrassing him. As she often did whenever she talked about how quickly he was growing up. Becoming a man. Neither of them was quite ready for it, but that didn't matter.

She put her arm around him but felt him struggling with the idea of pulling away. Reluctantly, she let him go, knowing it was only a matter of time before he wouldn't need her at all.

"Order whatever you want. Just don't complain about a stomach ache later."

"I won't." He ordered a hot dog, nachos and a root beer.

She stepped up behind him and ordered her hot dog, the garlic fries and a Diet Coke. She struck up a conversation with the lady behind the counter while they waited for their order.

"Geez, Mom. Why do you have to talk so much?" He'd waited until they were at the condiment station before complaining.

"I was only being friendly. There's nothing wrong with that." She unwrapped her hot dog and placed it under the mustard spout.

"Yeah, then why weren't you very friendly with Johnny Scottsdale?" He kept his head down, concentrating on his food. She'd learned to pay attention more when he seemed least interested in making conversation. "You actually knew him in college and you barely said a word to him."

She hit the pump on the mustard a little too hard and it splattered all over her sweater. She quickly grabbed a napkin to wipe up the stain.

"Is it… Is it because he reminds you of Dad? Does seeing him make you sad?"

"Oh, honey." She put her arm around him, pressing him against her. How could she possibly explain why seeing Johnny again was so painful?

"It seems kind of weird that they didn't keep in touch after college." Zach had no idea how weird it would have been if they had. The three of them had been the best of friends. How many times had they let Mel tag along on their dates? Or how many times had she made herself at home at their place? But Johnny had been at the heart of their little group. And when he'd moved on, she and Mel turned to each other.

"Johnny was trying to make it to the big leagues." She used the same story she'd told herself over the years. "He had to work very hard to get to where he is today. Mel had a job here in the city, and I was busy raising you. We just drifted apart, that's all."

"But, maybe you and Johnny can be friends again." He had a tiny hesitation in his voice. Telling her there was more to the story than he was willing to share.

She waited. Pushing him would never get him to open up.

"Maybe…" Zach took a long slurp of his soda. "Maybe he could tell me more about my dad."

* * * *

Well, that was a mistake. By bringing up his dad, he'd upset his mom. Zach could tell because she got really quiet. They sat in the stands to eat their lunch and watch the next round of interviews. She nibbled on her hot dog and absently picked at the garlic fries. He ended up eating most of them, which was fine. He loved garlic fries. But it was weird with her not talking. Normally she would chatter on and on about the upcoming season and especially all the new players. He'd expected her to be really excited about Johnny Scottsdale. She was probably an even bigger fan than he was.

She'd actually cried when he pitched his perfect game. Cried and hugged Zach like they'd been there. But she barely said a word to him when they met today. And they didn't even get an autograph.

Now, she was all quiet, and he wouldn't be surprised if she said she wanted to leave soon. He'd seen what he wanted to see. Johnny Scottsdale's first interview as one of the Goliaths, and then he'd gotten to meet him. Sort of.

Kip Michaels stepped onstage to introduce the next set of players. He was one of the best. He never had anything bad to say about an opponent, but he was a Goliath to the core. He also managed to throw out a few tips for young players during every game. He'd point out simple things, like keeping balanced in the batter's box or following through on a pitch. Plus, he'd been there. Way before Zach's time, but he'd pitched in the majors for ten years. So he knew what he was talking about.

"Thank you, San Francisco!" Nathan Cooper stepped up to the mic for his turn in the spotlight. "It's going to be a great season. I guarantee it."

Yeah, he was alright. Kind of a showoff, though. Like it was more about him than the team. Cooper played to the crowd, making them laugh and cheer and get pumped up for the season. Even if he was kind of obnoxious, he was a pretty good pitcher. Most of the time.

Zach glanced over at his mother. She was trying to rub the mustard stain out of her sweater. He wondered if that would be her excuse for leaving early. He wouldn't mind. Not really. He just wished he could have talked to Johnny Scottsdale more. He had a lot of questions. Mostly about baseball. Like what it was like to pitch a perfect game.

He had questions about his dad.

He barely even remembered him. Only a few fuzzy memories—mostly good—of a guy in a suit taking off his tie and getting down on the floor to play with the Thomas the Train set. He remembered watching movies and going to the park, but he didn't think he'd ever played catch with his dad.

He'd played catch with a few different major leaguers. As part of the minicamp. He never really felt like he was part of the program though. It was more like he tagged along, just because he could. Because his mom ran the show and his grandparents had started the whole charity thing after his dad died.

Some of the other kids had it real tough, though. Single parents who worked two jobs just to pay their rent. So they didn't have time to play catch with their kids. There were foster kids who never lived in one place long enough to be part of a team. Some of the kids had dads in the military, serving overseas in Afghanistan or places like that.

Zach felt kind of bad, taking up a spot for a kid who needed it more. At least he didn't have to worry about money. Or his mom didn't have to worry, anyways.

"Hey Mom?" He had an idea.

"Don't tell me you're still hungry." She smiled at him, but she was kind of distracted.

"No." Not really. But he would be after dinner. They'd probably have a big salad or vegetable stir-fry—something healthy to make up for all the junk food. "I was just thinking. Maybe I'm getting too old to be in the minicamp."

"You're not too old." She folded up her napkin and wrapped up the last of her unfinished hot dog. "There will be plenty of other kids your age."

"I guess." He wasn't as excited about it as he'd been the last few years.

"You don't have to do the minicamp." She tried to sound like it didn't matter to her, but he knew she'd be disappointed if he wasn't there. "I hope you're not quitting because I haven't asked Johnny Scottsdale to join us."

"That's not it." He grabbed the last garlic fry. Except maybe that was part of it. "I just don't know how much more I can learn from the same guys."

That kind of made him sound like a jerk. Like he thought he was some great baseball player already. That's not what he meant. He just didn't know how to say it without sounding like he was spoiled or something.

How many kids got to work with real Major League baseball players every year? Not many. For most of them it was a once-in-a-lifetime kind of thing.

"If you don't want to come, that's okay. You won't hurt my feelings." She said that, but she didn't like when he didn't want to do stuff with her. It was hard for him to tell her he'd rather be with his friends. She always worked so hard at finding fun things to do together. Maybe it was because he didn't have his dad around anymore and she felt like she had to make it up to him. Or maybe it was because she didn't have his dad around and she was lonely.

"I'll come," Zach said. But he didn't really want to.

* * * *

Johnny plopped down in front of his locker to change out of his jersey and into his street clothes. He was wiped out, but not in a good way like after a game. His muscles were sore from tension, not exertion. He was still reeling after his encounter with Alice. For years he'd pretended they were both dead to him. Come to find out, Mel had died. And even though they hadn't spoken in years, it still came as a big blow. The man had once been Johnny's best friend. Almost a brother. And now he was gone. Was it an accident? A long and painful battle with disease? Whatever the cause, Alice was left to raise their son alone.

Alice was a mother. Not a big surprise. She'd always loved kids. She was going to be a teacher. Until she'd married Mel and didn't have to work. Mel was rich. Came from money and probably couldn't help but make even more money once he graduated and went to work for his father, helping make other rich people richer.

It bothered him more than he wanted to admit. Her having a kid. Not that Johnny had ever really wanted to be a father. But maybe a part of him would have wanted to be the one to give her that gift.

He was wrestling with that thought when his manager, Juan Javier, approached him.

"Just the man I need to see." Javier had been a catcher during his playing days. A pretty good one too, until his knees gave out. But he was still in good shape. Still had a commanding presence.

"Sure, what do you need?" Johnny didn't know the man well enough to determine whether he should address him by his first name, last name or just call him "Skip." His reputation around the league was that of a player's manager. Well respected and well liked, with a thorough knowledge of the game and an uncanny ability to get the most out of his players. Johnny looked forward to working with him.

"I need a hero." Javier parked himself next to Johnny. "Got word this morning that Nathan Cooper didn't pass a drug test. He's out fifty games, unless he appeals."

Did that mean Johnny would be moved to the bullpen? Cooper was a relief pitcher, a left-handed specialist. Johnny was a right-handed starter. At least he had been his entire career.

"Don't worry, you're still a starter." Javier clapped him on the back. "This is a PR nightmare. At least it didn't leak out this morning. That would have put a dark cloud on the Fan Fest."

"So what can I do?"

"Your reputation is spotless. It's one of the reasons the team was so interested in signing you." They didn't call him The Monk for nothing. His composure on the mound was only part of the story. "We had a few years where...well, you catch the news. The fans are sick of this stuff. Sick of the cheaters. We need someone like you. Someone the kids can look up to."

"I try to be one of the good guys." Johnny shrugged. It's all he'd ever wanted to be. He wanted his name to be associated with honor, integrity and respect.

"Russ Crawford, from the front office, had Cooper lined up for this charity event." His manager placed a sturdy hand on Johnny's shoulder. "We don't want a guy suspended for drugs representing us to the community."

"No. We don't." Johnny never understood what would drive a guy to take such a risk. Or why there were still guys who felt they could get away with it. He balled his fists, thinking about how much harder the rest of them had to work at proving they were clean.

"We need someone to take his place. I thought you'd be perfect." He gave Johnny a friendly pat on the back.

"I was perfect once in my life." Twenty-seven batters had faced him. Every one of them had walked back to the dugout shaking their heads. None of them had reached first base. No hits, no walks, no errors.

"You and only about twenty-three other guys." Javier gave him a smile of admiration. Of respect. Not only for Johnny, but for all the players who'd come before him. "But you're not just perfect on the field."

That was his reputation. No wild parties, drugs or women. When he went out with his teammates, he stuck with one beer. Just to be one of the guys. Then he would return quietly to his room. Alone. He politely refused advances and room keys from his female fans.

"What kind of charity thing are we looking at?" *Let's get to the point.* What really mattered. As long as it wasn't a speaking engagement. He could pitch in front of a sold-out stadium. Or an empty one where the few fans in attendance tried to make up for the lack of numbers with an abundance of noise. But talking to a room full of people? No thanks. He'd much rather run the bleachers, drag the field, or even cut the grass by hand, one blade at a time.

"It's a minicamp for youth players," Javier explained. "They come to the ballpark after school and we take them through a few drills, demo mechanics and basically share your knowledge of the game."

"That sounds like something I could do." Johnny was just beginning to think about what he might do after his career was over. Coaching was something to consider; it would keep him in the game. But he wasn't sure if he'd be any good at it. He didn't know if he could explain things in a way others would understand. He could show them, though. He could demonstrate what worked for him.

"So you'll do the pitching clinic." It wasn't a question. The new guy on the team had to prove himself, no matter his reputation, and picking up a teammate was a good way to do just that.

Johnny nodded. Why not? Anything to keep his mind off Alice and Mel. And their kid.

"Tell me about the kids." Johnny didn't have a lot of experience with kids. Like, none. Even when he'd been a kid, he didn't really know how to relate to them. He was the quiet boy in school and in the dugout. "How old are they?"

"I think anywhere from about nine to twelve or thirteen."

"Old enough to tie their own shoes, then." In other words, about Zach's age.

"Yet still young enough that they don't think they know everything," Javier added with a slight smile. "About baseball, at least."

"So these kids should be coachable." When he'd been that age, he'd soaked up every tip and tidbit of information about the game. He'd been eager to learn and apply the knowledge to his rapidly growing skills.

Could he be the kind of mentor he'd had back then? Could he pass down his knowledge of the game to the next generation? He hoped so.

"They're good kids. Some of them may have caught a bad break. Single parent homes, families fallen on hard times. Some of these boys might be homeless or in foster care." Javier was starting to make Johnny a little nervous. He'd been one of those kids. He'd known hard times.

Lived with a single mother who'd worked too much. Without a father or a man to look up to.

Until his coach had stepped up.

"I guess you've got your man." Johnny hoped he could be the kind of man these kids needed. "Just give me the time and place."

"I knew I could count on you. The camp starts Monday. Here's your contact at the Harrison Foundation." The manager handed him a slick business card. Johnny's heart seized as he read the name.

Alice Harrison, Director

"She's a great gal. Professional. Knowledgeable." Javier seemed not to notice all the air had been sucked out of the room. "You'll love her."

Oh yeah. Johnny had loved her. He'd once loved her even more than he loved the game.

www.ingramcontent.com/pod-product-compliance
Lightning Source LLC
Chambersburg PA
CBHW021239260626
47155CB00004BA/1226